CRAIG MARTELLE

STARSHIP LOST

ENGAGEMENT

aethonbooks.com

ENGAGEMENT
©2024 CRAIG MARTELLE

This book is protected under the copyright laws of the United States of America. No part of this publication may be reproduced, stored in a retrieval system, or transmitted, in any form or by any means, without the prior permission in writing of the publisher, nor be otherwise circulated in any form of binding or cover other than that in which it is published and without a similar condition including this condition being imposed on the subsequent purchaser. Any reproduction or unauthorized use of the material or artwork contained herein is prohibited without the express written permission of the authors.

Aethon Books supports the right to free expression and the value of copyright. The purpose of copyright is to encourage writers and artists to produce the creative works that enrich our culture.

The scanning, uploading, and distribution of this book without permission is a theft of the author's intellectual property. If you would like to use material from the book (other than for review purposes), please contact editor@aethonbooks.com. Thank you for your support of the author's rights.

Aethon Books
www.aethonbooks.com

Print and eBook design and formatting by Josh Hayes. Artwork provided by Vivid Covers.

Published by Aethon Books LLC.

Aethon Books is not responsible for websites (or their content) that are not owned by the publisher.

This book is a work of fiction. Names, characters, places, and incidents are the product of the author's imagination or are used fictitiously. Any resemblance to actual events, locales, or persons, living or dead is coincidental.

All rights reserved.

ALSO IN STARSHIP LOST

Starship Lost

The Return

Primacy

Confrontation

Fallacy

Engagement

Check out the entire series here! (Tap or scan)

SOCIAL MEDIA

Craig Martelle Social
Website & Newsletter:
https://www.craigmartelle.com

Facebook:
**https://www.facebook.com/
AuthorCraigMartelle/**

Always to my wife, who loves me even though I work every day writing stories.

ACKNOWLEDGEMENTS

Beta Readers and Proofreaders - with my deepest gratitude!
James Caplan
Kelly O'Donnell
John Ashmore
Rita Whinfield

Get ***The Human Experiment*** for free when you join my newsletter. There's a zoo, but the humans are the ones being studied.
https://craigmartelle.com

PREVIOUSLY FROM STARSHIP LOST

Ever tried. Ever failed. No matter. Try Again. Fail again. Fail better.

"Ninety-nine percent, Captain," Taurus called. "Ready to fire on the cruisers."

"Light them up," Jaq said. They were less than two minutes out. It had taken that long to acquire the optimal firing solution.

"Fire!" Taurus beamed with the order. The E-mag batteries barked in a low rumble as they delivered a series of programmed volleys. The active sensors tracked the rounds to the bays in the shipyard where the two cruisers were being repaired.

A bright light shone and flashed with the impact.

"What was that?" Jaq wondered.

A second volley accomplished the same thing as the first.

Two cannons each delivered minimum fire on the two

gunships, blasting them off their airlocks. The debris of the shattered frames drifted away from the station

Jaq didn't care about them. Gunships attached to the station were no threat, but the cruisers were. "Hit them with everything we have!" Jaq ordered before the ship passed them completely.

"Adjusting." Taurus frantically tapped her keys. The other barrels slewed around to join the firing batteries. They cycled at the maximum rate of fire.

Out of habit, Jaq glanced at the energy gauge to find they were still at ninety percent. A grim smile crossed her face as the E-mags shook *Chrysalis* like never before. Too much damage upset the ship's balance. Too many batteries firing at once on a single target.

The light flashed and sparked.

The E-mags hammered away, creating a whine instead of a steady vibration.

"Overheating cannons, twelve, fourteen, and fifteen."

A gunship appeared from behind the station and fired into the space that *Chrysalis* would soon occupy. There was nothing they could do. There wasn't enough time to slew the batteries back to engage.

The E-mag fire penetrated the light and pounded the defenseless cruisers. One split in half and broke free from its mooring. The other ship exploded with the fury of a breached power plant.

The impacts screamed and ripped at the very fabric of the Borwyn flagship.

Red indicators appeared on the main board from breaches and system failures, electrical relays exploded from overloads, but the engines continued to drive the ship forward. The Malibor power plants had been ninety degrees to the incoming attack and were safe. Energy and drive. The air handlers processed air and pumped it throughout the ship.

Emergency bulkheads slammed shut and separated the breached sections to retain as much atmosphere as possible.

A line of E-mag rounds trailed *Chrysalis* and slammed into the gunship.

"Got you!" Taurus cried out.

The overfire hit the space station, but it was inevitable that would happen when the Malibor used the station to hide their ships.

"Invert and slow us down for a return trip to the station. Was anyone else shooting at us?" Jaq asked.

"No other shooters observed," Slade said.

"Brad?" Jaq wanted his input. Did they follow their plan?

"Stay the course," Brad replied. "I'll get the damage control teams out."

"Not yet, Brad. High-gee decel incoming. Ferd, you have your orders. Seven gees."

The ship inverted and the engines accelerated it to seven gees. The slowdown process began.

Alby, Slade, and Taurus worked to identify new targets. Alby slewed the cannons to cover all directions in case they needed to engage quickly, but no target presented itself.

"Review," Jaq grunted. "Was that an energy shield over the shipyard?"

Brad replied, "It had to be, but we beat through it. Ineffective if we can hold rounds on target for five to ten seconds. It's probably experimental, using the limitless power provided by the shipyard as opposed to the extra power available on board a ship, which isn't much."

"So, don't worry about it," Jaq said. "Concur. Too little, too late. Alby, order of battle review. Do they have any damn ships left?"

"They may have one cruiser and a few gunships as their order of battle has changed from our expectations. I calculate one cruiser and five gunships, but we aren't sure about the three on Septimus. I feel in my gut that they have no ships to throw against us. They have expended the last of their combat power. Think about the one gunship that was flying. All the rest were moored, even though they saw us coming from at least an hour away."

The energy gauge showed eight-six percent. It would drop a few more percentage points by the time they turned around, followed by a few more in the return trip to the station. Red lights dotted the status board, but none of the major systems had been impacted. Damage reports had not yet been submitted.

"Ship-wide, please," Jaq requested.

"Go," Amie called out.

"All hands, we took some damage and to the affected crew, we'll get to you as soon as possible. Until then, help yourselves as best you can and help each other. We're going to pull seven gees for sixty-four minutes. Your bodies will be under a great deal of stress. We'll slow to zero-gee. We'll do a quick damage assessment and then get back underway to return to the space station located at the zero point between Septimus and Alarrees. We're going to take control of the space station and from there, we're going to order the Malibor to surrender. It seems that they are out of ships to fight us. After fifty years, the Borwyn have returned to claim what is ours. All we have to do is clean up their mess and crush with finality any hopes they had of standing up to the Borwyn fleet. Captain Jaq Hunter out."

"Nicely said, Jaq," Brad offered. "They might have some ships in hiding, but they are better off staying that way. How long are you going to give us when we hit zero KPH?"

"Five minutes? I don't want to give the Malibor too much time to regroup and get ready to fight us. They'll get frantic when they realize we're returning and will be stopping. They'll know for sure when we start to slow down."

"Until then, they're cut off from the planet, I hope. Amie, can you raise *Matador*?" Brad wondered.

"I have been trying," Amie confirmed. "No joy. And not the ground station, either, but it's twelve hours from our normal contact window. It's early morning in Pridal."

"We don't know anything that's happening on the ground. I don't want to assume they've been successful." Jaq sighed. "Keep trying, Amie. We need to make contact with the combat team."

Sirens sounded in the city. People ran until the streets were deserted.

"Looks like the Borwyn are winning," Max said.

The others stared out the front windows. "Is this the end?" Lanni asked.

"The beginning," Deena said. She moved close, but

Lanni shied away, avoiding her touch. Deena knew what they wanted for the city and for the planet but not how they were going to accomplish it without the cooperation of the Malibor.

She could have been right that the real war had only just begun. To the citizens of Malipride, they'd been insulated from the battles that had been fought in space. They could no longer revel in their ignorance. The attack on the spaceport had put the war front and center in the civilians' lives.

"What are you going to do with us?" the general asked.

"It's too late to send you into the street. It's probably shoot-first out there right now. They'll think everyone they see is a Borwyn infiltrator. Maybe we can have an honest conversation about how to make Pridal a better place, welcoming to all."

"BOGSAT," the general tossed out. "It's just a BOGSAT. Bunch of guys sitting around talking."

"Like I said," Max began, "there aren't very many Borwyn. We're the first ones into the city, but Deena is the person who bridges both cultures. She's been less than welcome in yours and she's had her problems with ours. Who better than her to lead this city to a better place for both our people?"

"Don't you have a ship's captain and a fleet commander?" the general asked.

"We don't work how you're thinking. The right person in charge in the right place. To me, and probably everyone else, that's Deena."

"I don't want to be in charge. Pap could do it. He's never fought the Borwyn."

The general smiled. "But I have. We attacked the forests with some regularity when I could order troops around. We didn't want the Borwyn to gain a foothold too close to the city. But eventually, they took control over the entire forest on the western flank. I have fought the Borwyn but not successfully."

"I've fought Malibor, successfully, but I'm okay not killing more of you," Max shared.

"You're going to have to. They are not going to relinquish their authority easily. Turn on the radio. I guarantee the nationalist fervor is being spread across all the channels. They're coming for your children! The propaganda machine is running at flank speed. That was always the plan to whip up the population to fight an invasion."

Max looked at Deena and laughed. "An invasion. A couple hundred Borwyn soldiers. An invasion. No, General Yepsin. It's a removal of combat power followed by suing for peace. If the Malibor wanted to make problems, there wouldn't be anything we could do about it, but know that your ability to tell others what to do has come to an end. You can't order the Malibor around who are on Sairvor. Farslor is all but abandoned. There are some good people on that planet."

"You've been on Sairvor?"

"Yes, and we lost two of our soldiers there. The survivors aren't happy about their plight. They've been reduced to wearing furs and carrying bows and arrows. My friend Crip traded them a pulse rifle for a fur. That thing is ridiculous. It stunk up the whole the ship. Jaq threatened to send it out the airlock." Max chuckled at the memory.

The general and the boss looked at each other. "You don't strike me as baby eaters."

Deena laughed. "You've been lied to your entire lives. This is who the Borwyn are. They don't want to get into your lives. The Malibor leaders have accused the Borwyn of doing everything that they do themselves. The Borwyn aren't your enemy."

"That's a hard pill to swallow," the general replied. "But you're not what I expected. Is that why you're a good fighter?"

Deena nodded toward Max. "He and Crip taught me how to fight and fight well."

"You two are married?" Lanni asked, coming out of her shell for a moment.

"Newlyweds," Deena replied. "We got married on the mess deck of the Borwyn flagship, *Chrysalis* with as much of the crew as would fit sharing the moment with us, although they were there for Max. They didn't know who I was. We were at zero-gee, so more people stuffed themselves in there."

"I can't imagine what that would be like," Lanni said softly while staring at the floor. "People who don't know you accepting you."

"But you do know what that's like. Moran asked me to watch over you, and I have."

"The Borwyn are evil!" Lanni blurted and threw her hands up. "I don't know what to believe."

"If we can get out of the city, we can take you to him," Max offered. "You have a baby, don't you?"

She nodded. "I need to get home to her."

Deena pressed her face against the front window to look

into the street. A group of four soldiers marched down the center of the street. Deena opened the door. "We have a woman in here who needs to get home to her baby," Deena called.

"Get back in the building unless you want to get yourself shot!" one of the soldiers snapped.

Deena backed inside, closing and locking the door. "Not now," Deena told her. "If anyone goes outside, they're going to have a real bad day."

The general moved behind the bar and poured himself a stiff drink. "Before you talk about how early it is, I don't care." He drank it in one gulp, then poured another. "What's for lunch, Boss man?"

The boss shook his head. "Is this it? My restaurant is ground zero for the uprising? I'm not good with that."

The general snorted. "Makes no difference if you're good with it or not. This could be the safest place to be or the most dangerous. I, for one, was thinking about how I could escape, but I think I'll settle for keeping my head down. If the Malibor fleet is destroyed, then we have no options. The Malibor takeover of Septimus was based on having the strongest fleet. And yes, I know that we wrested Septimus from the Borwyn, although the history books teach it differently. Winners write the history, don't they?"

The general sipped from the second drink.

The boss joined him by pulling beer into a pitcher. He took a drink straight from it, claiming it as his glass.

"Are you okay?" Max asked Lanni.

"I'm not," she replied honestly. "In the course of an hour, my entire world has been turned upside-down, and here I sit with the man who killed members of my husband's squad."

Max frowned. "I haven't lied to you, and I don't intend to start. The Borwyn didn't start this war, but we are going to end it. If Chrysalis has done what it planned, then the end is going to come sooner rather than later."

"Yes, Madame President's husband." The general toasted Max and Deena by raising his glass and taking another drink.

"A politician through and through," the boss said with a snort. "I'm not taking the Borwyn's side, you traitors!"

"Then take my side," Deena said.

"You're making this too hard," he grumbled. "I'm not traitor."

"Traitor to whom?" Max said. "If it's the Malibor people, then the leadership, the same ones who ordered fighting other Malibor five times in the past fifty years? Is that who you're loyal to? You've fought only your fellow Malibor. Maybe the traitors are the ones who are in charge. We don't want any fighting at all. Killing your enemies isn't all it's cracked up to be. I'm tired of it."

"How many people have you killed?" Lanni asked.

"Too, as in too many. I don't have a number because keeping track would be traumatic. We fight battles and move on. It sucks. My wife is incredible. I'd like to spend time with her hiking and looking at nature. Dining on the incredible food she says is served here. Is that too much to ask? Is it too much to ask that you have the same opportunity?"

Lanni ducked her head and stared at the floor again.

"What do we do now?" Max asked. "I'm not going to

shoot any of you." He slung his rifle over his back. "I'm hungry and am going to get something to eat."

He strolled into the kitchen. Deena walked in after him leaving the three Malibor behind.

Lanni took one step toward the door, but another patrol was coming, so she thought better of it. "I could use some ranji juice." She headed for the kitchen.

The general and the boss looked at each other.

"If I had known it was going to be like this, I would have demanded the Borwyn invade and take over decades ago. I'm not a traitor, but I want more for my people. We've been holding them back. That revelation is sitting in my gut like a ten-kilo boulder. I was in a position to make a difference and didn't."

"Were you really? If you had made waves, they would have launched you out an airlock," the boss said. "Come on. I have to keep them from messing up my kitchen. Deena doesn't know the first thing about cooking, and I don't think space-boy does either."

They joined the others, and the boss started howling for everyone to stop touching his equipment. He belted out orders for a steak and egg late breakfast with a side of cinnamon rolls. He let everyone know in no uncertain terms how incompetent they were.

Halfway through preparing their meals, gunfire sounded nearby. An explosion followed, and the lights went out.

"That wasn't us," Max said. "The Borwyn aren't in the city, and we're definitely not blowing up power plants."

"Keep your heads down," the general advised. He

crawled out of the kitchen and to the front window. He cried out in anguish before crawling back.

"The war has started, but it's the one we know best. The soldiers are shooting their fellow Malibor."

A trail of smoke rose from the distant city. Crip stared at it. He thought he'd seen the dart of a gunship racing back and forth, but they were too far away to get a good look. The western Borwyn had the binoculars not the combat team.

"What do you think?" he asked.

Larson was the closest. "I think we're attacking the city with the gunship, or Max is a one-man army. I prefer the former explanation."

"I do, too," Crip said. "We're hanging out here blowing in the wind. We don't have the radio. We don't have any information. Dammit, Max!"

"Incoming," Danzig interrupted. "Commander Owain is here with his people."

Crip stood. "Make sure we don't get overrun by the Malibor army," he told Larson, using the running joke they'd had since setting up along the edge of the forest. In three days, they'd seen four total workers in the farthest fields and no soldiers.

Glen approached looking ragged from a hard hike.

"Max has gone to the city," Crip reported as the two shook hands.

"I expected. We heard from Chrysalis. They attacked

less than an hour ago. We were held up when we misplaced our prisoners."

"You brought the Malibor?"

"I thought it was a good idea, but the second we took our eyes off them, they bolted. We caught them, dragged them back to camp, and dug a hole in the ground to throw them inside. That was the deal if they tried to escape. It was the stupidest thing I've ever seen, but there's no accounting for Malibor intelligence. In any case, we're here."

"Did Chrysalis request anything? Give direction on how we can help?"

"Take out the three gunships, the comm relay, and the headquarters. It looks like Tram and Kelvis have done that. Begs the question: now what?"

Crip shook his head. "I honestly don't know, but I expect the people in the city are a little spun up."

"Just a little." The two looked at the tallest buildings that stood out over the horizon. The city was distant, even though it felt closer. With the smoke rising over the spaceport, it reinforced the fact that the war had come home.

The Borwyn were attacking Septimus.

"We brought your radio," Eleanor said as she approached.

Crip nodded in appreciation. "Larson, get it set up. I have to talk with *Chrysalis*."

CHAPTER 1

When the world looks to collapse, it starts with our small piece of it.

Captain Jaq Hunter was itching to get out of the captain's chair.

"Ten minutes to thrusters only," Ferdinand, the thrust control officer, stated.

"No one is shooting at us," Alby said, "but weapons are hot. We are ready to return fire."

"Heading over the top of the spindle on our way to the airlock designated G-Seven," Mary, the navigator, reported. "Ten minutes."

"Active scanning. No foreign objects. No ships," Chief Slade Ping announced. He finally looked up from his screens.

"Looks like your plan worked flawlessly, Captain," Alby stated.

"That's what scares me. The Malibor always toss a spanner into the works. What are we missing?"

"We either take that energy screen technology or we destroy it. We can't let the Malibor have it," Brad said.

"Add that to our list," Jaq replied. She had a list in her head but nothing in writing. "Space station. Are we seeing any movement?"

"Infrared is inconclusive at this distance," Slade answered. "Here's what we have, sharing to the main screen."

Slade sent the consolidated image to the screen. The station was a wireframe representation. The target airlock had been highlighted. Infrared showed the entire station to be slightly warmer than ambient space. It rotated quickly enough to keep it from overheating due to absorbing the star's radiation.

Inconclusive was a tactful way of saying it didn't show anything they could use.

"We have a couple landers filled with explosives," Brad suggested. "Benjy can fly one over to that big ship and lay waste to it along with the energy generation system. It'll take all of us to clear and control the space station. We only have pulse rifles for thirty-five. Trying to seize that shield without weapons or reducing our manpower on the station will lead to challenges we don't want."

Jaq saw the team as having too little with too much to do. Taking on multiple enemy ships was a three-dimensional chess match that Jaq enjoyed. Talking about how soldiers would move through the station to secure the command center wasn't anything in which she wanted to invest brain power.

She remained concerned about keeping her people alive. They needed to put the damage control teams to work as soon as possible. Seal the breaches and open the emergency bulkheads. Get air flowing through the ship again and repair any impacted systems. She wasn't about to leave the ship damaged in the hope that it wouldn't have to fight any more battles.

"Zero-gee," Ferd reported.

No one had to tell the captain. She was already unbuckling to free herself from the seat. Five minutes at the turnaround point hadn't been enough time to stretch after a seven-gee deceleration, then more acceleration followed by more deceleration. They'd worked the engines hard, and they had responded.

Jaq wanted to go to Engineering and personally thank Teo, but she needed to stay on the bridge because of everything they didn't know. With Brad leading the boarding team, she didn't have her deputy to manage the damage control teams. She wanted Alby, Taurus, and Gil focused on external threats.

She accessed her comm system and called down to Engineering.

"Teo," the chief engineer answered.

"Jaq here. I wanted to tell you thank you for the perfect performance of the engines to get us here."

"My pleasure. I expected the bio-pack to go belly up, but it continued to work. I'm declaring it proven technology. We can replace a couple other chip- and transistor-based systems. I'll grow what we need and set up the next system."

"Excellent work. Maybe we'll be able to export that technology to the planet when the time is right. What has Bec been doing?"

"He was fascinated by that energy screen. He's disappeared, so I think he's probably working on something related to it. He might be on his way to you to offer his services to recover that system from the shipyard."

"I look forward to it," Jaq lied.

"That answers your question," Alby offered. "Maybe you can send him over there on the explosives-laden lander. If he snags the energy thing, then we don't have to blow it up, but we can still use the lander to blow up that big ship. I'm not sure we want it hanging around."

"It could make for a nice flagship," Jaq mused. "Although it's Malibor design, so it could be a little more austere than we would like. I don't want to blow it up out of hand. That could be a good exploration and research ship. Thanks to us, there aren't a whole lot of surplus ships flying around the system."

"Freighters and shuttles, but why haven't we seen any freighters?" Alby wondered.

"The Malibor aren't big on resupplying anyone who isn't them. Just the boxy shuttles between here and the planet. That's all we can see. They are highlighted on the board as green dots. As long as they steer clear of us, they'll remain green," Alby explained.

Jaq acknowledged the info and checked the board to find what she hadn't previously noticed. "I think we took their last freighter and destroyed their last troopship. We'll contact *Cornucopia* to join us as soon as the space station is secure."

"That'll be good," Alby said. He tried to hide it, but he wanted to see Godbolt.

Jaq liked having the big ship nearby. It gave her options she wouldn't have otherwise, like giving an attacker two targets instead of one. And the food was incomparable. The crew liked it. She preferred it over the sustenance they manufactured. And spare parts, too.

They had transferred much to *Chrysalis*, but the cargo ship had vast quantities of supplies, even after filling the cruiser's corridors and sending pallets of food everywhere they were needed.

Chrysalis closed on the space station. They were going over the top to scan the void in the heart of the spindle.

"Prepare to fire," Jaq said.

"We've *been* ready," Taurus said. "Cruisers and gunships are valid targets."

The space station loomed massive across the ship's visual view. The infrared data populated the tactical board. The wireframe overlay showed warm bodies behind windows.

"Watching us arrive. That'll be an image forever burned into their minds," Jaq said. "They'll tell their kids and grandkids about the day the Borwyn arrived."

The ship eased toward the upper part of the station spinning before them. *Chrysalis* would match the spin to dock once the ship had scanned the interior void.

"Two meters per second," Ferd reported.

"Increase to five," Jaq said. She didn't want to remain a target for too long if there were ships ready to fire on the inside. Then again, even five wouldn't be fast enough.

"I got it, Captain," Taurus said, never taking her eyes off her screens. "Cannons are pre-aimed." Her finger hovered over the fire button.

As the nose of the ship passed, the operational transmitters radiated into the center of the spindle. A cover was in place over the void, but it didn't affect the radar.

"Getting a picture—mostly shuttles, a possible gunship, nothing facing us."

"Can you target that gunship all by itself?"

"Possible gunship. There's a lot of interference. We need to slow down," Slade insisted.

"Slow us, Ferd. Two meters per second should give us time to resolve the data." Jaq floated toward the battle commander.

Alby gave her the thumbs-up. "If anyone shoots from in there, they all die."

Jaq winced. Cargo shuttles would be important for the future viability of the space station and shipyard, if the Borwyn were to move forward as a race to explore the system and reestablish contact with lost colonies. To be a peaceful group of explorers and not expansionist invaders, like the Malibor had been, moving from Fristen to Sairvor to Septimus.

"Belay that. We're not going to destroy the space station and all the shuttles. Bring the engines online and prepare to accelerate at two gees," Jaq ordered.

"Standing by. Engines are hot," Ferd said.

"Course laid in to clear the area," Mary confirmed.

The ship veritably crawled past the station. It continued to rotate, which helped clear up the data.

"Not a gunship. I say again, not a gunship. Looks like a gantry attached to a shuttle. I count seventeen cargo shuttles in the interior. Four gantries. Unknown number of airlocks. Support structure throughout. A gunship would fit but a cruiser would not, contrary to my previous assessment."

"Roger," Jaq said. She could see the information on the screen as the sensors updated. She had no recriminations for Slade. He had a tough job and gave her everything she needed for the ship to fly and fight.

Slade pointed the infrared sensors at the shuttles to discover most of them had hot engines.

That told Jaq one thing.

"They're evacuating the station?" Alby asked. "We have a perfectly good lander loaded with explosives we could station at the opening, but we'll need to launch it within the minute before we clear the station. It can be on station in seconds. That would be a good threat to keep them from flying off."

"A threat is only good if you're willing to carry it out. I am not willing to blow up the station." Jaq chewed on her lip and then signaled to Amie. "Give me a broadcast channel to the Malibor."

"Ready," Amie confirmed.

"Malibor of the space station and most particularly the shuttles preparing to leave, we will shoot you out of the sky should you exit the spindle. We request that everyone at the station remain at the station for the time being. We do not want to damage the station. We do not want to kill innocent bystanders. Return to your quarters and secure yourselves inside until we give you the all-clear. This is Jaq Hunter, captain of the Borwyn flagship." Jaq drew a finger across her throat, and Amie closed the channel. "Put that on repeat for the next few minutes."

"A little psychological warfare," Alby said. "Do you want us to destroy shuttles that try to skip out?"

"If we have a shot, yes. If we don't, no."

"That sounds more profound than it really is," Alby replied.

Jaq shrugged with a smile. She was serious about not wanting to cause collateral damage.

"Rotating and aligning," Mary said while her fingers danced across her screen.

"Stand down the main engines, Ferd."

"Taking them offline but keeping them warm, Captain."

"As you do, Helm."

"Aligning and matching speed," Mary said. "Command deck airlock is coming into sight."

Jaq accessed the intercom. "This is it, people. Brad, we're aligning with the airlock now. Will dock shortly. Secure the command center as quickly as possible to avoid unnecessary engagements. It's your call as to whether we undock and maintain an overwatch position. Please stay in touch."

The channel crackled as Brad replied using his tactical radio. "I'll probably recommend undocking. That removes the threat to our rear area or a counterattack into *Chrysalis*. Better to sacrifice us than lose the ship. But, if we don't have to secure the corridor from the airlock to the command center, then we'll be able to maintain unit integrity. That will help us fend off any heroes who think they have a chance."

"The battle is joined," she said softly.

"Victory is ours, Jaq. I'll be back in touch. Need to rally the troops now." The static from the old radio disappeared as Brad released the transmit button.

Jaq glanced across the screen. Damaged areas flashed red. With the delay in making repairs, neighboring sections were losing atmosphere. The physical damage hadn't been secured with the automatic foam dispensers. After all the damage they'd taken, she wasn't surprised but thought they had enough left to seal most small penetrations.

"Damage control teams, all hands deploy. Priority to midship," she ordered.

"That's one big ship, Jaq, and its engines are hot," Slade reported.

Jaq looked where he was pointing. The Malibor new design showed the engines hot. "That ship's not finished. It's missing too much of its hull to be spaceworthy."

"Maybe it's generating the field," Slade guessed. "The field is drawn tightly to it. It shows up on a resonance scan."

"That ship is generating the field? We probably need to blast it."

"Lander number three has launched!" Alby nearly shouted.

Jaq jerked her attention to her battle commander. "What?"

"Rotational speed is matched. Docking alignment is complete with the port roller airlock," Mary announced.

Jaq turned her attention to the board with the visual inset showing three meters, then two, and finally, contact.

"We have a secure connection. Airlock is equalizing."

"Get me Benjy." Jaq gestured toward the comm officer.

"Benjy here," came the quick reply since he was at his station.

"What is that lander doing? I haven't authorized any departures."

"Bec said the launch was authorized. I'm sorry, Captain. I'll bring him back," Benjy apologized.

"What the what, Bec! You picked now to run off?" Jaq groused.

"He's cut the link and is manually flying the lander," Benjy said sheepishly.

"Thanks, Benjy. He's on his own. We have boarding operations that take precedence. In the meantime, clear the explosives from one of the landers in case we need to go after him."

"*Starstrider* is available. Brad's ship has been disconnected from providing power."

Jaq hadn't considered *Starstrider* as an available asset. She wasn't sure if there was anyone else who could fly the scout ship, and Brad was busy. She turned her attention back to the inset showing the live view of the breach. The outer hatch popped. Brad dropped to a knee and started firing his pulse rifle.

CHAPTER 2

Fire and maneuver to deliver a devastating blow to an entrenched enemy.

"I was born and raised on this thing," Brad said softly while they prepared to board.

Edgerrin, his nominal number two for this operation, paused for a moment. "Is there anything we should know?"

"There are a lot of places to hide on that thing." Brad tipped his chin at the hatch. It was time to go.

Brad raised his pulse rifle and looked down the sights while Edgerrin opened the hatch and stepped out of the line of fire.

A barricade had hastily been put in place, judging by the random items it consisted of—chairs, a desk, a cabinet. They'd shifted an office into the corridor. Brad wanted to convince the defenders that the safest place to be was somewhere else. He fired into the deck at the base of the barricade to create chaos for any defenders hiding behind it.

Instead of digging into the deck and making Septiman's own noise about it, the rounds skipped and ripped through the bottom of the barricade. Screams of pain and fear reached them but no return fire.

"Go!" Brad ordered. He and Edgerrin jumped up at the same time and moved onto the space station, hitting the deck heavily. The corridor ran along the outer edge of the hull. The spin created centripetal force to give the appearance of gravity. It was less than Septimus normal but not by much.

Brad stopped and lowered himself to the deck while the much younger Edgerrin dove to the deck and took aim the instant he hit. Brad knew if he did that too many times, he wouldn't be able to stand or keep moving. He applauded the younger man's zeal.

They studied the gaps in the barricade to assess the defenders, but there were two who lay on the deck unmoving. They saw no others. Brad stood and strolled the last few meters and kicked at the obstacles. It came down in a heap. He cleared a path along the side by bumping the lightest pieces out of the way.

The first shots of the boarding process had killed the two unarmed defenders. They wore jumpsuits similar to the Borwyn uniforms on *Chrysalis*. He had no material to cover them. He checked the corridor ahead before arranging the two bodies with their arms across their chest and legs straight. He wanted to give them some dignity in death. If any Malibor were watching, they'd see that the Borwyn weren't spitting on the defenders' corpses.

It was the least he could do.

He waved the next team of two past. They ran down the

corridor before hugging the bulkhead and aiming ahead. Then the next two ran forward.

Soon enough, thirty-five soldiers lined the corridor for a hundred meters from the airlock.

Brad activated his radio. "Jaq, we are on board. You can secure the airlock and stand away. We'll continue to the command center. All things being equal, our next call will be from there."

"Carry on," Jaq replied, which was what Brad was going to do anyway.

He motioned for them to secure the airlock from this side. "You have Tail-End Charlie," he told the last group, which included the welder, Phillips, who lugged a plasma torch.

"Who's back there?" Brad demanded of the figure behind the elder Phillips.

"My boy. We're the two best welders on the ship."

"Then you should be on *Chrysalis* helping to repair it," Brad argued.

"We're going to do something to win this war. We're here to fight," the elder Phillips declared.

Brad looked at the thirteen-year-old and shook his head. "Do not stray from them. Keep your heads down!" He waved angrily at the three soldiers that made up Tail-End Charlie. Brad left them to move forward. He tapped shoulders as he moved through his teams until he and Edgerrin were close to the front.

"What's the holdup?" he asked, although it was apparent. An emergency bulkhead was in place and nothing was moving it.

"Cut through or go around?" the lead team requested.

Brad rapped the butt of his pulse rifle on the metal. He didn't get the hollow sound of thin plate. It thudded with the density of *Chrysalis's* nosecone. "Go around."

He had prepared for this eventuality. The map in his mind left him no choice but to go up. The lower level was the outermost of the station and acted as a second hull to help fight off breaches from micro-asteroids. It held equipment and storage but nothing critical. It could be harder to move through and could also be isolated easier. Brad couldn't give the Malibor a chance to isolate them and vent them into space.

No. The only option was to go toward the station's inner area.

Brad backtracked to the stairwell. He motioned for Edgerrin to open the hatch. Brad looked down the barrel of his pulse rifle, finger on the trigger. The hatch popped open, and Brad pointed the barrel up the stairs, where blankets and mattresses blocked their way.

"We'll cover you," he told the team behind him. "Clear the stairs."

Brad and Edgerrin moved to the landing inside the door and aimed up the stairs. The soldiers behind him slung their rifles and turned to, tossing the mattresses, blankets, and pillows down the stairs to the landing below.

"Wait one," Brad told them. He and Edgerrin stepped carefully up the stairs, aiming upward, past the next piles.

"I'm not sure they're armed," Edgerrin whispered. "Why would they do this?"

"Slow us down. I suspect they have a limited number of

weapons and they're slowing us down to give themselves more time to set up a full ambush with a proper kill-zone."

"Let's not get caught in that," Edgerrin suggested.

"We'll do our best not to. We need to pick up the pace. Our best weapon at this point is not giving them enough time to erect a barrier we can't get through. Hurry," he told the pair removing the debris. They threw it down to the next landing and another team tossed it farther.

As soon as they had a path through, Brad and Edgerrin continued up the steps to the next level.

"Only a hundred meters to go," Brad said hopefully. They popped the hatch and looked through by ducking out and pulling back. "It's going to be a slog."

Heavy cables crisscrossed the corridor, and Brad could have sworn some of them were energized.

―――――

Deena and Max sat at the bar with the restaurant's owner, the former Malibor general, and Lanni, spouse of a soldier that the Borwyn had taken captive. It was a menagerie of personalities, all of them related to the military in some way.

"I guess there are worse ways to go," the general said. "We have plenty of food and booze. That wasn't something we contemplated. I always figured the final battle would come with more austerity." He toasted the group and took another drink. He'd had most of the bottle already and swayed as if moving to an unheard rhythm.

"If we have to fight, you're not going to be ready," the boss chided.

Max laughed. "There's no fight with the Borwyn. If any Malibor try to loot this place, Deena and I will finish them. It will be the last time they cross us."

The general gestured toward the door. "Looks like you'll get your chance."

A mob of ten men dressed in a mix of military uniforms and civilian clothes moved down the opposite side of the street. They kept close together. Four carried blasters. The group stopped and huddled next to a wall.

A voice carried down the street. "Ho there! What are you doing out?" A corporal leading a four-man patrol hurried them forward, spreading them out as they ran to present less of a target.

The mob aimed, but the soldiers fired first.

If the mob had any discipline, it evaporated when four of their number fell in the first volley. Three had been carrying the acquired blasters. The fourth fired back, but his shot was wild. The jostling ended in a run for their lives. The soldiers fired once more, taking out three more.

Only three men ran from the engagement.

The soldiers moved to the bodies and recovered the blasters. They saw the group watching them from inside the restaurant. The corporal aimed his weapon. Max and Deena dove to the floor. The general waved his arms, using a signaling technique from the army.

The corporal raised his weapon and jogged to the entrance, where the general opened the door. "General Yepsin, retired, at your service. I want to compliment you on the excellent tactics with your unit, Corporal."

"Thank you, General. Are you okay?"

"Besides having too much to drink because I'm sitting this one out, I'm fine. We're fine. Do you know if they'll restore power?"

"They'll work on it as soon as we gain control of the area. Mobs like that one are running around. We'll get the insurrectionists under control. And to think we thought the Borwyn were attacking. Just a bunch of ingrates. They even had a gunship, of all things. We'll regain control quickly, and you'll be able to go about your business. I suggest you've had enough, General. We might need a calmer head to help us through this. The others are a little excited owing to the destruction of the headquarters. No one is sure who's in charge. Hell, it could be you."

"I'm pretty sure it's not me," the general replied. "Stop by here tomorrow if they haven't decided. Until then, I wish you the best in putting down this insurrection."

He closed the door while the corporal was still speaking and returned to the bar. The general laughed. "You heard him. There aren't any Borwyn."

"That's good to know," Max said. "Thanks for not turning us in."

"And ruin the perfectly good delusion they're living? I wouldn't do that. They seemed happy to use their army training. Plus, you can't tell me you were comfortable with that mob roaming the street. They're better off dead."

Max shook his head. "A rather cynical view, General. I agree that the lawless have no place. How can society function?"

"Indeed. You may not like our methods, but they are effective."

Max winced. He didn't like their methods and didn't agree about their effectiveness. What culture would take advantage of a crisis to run rampant? They descended into chaos far too quickly, which meant that it was always boiling right below the surface.

Anarchy wasn't far away with the Malibor.

It was an opportunity for the Borwyn. It was better than what they hoped would happen.

Max smiled in satisfaction. "I'm pleased. Maybe I'll join you for a drink."

Deena shook her head. "We need to keep our minds clear. Have you ever had a drink before?"

"Have you?" Max shot back more harshly than he intended.

"Yes." Deena looked smug. "Well?"

"I have not."

"Then now is not the time. Keep your wits about you, Max."

The general threw his head back and roared with laughter. "You are married!"

"We told you we were," Deena said.

"Yes, but only an old married couple would have that conversation," he managed in between bouts of laughter.

"We *know* it is the Borwyn," Lanni interjected. "Why would they think it isn't?"

The boss answered, "Sometimes, truth is what people want to believe and what they don't want to believe. They do not want to think the Borwyn are here. It makes no sense. They don't know about anything that's happening in space.

The propaganda machine has woven a narrative that doesn't allow for the existence of a Borwyn fleet."

Max looked to Deena. "We never thought of that."

"Because it's nuts." She shrugged. "Once they restore power, we'll be able to move with impunity through the city. They won't be looking for us, a young woman and an old gimping man."

"I'm not that old." Max frowned. "But it could work. There's no benefit in staying here, is there?"

"Who's going to lead this new city of Malibor and Borwyn living together peacefully?" the general asked, throwing his arms up to help make his point of the helplessness of the situation.

"Not me, Pap. I've got a life to live, and I don't want to do it under constant scrutiny. Isn't that what the leaders get? Everyone trying to drag the offending individual from the pedestal to replace them with somebody even less worthy? There always needs to be a target of their ire. I don't want that to be me."

"You've thought about this for longer than two seconds," the general said. "You should reconsider."

Deena shook her head and crossed her arms.

Max continued to be amazed that the Malibor hadn't turned them over to the soldiers. "There's hope for you," Max told the group. "I hope that carries over to more of your people."

"I guarantee nothing. You'll probably die in a pillar of fire, but it won't be our doing," the boss said with a gentle, supportive nod.

Deena one-arm hugged him and returned to her seat.

The four soldiers patrolled up the street and back down it, staying close to the front gate and by extension, the restaurant.

No more weapons fire broke the calm. After another hour, the lights came back on.

"We can finish cooking breakfast," the general suggested.

"It'll be dinner," the boss replied. "Let's see if anything survived the power outage."

They headed to the kitchen to find that the refrigerator was still cold and the frozen foods were still frozen.

"We wait until it's dark and the military patrols are off the streets, then we'll leave. Straight to the wall and into the fields beyond," Max whispered to Deena. She smiled and nodded.

Despite the friendly banter, she was ready to leave this world behind. She was with Max and as much as she wanted to help the Borwyn cause, she wasn't cut out to be a spy. She was better by Max's side. She'd also had enough of food service. She didn't care to serve any more customers or wipe off one more table.

The boss had been watching her. "You were the best employee I've ever had, hands down. I know you need to go when the streets are clear. You do what you have to do. We won't tell the authorities about you, either of you. You're one lucky man, Max."

"I know that. We'll be out of your hair as soon as possible. We'll let the soldiers think it's insurrectionists. I still find that funny. No, Mister Soldier-Man, it really was the Borwyn." Max stood aside while the professionals dealt with the meal. That meant doing whatever the boss said.

"We need to get back to Crip so we can find out what's going on," Deena whispered.

"I hate not knowing, but I brought that on myself. Break out your radio. There's nothing preventing us from making contact."

Deena removed the radio set from her small pack and headed upstairs. Max blocked the stairs to give her privacy.

She set up in the bathroom as she had before. As soon as the power came on, she tapped the contact code and waited.

It took three tries over three minutes before she received a reply.

"Request voice," she asked.

"Granted," Commander Glen Owain replied.

"Chaos in the city. They believe an insurrection is underway, but they are violently putting it down."

"I see how that helps. Keep your heads down and don't become collateral damage."

"Max is with me," Deena stated simply.

"Good. We thought we'd lost him. We'll stop looking, then."

"We intend to egress the city tonight. The wall is porous, I hear," Deena added. "Any further instructions besides keeping our heads down?"

"None. We'll be along when we can. Remember the recce squad ambush site? We'll meet you there."

"Roger. Out." Deena pulled the radio apart and put it in her pack. She returned downstairs to find everyone at the bar, eating sandwiches and drinking beer, including Max. She gave him a withering side-eye that the general found to be the epitome of good humor. A plate and a beer waited for her.

"If you can't beat them, join them," she said.

"What's the news from home?" the boss asked.

Now, it was Deena's turn to find the humor in the absurdity of the situation. "They said they would stop looking for Max since we know where he is."

"Crip's going to be mad," Max admitted.

"Who's Crip?" the general asked.

"Ship's deputy and my best friend. He also runs the combat team, although I'm supposed to be the one who does that. It's okay. We make a good team."

"Combat team?"

Max took a big bite of his sandwich and chewed for an extended time rather than answer the interrogation.

"Make war, not love. That's the way I heard it," the boss joked.

"We've made war. We've won the war. The Malibor don't realize that they've already lost, but they'll figure it out soon enough. In any case, thank you for being decent. It gives me hope for the future," Max replied. He took small sips of the beer and decided quickly that he didn't like it. He pushed it aside and received Deena's approving nod.

They sat around the bar as the afternoon sun faded toward evening. The patrol disappeared from the street in front of the restaurant.

"We'll go out the kitchen door," Max said. "It's been real, and it's been fun, but it hasn't been real fun. I hope to see you again."

Deena hugged each person before joining Max. She faced them one last time. "It's not who we are that matters but who surrounds us. We are no more than the quality of our friends."

She waved and went through the door into the kitchen. In the alley behind the restaurant, she and Max found the darkness nearly complete. They waited outside the door for their eyes to adjust enough to make sure they were alone. It took fifteen minutes before Max was comfortable enough to walk away. He pulled the blanket over his weapon and his head while Deena walked at his side.

They were in the street for no more than ten seconds when a shout rocked their world.

"Halt or be shot."

CHAPTER 3

Patience is hard.

Crip stared at the radio, even though it was powered off. "I'll be damned. He found her in the middle of a city with a million people. That makes me proud of him instead of angry. Well, I'm still a little angry."

"Like when you took your squads from the camp angry, or just there's someone at the slit trench when you have to go angry?" Glen offered his version of the alternatives.

Crip smiled. "As long as people aren't getting killed, he didn't do any damage. If they're going to leave the city, two are probably better than one, especially if the Malibor are fighting each other. Did you see that as a possibility?"

"Not at all, although I should have. They are wildly distrustful, which has benefited us because they were worried more about internal challenges to their power than external. It's also why your weapons are far more advanced than theirs. Which reminds me, we brought a dozen pulse rifles that had been manufactured in the mountain. These are the first off the line."

"I heard that rumor. You want our people to have them?"

"Your people know how to use them, and they're armed with bows and arrows," Glen replied.

"The pulse rifles have a little more punch. A dozen, you said? That means you and Eleanor can get ones, too. How many power packs do you have for each rifle?"

"Just one," Glen replied.

"We have three each. We can share so everyone has two. That puts us with twenty pulse rifles, plus Danny Johns's weapon and power packs." Crip stopped. "Did I tell you about Danny?"

"Tell me what?" Glen's ears perked up at the change in Crip's tone.

"Died of what looked like a heart attack while we were looking for tracks up the cut. He was born on Septimus. He's now buried here."

"My condolences on the loss of your friend. I bet he enjoyed the twilight of his life, though, thanks to you and the other Borwyn. You gave him the greatest gift a soldier can have. You gave him a vision of victory."

Crip nodded. He wished Max was there instead of being the reason they'd been running. Otherwise, they would still be at Glen's camp. All of them together instead of Max in a city that was coming apart and Danny Johns in the ground. Crip was starting to feel bitter. He knew that wouldn't be good for the combat team, so he forced his feelings into the background.

"What's next?" he asked. "Are we going in?"

"Let's wait for Max and Deena," Glen replied. "They'll have the best perspective of the situation on the ground. Maybe now is the best time to sow discontent and wipe out the Malibor army."

Crip laughed. "I think they have us outnumbered."

Eleanor shook her head. "They used to send battalions against us, then companies, and now they send squads. We think their active numbers have decreased significantly. Something happened earlier this year that cost them dearly. I think that's why they recruited the Fristen mercenaries."

"We destroyed one of their troopships," Crip explained. "We saved them at great risk to *Chrysalis*. Jaq told them to return to Septimus, but they followed the supply ship that we had rightfully stolen and then tried to attack us, so we turned their ship and all aboard into space debris. We estimated over a thousand soldiers died. We didn't want to do it."

Glen and Eleanor looked at each other. "I'm not questioning you, but we didn't realize they had a thousand troops to deploy. They may have less than a thousand remaining. We can't be sure of the numbers since we gather no intelligence from within the city, but their once-massive army has disappeared. If they're fighting themselves, I wonder how many soldiers are dedicated to controlling the population. What does their military look like right now? They've lost the last two squads they sent out here. Maybe they're already in the death throes of the Malibor Empire." Glen grunted with the revelation of a mystery solved, but he had more questions than before.

"You're saying we have to sit and wait?" Crip asked.

"You don't sound like you want to," Glen replied. "Let me think it over. We need to talk with *Chrysalis*."

Eleanor waved over their radio operator. "Set up the space comm," she told him. "We're calling our friends, and if I'm not mistaken, the signal delay will be negligible."

"Your astrophysics calculations are sound," Crip replied. "*Chrysalis* is right there." He pointed overhead. Since they could see Alarrees, one of the two moons over Septimus, they had an unrestricted signal to the space station that sat in the zero-gravity gap between the moon and the planet. And the Borwyn cruiser was at or near the station.

Larson appeared. "Did someone say we were setting up the radio?"

Crip gestured toward Glen's radio operator.

Larson waved for Pistoria to join him. He'd been trying to teach her about technology. She was picking up on it much more quickly than Sophia had.

Glen looked toward the city. Another trail of smoke drifted skyward from a different part of the city than those from the gunship's attacks. He drew Eleanor's attention to it.

"Do we let them kill each other and then swoop in to reestablish order, save the day?" Glen suggested.

"An occupying army. I've read about that. One of the last reports from Septimus that had been received by *Chrysalis* before we lost the last battle fifty years ago. They suggested it would take a hundred thousand Malibor to pacify the city. The Borwyn intended to fight them from every street, every house, and every room."

"Nice thought, but from what we've been taught by those who survived, that resistance crumbled after less than a day.

They executed many, put others in camps for eventual execution, and the last, they assimilated to work in the fields."

"Did it take a hundred thousand?" Crip wondered.

"A few thousand determined souls without consciences. I hope they're all dead by now."

"Putting that behind us is a big ask," Eleanor added. "We're not looking for revenge, not anymore. That was costly. The first few years on the run out of the city cost hundreds of thousands of Borwyn lives."

Crip clenched his jaw. "We're not going to be brutal, and we have a total of, what, a hundred and fifty people if we completely empty the camp and logistics caravans?"

"It's a limited number," Glen admitted. "How much of the city will we have to control?"

Crip started laughing.

"What?" Glen was instantly angry.

"Here we are, already knee-deep in the final battles of the great Malibor-Borwyn war, and we don't know what we want to do. I laugh because I never thought this far into it. Maybe I didn't believe we'd get here. I don't know the reason, but now we have to do more than think about it. We need to execute a plan that we don't have."

"Sir, the radio is up, and the channel is live," Larson reported.

Crip whistled. "Maybe Jaq has an idea."

Jaq looked at the main screen and the status display. She had no idea what was happening on board the station. Brad hadn't made a second report. She expected he was knee-deep in problems. Taking three hours to stop and get back to the station gave the Malibor time to prepare defenses and rally their people.

Amie announced, "The combat team is checking in from Septimus."

Crip reported the status of the internal fighting in Malipride and that the combat team and assault brigade were standing by. Did Jaq have any ideas for a mutual engagement to liberate the city?

Jaq stared at the wall. "We can't leave here. We have Bec on his way to the shipyard in a lander and thirty-five hearty Borwyn souls aboard the space station. We intended to hover over the city and intimidate them that way, but that's not possible. You have to fill in for us, Crip. Do us proud."

Crip mouthed the words, "do us proud," and shrugged while making a face. "We have a hundred and fifty total people and thanks to good people supporting us, we have twenty-four pulse rifles but limited power packs. I'm not sure we have the means to fill in for a cruiser sporting sixteen E-mag cannons."

"Don't take me literally. I need to go. Bec is almost at the shipyard. Keep me informed of your progress. The battle is joined."

"Victory is ours," Crip replied weakly.

Jaq gestured to close the channel.

Alby cleared his threat.

When Jaq looked at him, he nodded toward the comm officer. Jaq lifted one hand while the other held onto the mid-rail. "What?"

"You kind of left Crip hanging," Alby said.

Jaq turned her head back and forth in contemplation of Alby's statement. "It's Crip. He knows ground operations better than I do. And Max is going to join him, if I'm not mistaken."

"Allegedly on his way," Alby stated.

"Then they'll get it done. They've got the assault brigade providing a tactical assist. I think they have a firm handle on it."

"Their plan involved *Chrysalis*. Without us, they lose that advantage. Do you think they can invade a city of a million people with a hundred and fifty soldiers carrying twenty-four pulse rifles? That's asking an awful lot."

"Don't they have the gunship in support?" Jaq asked.

"We haven't been able to raise the gunship," Amie interjected.

Jaq turned her attention back to the board. She had to maintain her situational awareness on the three fronts of her fight—the station, everything outside the station, and Bec in the lander. She didn't want to see the small ship impact the energy screen and be destroyed. She didn't want Bec killed. If he were to die, she preferred that it be her sending him out the airlock.

She thought of the irony of her misplaced anger at her genius brother. He'd kept them alive. He fixed things that no one else could fix. And now he was on his way to find the energy screen generator to figure it out.

Jaq wanted him to figure it out. Even if the war ended that very minute, they could use the technology for something. Flying through asteroid fields or exploring the outer reaches of the system. It was also the one military advancement in technology that was beyond what the Borwyn had discovered.

She wanted it, in case this wasn't the last battle.

Bec's lander eased close to the energy screen, then slowed until it stopped. Jaq had no idea how he knew where the screen reached, because the landers didn't have a great suite of sensors. They were limited at best, which was why they were flown by remote control, counting on the big ship's systems to see what was in and around the smaller ship's flight path.

The lander started moving again but perpendicular to its previous course.

Jaq was mesmerized by the small ship's movements. Bec knew something the rest of them did not. Jaq only had to figure out what it was.

The lander descended into the latticework of the massive structure. It worked its way through the support beams until it was inside the outer boundary of the energy screen, and then it continued to an airlock on the big ship.

"That ship is powered up with Malibor on board." Jaq wanted it to be a question, but she knew the answer. It was an active ship, although not all sections were completed. They'd built the new ship in such a way that the sections under construction didn't impact the spaceworthy nature of what remained. "That ship can fly, can't it."

Alby studied the images on the main screen. He was an engineer, but Bec and Teo were the ones who would know best. "I think so?" He made it sound like a question.

"Get Teo up here," Jaq ordered.

Amie called Engineering to deliver the summons.

The lander linked up to the airlock.

"No answer from the lander," Amie reported.

Jaq didn't expect that Bec would answer. He was singularly focused on finding the generator and learning its secrets. It was probably the most exciting thing in his life since his breakthrough with the ion drive.

"Get me Brad. I want an update." Jaq was losing patience, at least what little remained. This was going the wrong way. She had lost control.

"Malibor shuttles are leaving the station," Slade announced loudly to get everyone's attention.

"Move us where we can get a better look." Jaq gripped the support bar and prepared herself for the acceleration.

Ferd chose the main engines to get them in front of the shuttles. They'd get the best look from there.

Jaq didn't object. The Malibor had given her the finger.

"Gil, prepare defensive systems."

"We're hot," he confirmed. They had been hot from before they arrived at the station on the first pass. The repeaters were loaded and ready to deliver withering fire on anything that approached the ship. "We'll have to be close to be effective."

"Accommodate the defensive weapons, if you would, Mary. Put us where we need to be to blow all of those shuttles out of space."

Alby sucked air through his teeth. "I bet these are all civilians running for their lives because they believed the propaganda about how evil the Borwyn are. Do we want to prove them right?"

"Of course, you are correct," Jaq said, speaking slowly and enunciating each word as she fought her anger, something she had been able to keep under control previously. "We will not be shooting those shuttles unless they are filled with soldiers or make an aggressive move, like trying to ram us."

Chrysalis surged past the boxy, slow-moving vessels, inverted to slow, and then shifted orientation using thrusters to present a broadside to the shuttles.

"A channel, please." When Amie confirmed it was open, Jaq continued. "I thought we talked about this. Where do you think you're going?"

Unlike last time, they responded. The replies stomped on each other and descended into singular, unintelligible shouting.

"Only one of you gets to talk. You decide who. You have ten seconds to explain yourselves."

The number of voices reduced to three, who argued until only one remained.

"This is Captain Saul Win. These ships are returning civilians to Malipride. This is an evacuation of a warzone. Even the Borwyn should understand the humanitarian nature of that request."

"The Borwyn understand it far better than the Malibor," Jaq shot back. "But we are our actions and not our words. Civilians are authorized to evacuate to the spaceport outside Malipride, but understand, the spaceport has been attacked and facilities thereon are burning. We can see it from here."

"Then where will we go?" the captain snarled.

"Back to the station, which is what I told you to do thirty

minutes ago. Like I said, we already talked about this. Radio your people at the spaceport and see what they tell you." Jaq knew the radio station had been taken out because of the loss of datalinks to the space station. Slade had confirmed that on their first pass.

"We can't do that. Your soldiers are on board with ours. There will be fighting, and if it looks like we're losing, our people will destroy the station and take all of you with it."

"Amie, mute us, please," Jaq whispered. "Do you think they're serious?"

"No way," Taurus said.

"I think the hate is so strong, they'll blow up the station. I also think they're cowards, so you'll find military on those shuttles. Might be good information for Brad. I bet the station's defenders don't know they'll be sacrificed on the altar of Malibor expediency," Alby offered.

"My thoughts exactly," Jaq agreed. "Give me the channel."

Amie signaled it was live.

"Listen up. I need you all to go back to the station. Anyone defying this order will be considered a military target and destroyed. Go back to the station right now if you wish to save your own lives. Captain Hunter out."

Jaq moved across the bridge to the defensive weapons station. "Gil, can you skip some rounds off the lead ship's hull? High angle of incidence so they make a hellacious noise inside, but we don't penetrate the hull. I want to scare them back to the station."

"That's a tough one. A skip shot is a much smaller target on a small target. I can try to walk a few rounds into it. I could miss, Jaq. Are we ready to destroy one of those shuttles?" Gil looked uncomfortable.

"We're not ready to let the Malibor blow up this space station. I'm not ready to lose thirty-five Borwyn if we have a choice. I'd rather the Malibor sacrifice than us. How many Malibor are on each of those shuttles?"

Slade answered, "Twenty-five."

Jaq clenched her fists. She looked at the screen. The shuttles had stopped but weren't returning to the station.

"They're stopped and we're stopped, Gil. Take the shot."

"Yes, ma'am." Gil looked to Alby, who nodded.

Gil leaned into his system. The main screen changed to show a live view of the nearest shuttle.

A short stream of rounds flew past the lead shuttle by a wide margin. The distance narrowed through four subsequent shots. The fifth stream of rounds barely missed except for one that clipped the front corner and set the shuttle into a spin.

"Stop shooting!" came the frantic cry from the lead shuttle.

"Return to the station," Jaq replied emotionlessly. "It is in your hands to avoid further weapons fire."

"It is in *YOUR* hands, Borwyn."

"I'm glad we understand each other. Return to the station. Right now, please."

The channel screeched from an angry Malibor who crushed his mic. The channel turned into static.

"Shuttles are moving, Captain." Slade nodded and pointed at the main screen. The small armada was turning around and heading back to the space station.

"How do we keep them from trying that again?" Jaq wondered.

"Park *Chrysalis* on top of the station," Mary offered. "We can clamp us down. Block them completely. There's an airlock up there, too, but we'd have to build something to use it from the ship or access it using spacesuits."

"That airlock is the entire station away from the command center. It'd be better to block it off," Jaq said. "We don't need access to the station until we have complete control. Then we can use the closest airlock. Park a lander with explosives up here to keep the retractable section closed. I'd say use one without explosives, but we don't quite have one of those, do we?"

Alby's wry laugh punctuated the order. "Those lander bombs have caused us some grief, haven't they?"

"It was a good idea at the time. Make sure they're disconnected so we don't accidentally blow the top off the station." Jaq waved her hand, dismissing the issue.

Alby called Benjy and made the arrangements.

"As soon as the lander is in place, return us to our previous position to keep an eye on both Bec and the airlock through which our boarding team passed." Jaq returned to her seat and strapped herself in so she could steeple her fingers under her chin. She had put things back to a status quo that she found marginally acceptable.

Keeping the civilians on board the station reduced one risk while raising another. The risk of collateral damage had moved from the station itself to the Malibor civilians.

"Unable to raise Brad," Amie finally confirmed.

Jaq had forgotten that she asked Amie to get in touch.

The silence caused her too much anxiety. But the shuttles trying to leave suggested the Malibor crew were worried about losing the station. She embraced that theory to allay her concerns.

Teo appeared on the bridge. "You called?" she asked.

"Tell us about that ship, Teo."

The chief engineer smoothly flew across the bridge to lean down beside the captain. "I'm sorry. I don't know anything about that ship."

"Bec did, enough to steal a lander and take it over there. He's linked it to the airlock and boarded it, after maneuvering around and through the energy screen that it generates."

"I haven't seen Bec in days. That ship is generating the energy screen? That could come in handy."

"My thoughts exactly, but Bec going over there by himself? That wasn't in any plan."

"Why do you think I would know anything about that ship?"

"Because you're the best engineer on this ship. Look at it. Can it fly? What else can it do? What is its purpose?"

"I'll need some time." Teo pushed off and backstroked to the sensor section, where Slade gave her Donal's position to review the sensor information.

CHAPTER 4

Curiosity moves us forward.

Bec linked up to the airlock on the big ship. He cycled the system to equalize the pressure between the two vessels. It did so without Bec having to increase or decrease pressure or gas mix within the lander. The Malibor were using the exact same parameters as the Borwyn.

He knew that because the original Malibor starship technology was based on Borwyn designs and Borwyn specifications. He expected the new ship's energy screen was running off a mutually compatible power source. That's what the data from the scans suggested.

Bec had tapped into the sensor stations and accessed their data on the screen. It had piqued his interest until nothing else remained in his mind.

He figured Jaq had already won the war and beat the Malibor into submission. He had to be first onto this new ship if he were to get an unvarnished view of the technology. It irked him that he didn't design it first, but he was convinced that he could build it better.

The corridor beyond was empty, but the lights were on. The heat was at a reasonable temperature, warmer than they kept *Chrysalis*, but he had already known that. The energy screen only deflected particles, not other energy. The scans had been uninhibited. There was a crew on board, but minimal. He had counted fifty warm bodies, concentrated in Engineering and what he thought was the bridge.

Bec was on his way to the engineering section to talk with his fellow engineers. He wanted to find the smart one, the one who had devised the energy screen, so they could have a conversation at the highest level. Teo was that kind of person. Her bio-pack was genius, but it was biologically based, which he didn't care about. He would have never thought of it himself, nor would he have tried.

But the energy screen. That was right up his corridor.

The ship was static, but there was a light gravity that pulled him toward the deck plate. What made the ship look different was that it was oriented horizontally with fewer decks parallel to the engine. Bec should have assumed that they'd conquered the challenge of artificial gravity, too. He stopped to bounce on his boots after disengaging the magnetic clamps. He guessed the ship was at point-two gees. Enough to keep him oriented the right way but not so much that it would wear him down.

He guessed that the gravity would increase with forward momentum, but from what he'd seen, this ship had never left the shipyard. Everything remained theoretical, but the artificial gravity and the energy screen were both implemented and operational. Could the ship fly, too?

Bec expected it could and could fly well. So many technological leaps in one ship. This was what Jaq had expected when they left the outer reaches to return to Septimus, that the Malibor would have advanced technology. She had been surprised to find out that it was inferior to Bec's creation and other advances, like the improved E-mags.

Five civil wars had held them back. Resources that could have been used to propel their technology forward had been used to build standing armies and weapons for traditional combat. Instead of moving forward, they moved backward.

But they had been moving forward, only in secret. This ship was evidence of their progress.

Bec strolled along, careful not to launch himself into the overhead. He passed a crewman working inside a panel in the main corridor running down the vessel's centerline. He stared at Bec.

"Good morning. Engineering is this way?" Bec asked pleasantly. The man nodded. Bec continued on his way. He took in the austerity of the ship's corridor and those spaces he could see into. It was not unlike *Chrysalis*. Utilitarian. Industrial. Sanitary even, before the rebuilt ship engaged the Malibor, then it became scarred and pitted. It lost its new smell. They ran out of paint to hide the damage. The look became inconsequential compared to the utility. Bec liked the Malibor ship. New and useful.

He especially liked the artificial gravity. So much new technology. A double-sized hatch was open into the engineering spaces beyond. Unlike the usual design where Engineering was toward the engines, this one was almost midships. The command deck was one level up and a little forward, but also mostly midships.

There was a great deal of steel and voids between the outer hull and the vulnerable areas.

The ship would be over a thousand meters long once finished. It was immense compared to the Borwyn cruiser. The flat shape meant it had more cubic meters of internal space. Far more. It also looked more intimidating with its aircraft style versus the traditional cylindrical form. Artificial gravity gave them that option.

Bec waved when he entered the engineering space. Two people stopped to look at him, and then two more, until the entire crew working there stared at him.

"Is your chief engineer available? I'd like to talk with him about the energy screen and the artificial gravity." Bec gripped his hands behind his back.

"Have we been taken over?" someone asked.

"No one told us that we've lost!" another cried. "I didn't feel the explosions. The Borwyn must have a secret weapon of terrible power."

Bec screwed up his face. "The what? I just want to talk to your chief engineer. I'm sure we have a lot in common."

"We won't go quietly!" A younger man jumped from a first-level catwalk to land on the main engineering deck. He carried an oversized spanner.

"No one is asking you to go anywhere. Keep working. Don't you have stuff to do?" Bec wondered. "You all seemed pretty busy. This won't take long, and then I'll be out of your hair."

The young man looked to the others, hands up and shrugging his confusion.

"I'm the chief engineer," a voice from behind Bec said.

Bec turned to find an older, heavy man with his arms across his chest. He looked uncomfortable.

"I'd like to talk to you about your energy screen and artificial gravity. Those are magnificent technological achievements. You should be proud."

The man stared at Bec. "You're Borwyn."

Bec nodded. "So?"

"How'd you get here?" the chief asked. He gestured to someone behind Bec.

Bec glanced over his shoulder. The young engineer was climbing a ladder to get back to where he'd been working.

"I walked because of your most excellent artificial gravity."

"Not here-here, but here, as in on this ship."

"I brought a lander over from *Chrysalis*. What do you call this ship, by the way?"

The chief engineer shook his head. "This is *Epica*, the greatest ship to ever exist."

"I believe it—once it's finished, that is. Shall we?" Bec gestured toward the hatch.

"Shall we what? And how did you get a lander through the screen? Lander. I'm assuming that's a small ship of some sort. And what's a *Chrysalis*?"

"*Chrysalis* is the flagship of the Borwyn fleet. A lander is a fragile craft but able to land on planets and return to the ship. Your energy screen has significant gaps that are easily exploited. I can help with that, I have no doubt. Let's take a look at it, shall we?"

The chief engineer unfolded his arms and let them hang at his sides while he stared at the deck.

"I still don't understand why you're here. Am I supposed to surrender to you or something? I haven't heard anything from the captain. Maybe we should go see him."

"I don't care to see the captain. He's probably ignorant when it comes to the finite details of the systems we work with. I find ignorant people tedious. I'm finding this conversation annoying. Just show me where it is and I'll look it over myself. I brought a system analyzer to help me understand the components, but I have to have physical access. Now, if you wouldn't mind. My patience is growing short. Are you smart enough to talk with me or not? If not, then point me to someone who is, like the one who designed the energy screen and the artificial gravity system."

Bec had tried to be pleasant for as long as he could, giving Jaq and Teo's advice about being nice to people a chance, but it hadn't worked. He had resorted to intimidating them with his intellect. It was a tried-and-true way to get to someone who could carry on a conversation about a complex technical subject.

The man stood there, staring in disbelief.

"Time is linear no matter how much we'd like it not to be. Until we can master it, if we waste time, we're not getting it back. Chop, chop." Bec emphasized his point by chopping one hand into the open palm of his other.

"Come with me," the chief engineer conceded.

Bec would have asked his name if he cared to know it, but

he did not. The man was a means to an end, nothing more. He struck Bec as a lackey and not the genius who created the device.

"Artificial gravity is my thing," the chief engineer said over his shoulder while leading Bec away from Engineering. They were walking aft toward the airlock where the lander was located.

Bec knew where he was because he had just walked it. He passed the crewman still working. "How's it going?" Bec asked, although he didn't care. He'd seen Teo engage with the crew using that phrase. She usually stopped and smiled as well. The crew responded well to her. He stopped and smiled.

"It's hard work. I need to concentrate," the man replied.

"Sure. If you need a hand, let me know." He parroted what Teo would tell the crew. They politely declined every time. She'd walk away still smiling.

That didn't happen here. "Are you serious?"

"Yes," Bec lied. The chief engineer crossed his arms and stared at Bec.

"Right here. This switching panel isn't switching. I can't find anything wrong with it." He pointed at the offending technology.

Bec looked at it. It was a circuit board, more advanced than anything on *Chrysalis* but still straightforward. It looked to be reversible, but the programming could need tweaking. Then again, he said that it should have worked.

"Try flipping it over. That'll reboot the firmware." Bec was winging it. He had no idea.

The man pulled it out, carefully turned it over, and placed it back into its slot.

The lights within the panel blinked before turning a solid green. The same light pattern the Borwyn used. Green was good.

"I'll be bin-funckled," the man stated. "Thank you, sir. I've wasted two hours here doing what you did in thirty seconds."

Bec felt like the intellectual superhero he knew himself to be. He beamed with the praise.

"Get to your next task. I'm sure there's plenty to do to bring *Epica* up to speed."

"There is, sir. Thank you, sir." The man looked to the chief engineer for approval, but he didn't get it. He only received a condescending stare.

"Shall we?" Bec asked.

"Back to that, huh? Yeah, sure." The chief walked them to the next interior doorway and walked through. A single panel stood between two cylinders attached to a network of chrome piping. "The anti-grav system."

"Gravity?" Bec asked.

"Anti-gravity. It pushes away instead of pulling down. We use it for the star drive engine, too. If my calculations are correct, we should be able to achieve acceleration of up to twenty-five gees."

"That would crush the crew," Bec said.

"Anti-gravity within the ship. It isolates the crew from the rigors of acceleration. The crew can go about their business unhindered even at twenty-five gees. This ship will be invincible."

"That it will," Bec agreed. *Too bad you didn't launch it before you lost the war*, he thought.

"I was hoping to see it fly. Damn. Am I your prisoner?" the chief engineer wondered.

"No. We're not playing that game. Cooperation is your key to survival. I don't see any reason why anyone aboard this ship needs to die," Bec said, looking around to check if anyone was listening.

"Thank you, sir," the chief engineer replied.

Bec thought, *I could get used to this.* "Tell me how it works, this anti-gravity generator."

The chief started to explain when two men walked in through the hatch.

"What do we have here? Is that a Borwyn? On my ship?" He strode forward and grabbed Bec's arm, nearly yanking it out of the socket to turn him around. "And what are you doing?"

Bec stared blankly at him with a hint of disdain, as he did with people who annoyed him.

"We didn't surrender?" The chief engineer was confused.

"We're fighting, you moron! Grab him and prepare the ship to get underway. We're leaving the yard."

CHAPTER 5

The time to act usually comes before you're sure it's the time to act.

Max froze but only for a moment. He wanted to see what they were up against. He had superior firepower, but only if he could use it. Were they aiming at him and ready to fire? He hadn't forgotten that Deena was armed, too. Were two well-practiced soldiers sufficient against four untested souls who were probably scared as well?

"Please, don't shoot!" he called out, raising one arm. The other held the pulse rifle and blanket.

Deena moved laterally away from Max. "I'm not with him. Please, don't shoot."

The soldiers relaxed when they saw her face.

In that moment, Max brought his pulse rifle up to snap-fire into the group of four soldiers. He brought his raised hand down to meet his rifle and aimed to rapid-fire six more times.

The soldiers never managed to get off a single shot. The pulse rifle echoed down the empty streets.

"We need to go," Max urged, but Deena was already running. She headed straight for the soldiers to pick up one of their weapons and extra reloads. She hugged the rifle to her side and jogged down the street to turn hard at the first corner. Max was right behind her.

"Did you need that?" he asked.

"If we're going to fight our way out of the city, yes. There are more soldiers out there."

"Where's the nearest wall?" Max asked.

"A couple blocks. This way." Deena took off at a dead sprint, carrying the rifle before her. Max carried the blanket over his rifle, but he also had to carry it before him. It was the only way he could keep his balance.

A civilian peeked out their back door.

"Get inside and keep your head down!" Deena shouted. She jumped toward him and he fell inside, slamming the door behind him.

She continued past. Max caught up with her. "Nice," he said between breaths.

They reached the wall but stopped and backed up.

Someone was walking along on top, but they had been looking out. At the sound of footsteps, he turned around, but it was dark where Max and Deena had been. He leaned forward to get a better look. He stopped searching the shadows and returned to looking into the fields beyond.

"I wish I had one of the bows," Max whispered.

"It would come in handy right about now, but there's no

way we would have made it this far carrying what we're carrying and a bow," Deena replied with a soft laugh.

Max smiled. "I missed you." He leaned around the building to check the soldier.

"I can disarm him," Deena said. "I'm a woman, and they discount us."

Max clenched his jaw. He didn't want to agree but knew he had no choice. "Good for us. Bad for them. I'll cover you." He took a knee. Deena braced her rifle against the wall and loosened the hand blaster in the back of her trousers.

She kissed Max, but with a promise of something more rather than good-bye. She had no intention of dying on that wall.

She walked slowly through the darkness, hiding in plain sight and using the slow speed to mask her movement. Nothing would catch the soldier's eye.

Deena reached the wall and pressed her back against the cool stone. Her blaster clinked softly. She held her breath and waited. She couldn't see the soldier above. He didn't lean over to look down. She listened carefully for any sign that he was walking.

Max showed her the okay sign with his hand, but she couldn't see him either.

Deena waited ten more minutes before taking another step. She needed her heart to slow down. When her hand no longer trembled from the adrenaline rush, she walked along the wall where the soldier wouldn't see her until she reached the stairs up. She had to climb over a rudimentary gate, but it was low and had been hastily installed. She walked up the steps and waited.

"How about a light," she said into the darkness without exposing herself.

"Halt! Who goes there?" The soldier brought his rifle up and tried to aim at the sound of the voice.

"Just a concerned young woman looking for the warmth of a soldier to protect her," Deena cooed.

"Get out of here! Take one more step and I'll shoot you." He was shouting. That wouldn't do.

Max aimed at the figure outlined above him. He squeezed the trigger, and the pulse rifle barked. The soldier was blasted over the wall and disappeared into the darkness beyond.

Max picked up Deena's rifle and ran for the stairs. "Sorry, but I couldn't let him shoot you," Max whispered.

Deena took her rifle. She didn't dispute that the soldier had been more excited than she was comfortable with. She thought the sultry voice would appeal to him, but it didn't.

Now, they had to run for it.

"Can you see a way down?" Max asked since Deena was first to the top of the wall.

"No. There are rocks here." She crouched and moved quickly down the wall. She wondered where the next soldier would be. He had to be there. They wouldn't put one by himself.

There wouldn't be too much distance between them.

Deena stopped and studied what she could see of the ground below. "Good enough." She eased over the top and executed a spider hang, clinging with one hand and one foot, holding her rifle below her. She let go and brought her legs together, knees bent before she hit to roll. She landed on dirt and rolled into a boulder. She grunted from the impact.

"Right there," she gasped. "It's good. Try not to roll."

They'd practiced the spider hang to come out of trees from higher branches without injuring themselves.

Max executed the same hang-and-drop. He didn't roll as he landed on all-fours. He stood gingerly. "I'm good," he announced.

"Hey!" a voice called from the top of the wall, a hundred meters away.

"Let's get out of here." Max slapped Deena on the shoulder to make sure she was okay. She grunted her confirmation.

Max moved into a jumble of rocks, having to climb over one half his height because there was no path. He wasn't sure this would lead to a cliff, but it was all they had. They moved carefully from rock to rock. Max ducked behind one that provided cover from the wall. Deena joined him right as a light shone on the space where they'd just been.

They were in the boulder's shadow. They tried to control their breathing as if the soldier was close enough to hear them. They'd covered twenty to thirty meters away from the wall. It had been rough going and wouldn't get easier.

The light continued to dance across the area. Near to far, the soldier searched.

"He's not coming down here," Max whispered.

"They'll send someone when they see the body." Deena leaned into Max's chest. "The nearest gate out is a thousand meters away or farther, somewhere in the spaceport."

"We're that close?"

Deena nodded. Max felt it more than saw it.

The light stopped panning the area. They waited and listened carefully. The light stayed off.

Max risked a glance over the boulder. He could see nothing on the top of the wall. He leaned down, waited a moment, then looked toward the wall once more.

When he was satisfied the guard was finished looking, he gestured that it was time to go and for Deena to lead the way.

She picked her way carefully between boulders when she could and over them when she had to.

They made good progress and were soon far from the wall, but the open approaches funneled them toward the spaceport, which was the wrong way from the forest where Crip had instructed them to go.

They were hell and gone from where they needed to be, but to survive the night, they needed to get as far from their eventual pursuers as they could get.

Once they reached open ground, they decided to run. There was no other choice. Deena ran slower than Max, but she was hunched and favoring her side. Max had to slow, turning their progress from a run to a crawl.

Max let her put her arm over his shoulder, and that improved their speed but not by much.

"I got hurt more than I thought," Deena said apologetically. She favored her left side, hunching more and more with each step.

"We'll look at it in the daylight. Let's find a depression to hide within and stop doing any more damage to it." Max held her closely. Her pain was his pain.

Max checked over his shoulder as they hobbled over the fairly even terrain. He looked ahead for shadows that were darker than the darkness. He found one in less than two minutes. They angled toward it to find it was only a meter deep, but enough to hide them from wandering eyes and spotlights.

They laid down together. They had no ice or anything to put on it. The best Max could think of was to bind it, but they had only what they carried, which included the radio.

Max dug into the pack and removed it. "I need to check in," he said. They stayed prone while he set up the radio, raising the antenna above the lip to give it better range.

He sent the digital contact code and waited. He repeated the process every two minutes. Twenty minutes later, he received the confirmation. Max didn't want to push his luck. He sent the code for 'all is well and in a safe location.' He powered down after Glen's company acknowledged receipt.

"There we go. They've been notified that we're safe. It's the most I was willing to do. I don't want to lead them to us, in case the Malibor intel group doesn't buy into the hype of a civil war and focuses on looking for Borwyn infiltrators."

"They are paranoid enough to believe their own people are coming for them, but then again, they're also the ones who know the truth that the Borwyn have returned because Jaq told them we were back."

"*We*," Max repeated with emphasis. "Why don't you try to relax and get some sleep. It's been a long day."

Deena grimaced while she shifted around, trying to get comfortable. She settled onto her right side and breathed shallowly until it slowed. Max was happy to see her get some sleep. Any sleep. He had no way to comfort her. No medicines. No bandages. They were ill-suited to be on the run, but like too many things in life, they had few choices. The only one that mattered was to survive.

CHAPTER 6

Winning is mindset combined with action.

Crip shook his head. "They're on the run, but where are they that they're now safe?"

"Outside the city?" Glen ventured.

Eleanor shrugged. "That's what I'd guess, but where? He didn't say anything about meeting us, either."

"I can't even fathom where they are," Crip said. "Next time they contact us, we need to use voice. If they escaped the city, then they're probably going to need help. Food. Water. But we can only help them if we know where they are."

Crip was agitated. He'd lost control. He needed Max as his sounding board, but Max was doing what he needed to do.

Would Crip do the same for Taurus?

That's what grated on his soul. He didn't think so. He was married to the idea of the greater good. They could enjoy the distractions of each other's company, but only if those times didn't take away from their mission of liberating Septimus.

Crip nodded to Glen and Eleanor. "They'll be fine. They're adults and well-armed. They'll call if they need help. The question we have to answer is, how can the assault brigade best be employed to support the liberation of Septimus?"

"Look at you," Glen said. "I wish I knew, but when we called your captain, we got our asses handed to us. I'm inclined to wait, although I would like to update the leadership of New Pridal."

"Do you have directional comm?" Crip thought they'd used it before.

"We do. I brought the unit with us."

"What else do we have to do?" Crip asked.

Glen groaned and threw his head back to stare at the night sky. "We're running back and forth, always missing the last thing. That being said, we've already broadcast from this point to Max and Deena on their last transmission."

"But we haven't been struck since that, so we can assume they didn't target us. We can move five kilometers up the treeline and transmit from there. It might be better to relocate anyway because of that cut. It's the main trail from the city. They should assume that we have the end of it covered."

"Too much logic that took us too long to arrive at. You'd think we've turned our brains off," Eleanor said.

"It's the frustration of not being able to do anything while a lot of stuff is happening. None of us are the sit-back-and-watch type," Crip replied.

"And Max and Deena are your friends. We get it. Plan approved. Let's move the company south one kilometer while we take the radio five klicks north to talk with the mountain." Glen clapped his hands and gestured. Crip and Eleanor moved away to deliver to the orders.

Fifteen minutes later, everyone except Hammer, Anvil, Ava, and Mia were moving. Those four remained to watch the end of the cut.

Crip and Glen headed north with the company's radio operator. They hurried along using game trails without rushing. They didn't want to overdo it. It was dark, and they were going to cover the same distance when returning after they made the transmission.

"Are we too cautious?" Crip asked.

"Better safe than wrong," Glen replied. "I've lived my whole life doing everything I could to limit our exposure, give the Malibor nothing they could sink their teeth into. When they found us, we fought, and we died. We're far better off when we find them first. To do that, we have to be silent or never stay in one place for long."

"We haven't seen intra-atmospheric craft. You talked about missiles and bombings. When's the last time one of those happened?" Crip pressed.

"Before my time. We learned what not to do and we don't do it. Maybe they can't attack us anymore. Maybe they can't use radio direction finding equipment. From what you've said, I think they took too great of a risk sending such a force to Sairvor. They have handicapped themselves to a level where they may not be able to recover. If we keep hitting them, they may not be able to respond." Glen put his hand on Crip's shoulder. "I'm hopeful. What does the end of war look like? I can't fathom. We've been at war my whole life."

"I grew up on a spaceship. I'm on Septimus now. Anything is possible. I'm hopeful, too. But I want to do more."

"You want to be the hero in your story, Crip? I don't blame you. We name our schools in New Pridal after our heroes. Maybe it's time to add new names to the mix."

"Captain Jaq Hunter before anyone else. Even if we lose, she made a difference in all our lives."

"I think we should talk to the ship again, even if we catch her in the middle of something. There has to be someone who can talk to us. I want to know how they're doing. More importantly, I want to know what they're doing next."

"We can talk about the same things over and over again, or we can do something about it." Crip looked around conspiratorially and then whispered, "I brought the radio to talk with the ship."

Glen snorted. "What are we waiting for?"

Crip set up the equipment and checked it over. He'd seen Larson do it enough times. It was a simple system. He aligned the dish by eye, aiming it at the visible moon.

"*Chrysalis*, this is the ground combat team, requesting information update."

"This is *Chrysalis*. Standby."

"Come on!" Crip blurted.

"They could be in the middle of a big fight. Do you want to distract them?" Glen said.

"You were on board with this two minutes ago." Crip

wasn't the only one who wanted to know. "There has to be someone on board who is not engaged and can talk to us."

"Crip," Jaq said over the radio, "Sorry about being so short with you, but there's a lot of moving parts up here. Bec is on the big ship that we haven't been able to identify, and Teo is trying to figure out what it is and what it does. We just chased all the personnel shuttles back into the spindle void. They were trying to evacuate the civilians, supposedly, but they also admitted that they were willing to blow up the station. I figured they wouldn't if the civvies were on board. In any case, we haven't been able to raise Brad, but I don't think they'd have tried to evacuate the station if he wasn't making progress. We're at a standoff distance to watch the station, the shuttles, and the shipyard. But otherwise, we're doing a whole lot of nothing up here except worrying."

"Same here, Jaq." Crip updated her on everything he knew. At the end, he felt stupid for bothering her. He wasn't sure what he expected to hear, but it was same thing Glen had said earlier. Sometimes, there's nothing to do but wait. "What do you need from us?"

"Be ready to move to the city. If Brad is successful, we'll send the order from here for them to surrender, but they may not receive the message because the comm station has been destroyed. You may have to relay our message."

"We can do that from here, Jaq. We've talked with Deena inside the city from the forest."

"Then you don't need to move, but keep the radios on. We won't be able to communicate on a schedule because I have no timeline. Anything else, Crip?"

"I'm sorry to bother you. I was hoping for more."

"I'm sorry there isn't more information. You're doing a good job, Crip. I have no concerns that when we decide what we need, you'll execute in the best way to accomplish the mission. Until then, the battle is joined. Keep your eyes open and head down."

"Victory is ours, Jaq. Crip out." He looked at the radio. "We can't quite keep it on while we're moving, can we?"

"That's going to be a challenge." Glen turned to the radio operator. "We're going to make the call to the mountain from here and then we'll double-time it back to company. I figure we're at least two klicks from the cut, which means three klicks from the new deployment site. It's going to have to be good enough. We can't take the radio offline for any longer than necessary."

"Set it up," Crip conceded. "Let's get this done and get going."

The radio operator set up the unit and initiated the contact sequence. The mountain responded almost immediately with the challenge. The radio operator sent the appropriate response.

"Solid comm, Commander," the operator reported.

Glen picked up the microphone. "First Company, reporting. Movement complete. Standing ready to move to the city should the order be given."

"The order will not be given. Not after those ingrates stole the gunship and flew away. Should any of the spacers show their faces, they're to be arrested immediately and secured for return to us. Do you understand your orders, Commander Owain?"

Glen's mouth dropped open and he stared at Crip. He didn't answer.

"Did you hear me?"

Glen keyed the microphone. "Loud and clear. Arrest the spacers when I see them. As soon as possible, General. I better get going since this changes things." Glen reached over the radio operator and shut the unit off.

Crip's lip curled. He looked at the stars. "Up there, we have Jaq fighting on three fronts. Down here, we're fighting ourselves. Are we any better than the Malibor?"

Glen held out his hand. "We're not the Malibor, and I have no intention of arresting you. To win this war, we have to work together." They shook hands. "And from the sound of it, I don't think we'll get any support from New Pridal. The general may change his mind after he gets some sleep, or maybe he won't. We're on our course, Crip. The next time we go to the mountain, it better be to announce the Borwyn victory. Otherwise, we won't be going back."

"Does that mean we're cut off from supplies? No more horses or eggs or ammunition?"

"That's what I'm thinking. So, the elders didn't give permission for *Matador* to execute the attacks that Jaq needed. No risk, no exposure, but we know the truth. No risk, no reward."

"May Septiman give us strength. I'm sorry to put you in this position, Glen. We lost control the second Max went after Deena. I'm sorry for that."

"What?" Glen scoffed. "That didn't affect anything. From everything I've seen and heard, sounds like the Malibor are the ones who have lost control. All we have to do is keep our cool."

They collected their gear and stepped into the night, taking their first steps together as fugitives from the authority operating out of New Pridal.

―――

"Can anyone hear me?" Tram gasped. The control console held him in place under the collapsed outer hull. He felt his way in the darkness to a gap. He twisted sideways, wincing before he cried out in pain. He repeated himself, "Can anyone hear me?"

A groan from the overhead side, toward the front of the ship which was now ahead of him since the ship was on its side. There was nothing from the engine room behind him.

Tram pulled himself to his feet. He thought he was standing on the viewscreen. It didn't matter. The ship would never fly again. He climbed toward the hatch near the airlock with access to the engine room and felt his way ahead. He crawled through the hatch and took one step before slipping in something wet.

"No. Please say it isn't." He took a knee to search with his hands through the blood and gore of his friend. Kelvis's body had already turned cold. How long had he been out? Tram wept softly for a brief spell before he remembered that there had been a groan from the upper deck.

The women!

Tram pulled himself through the hatch and walked on

the wall to get to the upper deck hatch, where he crawled through.

"Hold on. I'll try to get to you." Tram felt like he'd been beaten, but the sharp stabs of pain were already fading into a single desire to not move. The pain in his head threatened to make him puke. It would have blinded him in broad daylight.

Tram forced his way forward, straddling the ladder to get through the hatch and into the forward compartment. He stumbled through the wreckage to get forward far enough to reach where the sound was coming from.

Two warm bodies were lying together on a side cabinet.

"Ladies, ladies!"

"It hurts," Evelyn mumbled.

Tram cradled her head. "Where are you hurt?"

"All over," she gasped between breaths. He checked on Sophia, feeling his way along her arm to her neck. She had no pulse. He couldn't reach her chest to begin compressions. He felt her lips.

"Sophia's not breathing."

"She stopped a while ago," Evelyn whispered. "Did you find Kelvis?"

She seemed to already know the answer.

Tram was crushed by the losses of his wife and his friend. He didn't reply for a while. He sat there, focused on breathing, nothing more.

"Tram," Evelyn whispered. "Please, help me."

He shook himself out of his reverie. Two of them had survived the attack and the crash. "We probably need to get out of here. If they sent someone after us, I'd be surprised if they're not waiting outside. Still, we can't stay here."

Tram felt down her body to find what was holding her down and couldn't find anything. "I'm going to pull you upright," he said.

She screamed and started sobbing when he pulled, but she hung on and he kept pulling until he could get an arm around her waist. They stood like that until she stopped panting.

"Is anything broken?"

Evelyn calmed enough to answer. "Left leg, lower, and left arm, upper. My harness came free, and I was bounced around when we hit the ground."

"Is that what happened to Sophia?" Tram asked as they straddled his wife.

"No. She was trapped in place when the walls caved in."

Equipment had torn free with the twisting and warping of the hull. The forward end took the worst of it, but in the engine room, the power supply had not been welded in place. It had been strapped in, and that hadn't been enough. It must have broken free and whipped around with the violence of the impact. That had nearly cut Kelvis in half.

"We need to get out of the ship," Tram said, focusing on one single thing to help them through the next few moments. After that, they could decide what they would do next. He stepped on a pulse rifle. He backed up quickly, and Evelyn nearly fell. "Better take this. I think we're close to the forest where we can hide, but we'll need to protect ourselves."

"We can't even walk," Evelyn grumbled.

"No choice," Tram said softly. "Lean on me with your broken left arm to take the pressure off your broken left leg."

Evelyn snorted and gasped to end it. "Is that a joke?"

"It's the best I have in the dark and with a crushed skull."

Evelyn felt his head until she touched the bloody mess on the side. "At least it's only your head."

Tram smiled in the darkness. It was the way of the warrior to make jokes in the darkest of moments.

"Ahhh!" Evelyn cried out as Tram straightened and put pressure on her arm. "That hurt a lot."

He pulled her body tightly against his and stepped away from Sophia. Evelyn grunted but managed to stay upright as she tossed a leg over the body in the wreckage. They made it to the hatch, which Evelyn hung on to while Tram crawled through. Helping Evelyn to the airlock took two tries and taking Septiman's name in vain.

Opening the outer hatch wasn't as easy as Tram had hoped. It had warped as well. He checked the port-side hatch, and it was wedged in the ground. He stopped by the bridge and pulled off a support leg. He returned to where he'd left Evelyn, gently moving her back to give himself room to lever the hatch open.

It took three separate efforts to get it open enough to get through. The good news was that they were only a meter off the ground. It was also night. "We'd been out for twelve hours."

Evelyn had lost track of time, too. It was a pain-infested blur.

He helped her through and sat her down to lean against the cool metal of the ship before reaching back in to grab the pulse rifle. Around the ship, he couldn't see any terrain features like trees or hills, but on the other side and behind the gunship, he could see lights from the city. They weren't as far away as he would have liked, but there weren't any Malibor soldiers waiting for them, either.

"Maybe *Chrysalis* followed up our attack and the soldiers are preparing to defend the city, or they've already surrendered," Tram posited. He sat down heavily, grunting when he impacted the dirt.

"What else is on the ship that we need?" Evelyn asked.

Tram started to shake his head, then froze. He held his head in both hands and groaned in pain. "Don't move head. Important safety tip."

"That bad?" Evelyn replied softly. "Is there a medical kit in the ship? Maybe we shouldn't let the other pulse rifle fall into Malibor hands."

"They're not out here, and I don't know how many trips I can make back inside. Not right now. I've been awake for a grand total of fifteen minutes, or that's what it feels like, and I'm exhausted."

"I know how you feel," Evelyn said. She hugged Tram to her with her good arm. "It's cold out here."

"I'm going to have to go inside again, aren't I?" Tram started to stand and stopped. He sat down. "In a few. I need to rest."

He closed his eyes and let his chin drop to his chest. He concentrated on nothing more than his breathing, trying to clear his mind from the hurricane winds within.

"Something hit us," he said. "I didn't just crash the ship."

"Why are you thinking like that? Of course something hit us. I thought it was going to rip the ship apart. Better to crash and limp away. Well, not all of us. Maybe it wasn't better to crash."

"Don't talk like that. Septiman chooses our time. It's not ours yet. We will mourn our spouses when the time is right. Until then, we owe it to them to survive. I'll go back in and find a blanket and the other pulse rifle."

"It was with us," Evelyn said.

Tram pushed himself up the side of the hull until he was standing. He took careful steps but even with gentle placement of each foot, it felt like his head would explode. Each minor shock sent dazzling arrays of sparks and color before his eyes.

He closed them. They weren't much help in the darkness, but that didn't stop the fireworks. He climbed inside and retraced his steps to get into the forward compartment. He felt around, taking care not to cut himself on the jagged metal. He stopped when he passed Sophia to rest his hand on her cooling form. He decided to take the light jacket she was wearing. It wasn't a blanket, but it was something.

Tram wrapped the coat around his hand while he continued to search. He found the pulse rifle under a cabinet where there was no hope of removing it. He took its power pack and reloads, stuffing them into his combat vest, which was mostly empty nowadays.

More important than the pulse rifle was their toolkit. Inside, he found an operational flashlight. The beam of light pierced deep into his brain. He cursed himself for looking at the light when he turned it on. He expected it not to work. He was happy it did, but the pain dulled the opportunity for joy. He scanned the area for supplies and found four Malibor meal packs and one blanket.

With his arms full, he made to leave the space but

decided to take one last look at Sophia. The damage done to her body was clear in the light. He turned away. That would be the last image in his mind of her. He regretted looking. With the light, it was easier to get out, but it amazed him they had made it in the darkness. The ship was destroyed. The fact that anyone survived was a miracle.

He draped the blanket over Evelyn and wrapped Sophia's jacket around his front. They leaned on each other in the dark of the growing night. They had nowhere to go and couldn't have gotten there if they did. Not until dawn showed them what they were up against.

Not until they decided what to do.

CHAPTER 7

Observe, fire, talk, move.

Brad hunched down in the stairwell. If they climbed higher, they'd move farther from the command center. Apparent gravity would be less the closer they came to the central ring, the one adjacent to the void of the spindle.

The Phillips family moved into the area with the cabling. Brad stopped them.

"Some of this stuff is live." He pointed to cables that ended with scorch marks. Most didn't, although Brad couldn't say if any of it was harmless.

"We figured all of it was live," the elder Phillips said. "Better safe than sorry."

"Can you cut it with plasma?"

"Cutting on live wires is strongly discouraged according to any safety measures we've ever embraced. That being said, we can cut from the top down. Live wires falling on live wires should prove to be exciting."

"Make sure you're not grounded. Path of least resistance and all that. How long do you think it'll take to clear this corridor? The command center should be on the other side of what we can see."

"An hour? Maybe two." Phillips leaned back when he made his prediction, as if Brad would be angry.

"We'll hold off the legions of evil until you've given us clear access from this end. We'll also look for an alternate way in, which gives us an alternate way out, too."

"It's nice to have options," Phillips replied. "If you don't mind, we'll get started."

"Do not get yourselves fried. I don't want to explain to Jaq how I sparked her best welders." Brad waved and returned to the stairwell. He sent an order down the chain. "Twelve soldiers to secure this stairwell, four to provide security for the two clearing the corridor, and I'll take the rest with me to look for an alternate route. Edgerrin, you stay here and keep in touch with me. If the Malibor try to counterattack, call me and we'll counterattack the counterattack."

"Splitting our forces, Captain," Edgerrin said.

"It's what Jaq cautioned me against doing," Brad admitted. "But I don't see standing around and making ourselves targets as a viable alternative. We can't budge those bulkheads, but we can cut lots of wires."

"How about tapping into the control system and activating an override?"

"Do what you can. If overriding is an option, then let's make it happen. Check in with Phillips. He's been working on the bulkhead overrides on *Chrysalis*. If you have someone who can drive a plasma cutter, then swap out. Phillips will be able to help."

"Why didn't we bring more engineers from *Chrysalis*?" Edgerrin wondered.

"Because they're fighting the war. We're fighting one small battle. They have it all and need every asset available to them. That's why we pulled the volunteers from New Septimus as the next combat team. *Chrysalis* had no one to spare. We should feel lucky that they lent us the Phillips boys."

Edgerrin left to make the arrangements with the soldiers. He kept his head down and rushed from one spot to another as if there were incoming fire.

It's how Brad would have moved. The attack had gone too easily so far. They hadn't come under fire like he'd expected, despite Jaq's argument that they might not have weapons aboard the station. The Malibor's distrust of each other was so great, it handicapped them.

The real enemy had arrived, and the Malibor couldn't protect themselves except with tricks and traps.

"The sooner we can get to the command center, the better off we'll be," Brad said to himself.

The boarding party reoriented itself to cover the stairs and the outer ring along with the second deck where Phillips and his son were working. They had established a foothold on the space station. Brad took a moment to study the bulkheads. Utilitarian with markings that showed ring, deck, and quarter. They wouldn't have to question where they were. There was a map at every hatch.

Edgerrin returned. "The last of them are coming forward.

We don't have anyone at the hatch, but it is within sight of our rear guard."

"Look at this." Brad pointed to the label on the access to the stairway.

"All the hatches have them," he replied. "No reason to ever get lost."

"Exactly. Make sure everyone knows. Looks like our rally point is *Ring Nineteen, Section Twenty-four, Deck Two, Q-One*."

"Three decks per ring? That means fifty-seven total decks. We'll be spread thin." Edgerrin looked skeptical.

"That's an understatement, Edgerrin. That's why we're trying to take over the command center. We'll control what controls the rest."

"Good luck finding a way around."

Brad waved over his shoulder as he headed up the stairs. A large group of rifle-carrying refugees from New Septimus fell in behind him. Brad walked to the first landing, where six soldiers were arrayed, three by three. They nodded to Brad as he passed.

Two steps up and Brad decided to hug the bulkhead, stepping carefully, toe to heel. He had a sense of foreboding. He motioned for those behind him to stop. He listened. Boots scraping ahead. Material rustling.

His subconscious must have registered the sound outside of the other noises he heard.

The scrape and squeal of metal on metal. A grunt. The impact of something heavy hitting the stairs. It bounced past Brad.

"Grenade!" It skipped past. Two reached for it and

missed. Most turned toward the bulkhead and covered their heads. One young man threw himself at it and shoved it under his body. It blew up, tossing his body a meter into the air. He settled onto the stairs, a broken mess.

In the instant throes of shock, a second grenade hit the stairs.

Brad reacted with nearly unnatural speed. He grabbed the grenade off the first bounce, spun around, and sent it back up the stairs to bounce off the bulkhead before hitting something soft and exploding. Screams of pain followed the blast.

Brad ran up the stairs. The theory of an unarmed crew had been incorrect. They had deadly weapons that included worse than he imagined. In that moment, he decided on the need to deliver overwhelming force to the enemy.

He jumped across the next landing, aiming his pulse rifle into the area ahead. Two Malibor security guards stood at the front of a group. They tried to duck, but Brad was already firing. Sending more rounds up the stairs than was prudent. The bloody smears on the bulkhead marked where the two Malibor had been. Their lifeless bodies had fallen onto the stairs where he could no longer see them. He backed up, aiming into the gap above where he could no longer see any other Malibor.

The Borwyn soldiers eased up behind him, hurrying as much as they could while being careful and increasing the spacing between them.

Brad changed his aim to the metal stairs above him. He thought the rounds from the pulse rifle would penetrate. If he was wrong and they bounced back, he and his team would suffer greatly. He aimed and fired. The first round cut through, leaving a neat little hole. He walked the rounds up the stairs.

"Fire!" he shouted over his shoulder. The handful of soldiers in the space behind him, and with an angle at the stairs, took aim and fired in a cacophony of echoes and shearing metal.

Screams from above punctuated their success. Brad waved for them to follow as he ran through the next landing and halfway up the next flight. He took aim again, but his targets were scrambling. A grenade skipped off the bulkhead behind him and bounced away before he could grab it. It went over the edge of the stairs and into the group behind him. He turned to find the one who threw it.

The grenade exploded. Borwyn soldiers screamed and fell. A couple behind the explosion ran. The two nearest to Brad ran toward him in a panic. He had to trip them to keep them from getting past and running into the Malibor above.

He held onto them. "Settle down. Focus on the Malibor or they'll kill us all," he snarled.

Their eyes remained wide, but their frantic movements calmed.

"If the Malibor pop up, shoot them. Can you do that for me?"

The two men nodded.

Brad glanced over the rail at the carnage below. He counted five dead and at least another five injured. The other members of the team were moving in to help them.

"We need to create a stand-off distance, give ourselves time to recover." He took two steps up and stopped. The two men behind him were afraid but moving. He couldn't ask for anything more than for his people to overcome their fear. They hadn't actively fought in the war. None of them were members of the scout crews. All they knew was life on New Septimus.

The rigors of war had been lost on the young. Their all-too-sudden lessons had cost Brad the momentum he hoped to gain through a rapid thrust into the station. Suing for peace was easier when one maintained the upper hand. The longer it went on, the more of Brad's people would die until there were none left to prosecute the engagement.

"If you see any grenades, we'll want those." He continued up the stairs and through the bodies scattered along them. He watched his step with the slickness of blood and tripping hazards throughout. Brad took a step, searched for the enemy above, then checked within arm's reach for anything worth taking.

The two behind him were more thoroughly searching. They were perfectly happy allowing Brad to do the hard work of fighting the enemy.

Brad stopped glancing around and focused on the way ahead. Step after painstaking step. He wasn't glad of the gore, but he was gratified with the effect the pulse rifles had through the stairs' thinner metal. He stopped and tried to think. How many rounds had he fired from his first power pack?

He raised his fist for those behind to hold up. He dropped the power pack from the rifle and replaced it with a fresh one. That left him with one recharge.

As morbid as it felt, six dead left him with eighteen power packs. He would marshal his resources first and mourn the dead later, if he was able to defeat the defenders and take over the station. He was down to less than thirty fighters and was no closer to the command center than he'd been an hour earlier. The delay frayed his nerves.

He looked for a way to block off the inner rings. Ahead, he found that the Malibor had done that for him. In between each of the nine rings was an emergency bulkhead. The one above him had closed off. Decks one to three were available to him while the upper decks were blocked.

Brad made it without issue. The two soldiers covered the exit hatch to the third deck while Brad examined the bulkhead. He stepped back, took aim, and fired a few well-aimed shots at the seam to block it in place. If they could do that in each of the quarters, they'd cut off the Malibor reinforcements.

That gave Brad a new plan, but it counted on him moving fast. He'd take four soldiers with him and run.

"Four grenades," the soldiers told him. "That's all they had."

"They should have used them," Brad said, "but I'm glad they didn't." He looked below. "Stay here."

Brad moved down the stairs to check on his soldiers. They were scared. He remained upright as he walked. The bodies of the fallen had been covered by what remained of their shirts. It was an ugly mess. Bloody hands hung by the sides of those who helped. Three of the soldiers were prone and unconscious. The other two injured wore bandages on their arms from where they'd covered their faces from the blast.

They must have been farther away from the explosion.

Brad touched each of the wounded and said a few kind words. The two with wounds on their arms promised that they could keep fighting. "Take your weapons," he told them. "Parcel out the spare power packs from the fallen."

"Most of them are damaged beyond utility. Only a few survived."

Brad frowned. The impact of the losses weighed even more heavily. He found his legs sluggish as if the gravity on the station had changed. But it hadn't.

"I need four who are ready to run. Someone looking to help us seal this ring off from the others, maybe get a little payback for this." Brad wanted them angry. He couldn't think of any other way to motivate them. He was angry, too, looking at the bodies of those he'd seen born and raised on New Septimus.

What did he expect?

Brad's inner monologue had long been a trusted friend. He had spent so much time alone, he learned to trust his own counsel. This was different. He needed the training and experience that Crip and Max had. Flying alone didn't give him any of the skills necessary for combat like this.

He was making it up as he went, and he'd gotten people killed. Jaq would tell him that he was doing the best he could with the information and time available to him.

It didn't make him feel better.

"Come on," he called to the four who stepped up. He took the stairs two at a time until he reached Deck 3. He stopped at the two soldiers who'd been guarding the hatch. "We're going through. You watch our backs. Don't let anyone try to sneak through this hatch after we've gone around the bend. Get someone up here to collect the Malibor weapons. We will need them if this goes on for too much longer."

Brad turned to study the faces of those who had followed him up the stairs.

Pickford, a legacy family that had been wealthy on Septimus. That was a long time ago. Their privilege ended with the loss of their planet, but their pride remained intact. Maybe he was going because he thought he needed to in order to restore honor to a once-proud family. The same reason he argued to be included in the group that left New Septimus.

Gristwall and Crombie. Farmers, not by choice. They were happy to leave New Septimus when the opportunity presented itself. Brad had no idea what they wanted out of life. He hadn't gotten to know the newer generation as much as he could have because he was away on *Starstrider*. He avoided having to know anything about the people he claimed to lead.

Another failure. Brad gritted his teeth and tried to change his focus after the inopportune time for deep self-reflection.

The final member of the group was from the second generation of refugees. Barely more than eighteen years old, Zin had no resumé. He recently completed his studies, engineering and math, like most of them. He wasn't a very big lad, but he carried his pulse rifle with confidence. The combat vest hung on his slight frame.

"Are you ready? Here's what we're going to do. We run. We kill any Malibor we see and keep running. Our mission is to secure the stairwells leading up to the next ring and all the decks above. Once that is done, we'll return here to coordinate the clearing efforts until the command center has been completely cut off from the rest of the station. Then we'll clear the command center by any means necessary."

The more Brad talked, the more intense he became and the more he bought into his own statement.

"What if one of us is hit?"

Brad clapped him on the shoulder. "Then you defend your position while the rest of us keep running. We may not come back from this. Are you okay with that?"

They nodded.

Brad raised his hand but only barely before his radio buzzed again. It was nearly endless. He hadn't had time to answer, but Jaq wanted to know.

Jaq deserved to know.

He answered. "*Chrysalis*, this is the boarding team, over."

"Status update, Brad, please, but first, we're going to maneuver since that big ship is coming out to play. We don't even know what weapons it has, but it's the reason for the screen. We may have a hard time with it, and Bec's on board."

Brad tried to parse the flurry of information, none of which was expected. "How did Bec get on board?"

"He stole a lander. What's your status?"

"We've lost six, five wounded. We're going to clear the third deck in the outer ring as soon as I'm done updating you. The Malibor have thrown obstacles in our path, but we're pressing forward. We expect to cut off the command center from the rest of the station in less than two hours. We'll see what we can do about getting them to talk with us at that time. I'll update you then, or someone will. Brad out."

Brad wanted to turn his radio off, but he had responsibilities. He turned the volume down so he wouldn't have to listen to it buzz when someone called.

He finished giving the hand and arm signal for the group to depart. Out and to the right. Pickford secured the corridor to the left while the rest ran to the right. After ten seconds, he'd run to catch up.

"Speed is our advantage," Brad reiterated. He nodded to Pickford. "You're up."

The soldier jumped through the hatch, aiming his pulse rifle down the empty corridor to the left. Brad stepped through and ran to the right. The corridor ahead disappeared into the overhead as it rose before him. Centripetal force kept them in place, the station's rotation providing the apparent gravity. That meant they were walking on the inside of the outer area.

Where the orientation appeared to be vertical from the bottom of the spindle to the top, the orientation inside the station was outside in, aligned toward the void at the center.

The doors along the way were closed. According to Brad's math, they had a three-kilometer run ahead of them. A thousand meters across. Three thousand meters tall. Rings stacked on top of rings with smaller rings inside them. Stairs went up while access points opened sideways.

The Malibor had evacuated most of the outer sections because of the threat from the Borwyn attack. They wanted to avoid collateral damage as much as Jaq wanted to.

Did it apply to Sections 1 to 48? Brad hoped it did but wouldn't rely on that. The Malibor weren't going to surrender their station without a fight. The little resistance they'd encountered so far wasn't the main event. There was more coming. By running, he wanted to head off the worst of it.

A hatch opened to their side. Brad fired the instant he realized it was an adult. He wouldn't shoot children, even if they were shooting at him. That was where he drew the line.

He embraced the philosophy that one deserved to win, unlike the Malibor who had won but didn't deserve it.

The body blasted backward. The force of the pulse rifle's single round was enough to end him.

Brad kept running. If there was someone else in the space beyond, the others would have to deal with them. Brad wasn't used to the cardio stimulation of running. He worked out and was in good shape, but he was also over seventy years old. The trials of the past few months had aged him. He felt aches and pains where he hadn't before. Zero-gee took its toll as well, reducing muscle mass enough to be noticeable.

He had to slow because his hands started to shake. He needed to be able to aim, even if he was snap-firing at targets.

Someone behind him fired two shots. He didn't look back.

No distractions. Brad listened to make sure they were still coming. Lots of feet pounding the deck. He couldn't tell if it was four or more. It sounded like too many. He risked a glance over his shoulder.

It was just the four volunteers, jogging easily. They'd nearly caught up with him. He wanted to give them the thumbs-up, but his hands held his pulse rifle. He needed both to make sure he didn't drop it.

He snarled himself back to focusing on the way ahead,

looking up, down, left, and right. Repeating the pattern, then mixing it up but checking all four points for threats.

Lenses peeked at him from panels beside the doors, and the overhead globes undoubtedly contained more video capture equipment. The command center most likely watched their every step. He didn't have enough rounds or power packs to shoot them out, but between the five of them, they did. He slowed even more.

"Shoot out those globes. One round each."

The first shots were errant. Close didn't count. They slowed even more. The soldiers blasted the globes from directly below, holding the pulse rifle in one hand and extending the end of the barrel to the globe before pulling the trigger, which showered the entire team with glass shards. The next one was blasted at an angle, sending the remnants into the bulkhead.

They adopted the side-shot strategy, but it caused them to slow more than Brad was comfortable with.

Zin asked, "Want me to go back and blast the ones behind us?"

Brad couldn't split his force any more. "We'll get them on the way around." He continued forward. The pace treated his body well, but his mind raced ahead, imagining traps the Malibor had time to set for them. Subconsciously, he increased speed, which left the globe-shooters farther behind. They were stopping at each and then racing ahead.

He looked over his shoulder to see them thirty meters behind him. He turned forward again to find a Malibor aiming a weapon at him.

"Incoming!" he shouted and dove to the side. Five meters

behind him, a bulkhead slammed down. He looked ahead in time to see the spark of a round impacting in front of him and skipping over his prone body.

Brad fired.

The roar of the pulse rifle drowned out the pops of the lesser Malibor weapon. The Malibor tried to get out of the corridor but didn't make it. He twisted and spun, crashing to the deck when a round from the pulse rifle tore through his chest. Another round pinged off the bulkhead to Brad's side.

Need to get out of this box, he thought. A hatch stood to his left. He bounced to his feet and threw himself at it, into the darkness beyond. He jumped to the side and dropped prone. Listening for the sounds of an enemy waiting within.

A scrape and click caught his attention. Brad felt around for cover, but there were only pedestals and legs. Maybe chairs. Maybe tables. Nothing that would stop a Malibor round. He controlled his breathing and listened like his life depended on it.

CHAPTER 8

The greatest feats in history require that we turn our fear into courage.

"E-mags are hot," Taurus stated.

"Prepare to fire," Jaq said. "Maximum rate, all batteries. We have to beat through that screen."

"Hold up," Alby called. "Bec's on that ship."

"He's there by his own choice. We can't let that ship get out into open space where it can maneuver. Teo? What weapons does it have?"

"I see missile tubes. A lot of tubes. Not many railgun batteries, but it has other directional turrets. Lasers, maybe? Other kinds of energy weapons? The one thing I can guarantee is that ship generates more power than every other ship in both our fleets combined, when we both had all of our ships."

"Then we need to kill it before it kills us," Jaq argued. "Fire!"

"Hold!" Alby shouted.

Jaq turned on him, her hair on fire. Her glare could have melted steel.

"It's accelerating. Three gees. Five gees... Captain?"

"Alby?" Jaq focused on him while waving frantically at Taurus.

He stabbed a finger at the screen, and his lips mouthed unintelligible words. He withered under the spotlight she cast on him.

"Firing," Taurua finally conceded.

The ship thrummed with the violence of a full broadside fired at the cyclic rate. Rounds flashed through the dark of space and impacted the energy screen. It lit up like a green globe around the massive vessel.

"Focus your fire on a smaller spot."

"Calibrating. Retargeting."

The big ship moved beyond the shipyard and toward the moon, Alarrees. It was already past five gees and accelerating.

"Alby!"

"Would have made no difference. We can't penetrate the screen when it's reduced to cover just the ship," Taurus explained. "Firing earlier would have made no difference."

"Get us out of here," Jaq called.

Mary and Ferd's hands danced across their screens. "Angling away."

"Accelerating at three gees."

The green bubble lessened, and a pulsed light flashed through like a string of loosely knotted pearls.

"Thrusters at maximum," Mary said. "Changing orientation."

"All ahead flank!" Jaq ordered.

"Hang on!" Ferd shouted. He jammed the accelerator to maximum. Jaq was caught between the battle commander's station and her seat. She slammed to the deck with a grunt, rolling flat on her back and staying that way as the ship powered to seven gees.

"Did you see that?" Jaq said with a groan. "They had to reduce power to the screen to fire. You know what that means?"

Jaq tried to project her voice, but she was being crushed to the deck. Blood was pulled from her head and into her limbs. Her ankles stung as they swelled.

"We make ourselves a target and then shoot them before they shoot us," Alby replied.

"That," Jaq confirmed. She tried to tighten her muscles to fight the gee forces. Relaxing was the last thing she needed.

The space station blocked the line of sight to the ship, then the moon blocked the ship and they were no longer a target.

"Fly behind that ship. Keep the moon between us and them until we figure out how to kill it."

Chrysalis inverted and accelerated in the opposite direction. When they transitioned through zero gees, they cut the engines for a few seconds. Jaq climbed into her seat and let the gel wrap around her tortured limbs. Her head remained muddled from the lack of blood.

"All hands, prepare for immediate acceleration," Alby announced over the ship-wide.

Jaq nodded. "Amie, send a message to Brad. The big ship

has escaped. Engaged in space. Will return once it's destroyed. Good luck."

"YOYO?" Amie asked.

Jaq knew what it meant. You're on your own, and that was exactly the message.

"Go ahead and send it," Jaq confirmed.

"We have to hurry," Max said. False dawn gave them enough light to see. They could put more distance between themselves and the city. After a fitful night where Max refused sleep in order to watch over Deena, he wanted to move before he passed out. The action would keep him awake.

Deena tried to look under her shirt, but it was still too dark.

"I feel like garbage," she said.

"How's your breathing?"

"Hurts, but I'm not coughing up blood, so that's good, right?" she joked.

"Probably just a broken rib. I'll carry you if I have to." Max was sincere in his offer, but he knew Deena wouldn't take him up on it.

"Let's see how the first twenty meters go," Deena said.

Max pulled her to her feet. She breathed quickly with the pain but relaxed into a slower rhythm. "As bad as trying to sleep on the ground was, I feel better. Let's go. You blaze the trail and I'll follow."

"Are you sure?" Max screwed up his face in confusion

and concern. He locked eyes with Deena, but she gave no quarter. He finally gave in. "I'll go slowly."

"I'll let you know," she confirmed.

Max moved out far slower than he wanted. He stepped carefully, one foot in front of the other, pausing with each step.

"You're killing me, Max," she said. "Pick up the pace or we'll be out here all day."

"That's the woman I married!" he said, moving out without taking the pause between steps. He glanced over his shoulder every fourth step. Deena waved at him each time.

He stopped to let her catch up so he could hug her. The coldest time of day was right before the dawn. The bitterness of the wind added to it, but their spirits were high. Max had risked too much to find her and then escape the city. They had been on the run, but not any longer.

"We need to get to the forest," Max said. "Why don't you go first? Set the pace you're comfortable with."

Deena rested her hand on Max's chest and smiled up at him. "That's a good idea." She moved out and kept walking, trying not to limp for Max's benefit, but her breathing sounded labored and shallow. It would catch in her throat each time she tried to breathe too deeply.

Max didn't say anything. He let her be stubborn, assuming she would let him know if she was hurt too badly.

She slowed after a solid thirty minutes. After another five minutes, she stopped and worked hard to catch her breath.

The first rays of light shone over the city. "We better go," Max said.

Emerging from the darkness ahead was the shadow of a wreck. "What is that?" Deena wondered.

It was barely a couple hundred meters away. "Let's see." Max couldn't see a way around. The wreck stood between them and the woods.

Max brought his pulse rifle up. He moved in front of Deena and hurried ahead. Deena pulled out her aged Malibor blaster and followed Max, but he was increasing the separation between them. Deena couldn't catch him.

"It's the gunship," he called over his shoulder. He'd seen it on the ground and been around it enough to know. He ran to it and worked his way around the other side, where he found two bodies huddled together.

"What?" Tram's gruff voice asked. "Who is that?"

"Max and Deena. What happened, Tram?"

"Where did you come from?"

"City. It's a long story. Are you hurt?"

"We're banged up. My head is still killing me. Evelyn has a broken leg, we think." He hadn't opened his eyes, holding his head in both hands. "We had to steal the ship. The elders denied our plan to attack the city."

Max looked to Deena. They grimaced at the news. They needed the support that New Pridal could provide. "Didn't Kelvis come with you? Or Sophia?" Max pressed.

"They're inside." Tram let go of his head and looked up through bloodshot eyes. "Don't go in there."

Deena rounded the corner of the ship. Max held up his hand to forestall her getting closer.

"I'll go inside. We might have a light. Deena?"

"I don't," she replied.

"Emergency gear in Engineering, right?"

"It's a mess down there, more than just the mechanical wreck."

"I get it," Max answered. He put his fingers under Tram's chin to better look into his eyes. "It's good to see you, Tram. You too, Evelyn. I'm sorry about Kelvis and Sophia. But you did a great job on the spaceport. You sent the Malibor into a frenzy. They thought a new civil war had started. People were taking sides."

"That good, huh? They still had enough firepower left to shoot us down."

Max and Deena stood there uncomfortably, not knowing what to say. Two of their people were dead and two injured.

Deena kneeled next to Evelyn and nodded toward the open hatch.

Max understood. He backed up until he reached the hatch. He worked his way inside through the hatch where the Malibor saboteur, Cryl Talan, had tried to damage *Chrysalis*. He stopped for a moment and steeled himself before continuing.

He felt his way toward the engine room. He stepped into a wet mess. Max knew what it was. He continued as far as he could into the space to feel for the emergency kit. Max went methodically until he found the canvas bag inside the netting that held it in place in zero-gee.

He turned on the flashlight and immediately regretted it. His boots, knees, sleeves, and hands were covered in blood. The worst of it was seeing what was left of Kelvis.

Max left Engineering to quickly check the rest of the ship, but the damage was too great to get everywhere. He recovered nothing else beside the flashlight and a pry bar. He found Sophia and a pulse rifle, but the ship damage blocked him.

Kelvis and Sophia were in their coffin.

Outside, dawn had broken, and the sun was climbing into the sky. He turned off the flashlight. He had three people with him, and they were all broken in some way. But broken was better than dead, like the two inside the ship. He manually cranked the outer hatch shut and locked it to let them rest in peace.

Max crawled up the side of the gunship to where he could get the best look at the city. Tendrils of smoke drifted into the sky. It looked calm, and most importantly, there weren't any soldiers moving across the open area toward them. Max watched for a solid ten minutes, looking for any movement. When he was satisfied they weren't being followed and that no one was coming out to check on the crashed gunship, he slid down and joined the others.

"We should probably get going," Max said.

Deena pointed to Evelyn. "Broken leg. We need to straighten it and then splint it."

Max held up the pry bar. With the medical kit already on the ground beside them, they got to work by removing the clothing covering her lower leg. The purples and blacks stood out. "At least it's not an open fracture," Max said, trying to sound upbeat.

Evelyn scowled at him.

"This might hurt a little bit, but try to relax," Deena said.

Max made a face.

Deena laid across Evelyn's lap and held her leg at the knee with both hands. She pulled toward her.

"Harder," Max whispered. He gripped Evelyn's ankle while on his knees, ready to use his body weight to pull the leg straight. Without warning, he yanked, nearly pulling Evelyn and Deena with him.

Evelyn screamed but cut it short by turning it into small gasps for air. Max studied the leg as best he could. "There we go. It's straight. Now, all we need is two months of rest and relaxation for it to heal." He put the cold metal of the pry bar against her leg. She flinched but settled in with the relief of the cold. It was better than ice, but only briefly.

They wrapped it tightly with gauze and tape.

"Now, we need to get moving," Max said. "I'll help Evelyn, and Deena can lead Tram. We won't go too fast. We only have a few klicks before we'll be under cover of the woods."

"And then what?" Tram asked. He kept his eyes shut. The look of pain on his face told the full story of his bruised brain. Tram needed rest in a cool, dark place.

"Then we disappear. You're out of the war, and so is Evelyn. You've done your part. Leave the rest to us. Once we're in the woods, I propose we build you two a shelter, kill a deer, and stock it with food. Then, Deena and I will find the western Borwyn so we can rejoin the combat team and add our firepower to theirs. Maybe it'll make the difference."

"I second the proposal," Deena said quickly.

"Look at us. How are we going to fend for ourselves? What happens if someone comes?"

"Surrender. You're in no shape to fight anyone. I doubt

you'll get company. The war isn't going to be fought over there." Max pointed to the woods. "It's going to be fought there." He pointed over the ship and toward the city. "That's where the enemy is directing the war, between that and the space station. Which reminds me, we should try to call Crip."

They removed the radio from Deena's bag and set it up.

Deena tapped the code and broadcast the contact message. "This takes time," she explained. "They aren't always listening."

Max started to get antsy until thirty minutes later, when they received an answer.

Deena asked for voice contact. She didn't have any codes for this situation.

Once granted, she handed the microphone to Max.

"Max here with Deena, Tram, and Evelyn. Gunship is destroyed. We lost Kelvis and Sophia. Three injured, one is okay. We'll make it into the woods to the southwest of the city today. Tram said the elders denied the use of the gunship. Request instructions."

"This is Glen. I'm sorry to hear about the two we lost, and that the gunship is out of action. Proceed to the woods at best possible speed. Get out of the open. We'll send a patrol to escort you to our position."

"Roger. That's better than our plan. See you soon. Max out."

Deena powered down the radio and repacked it.

"You heard the man. Get under cover and relax, which means I'm going hunting."

Deena smiled at him. He shook his head and tossed his

hands up in confusion. She pulled him close and whispered, "You look happy. Despite everything."

"We can mourn later. For now, we have to survive. Hunting is incredible. It gives me the peace I've sought my whole life, with the action that my body craves. I don't understand it, but with you by my side, I feel invincible."

"Invincible! Keep your damn head down or a Malibor will shoot it off," Deena quipped.

She let go and together, she and Max helped the injured to their feet. They set off at a glacial pace but soon moved more quickly. What Max had thought was a few kilometers turned out to be more than ten kilometers, and it took nearly all day to get there.

They hadn't been harassed by the Malibor because they hadn't been seen, as far as they knew.

Tram and Evelyn were exhausted when they reached the sanctity of the forest. They'd barely moved into the shade of the woods when they sat the injured against a tree trunk.

Deena was breathing hard but swore she was fine.

"You stay here. I'll scout the area, see if there's any ready-made shelter and maybe signs of life, like deer." He stared into the darkness of the deeper woods. "Or Malibor. Stay alert."

Max checked them one last time before silently disappearing into the nearby brush.

CHAPTER 9

You should always train when you're tired, because that is when you'll face your hardest challenges.

"We can't keep the E-mags energized all the time," Taurus said.

Jaq's lip rose in a half-snarl. She knew about the limitation but had no idea if they'd matched the big ship's speed until it didn't appear behind them or in front of them.

"The time for restraint is over. Slade, radiate all systems. We need to find this ship at least as soon as it finds us. Give us time to energize our weapons." Jaq remained in her seat. She was stiff and in pain from the bruising of the earlier acceleration. She didn't want to repeat that.

"Powering down," Taurus reported and leaned back in her seat. She threw her head back and stared at the overhead.

"Defensive weapons remain hot," Gil muttered.

Alby chuckled. "Did you see that energy weapon they fired at us? Anything you can do about that?"

"No. Admittedly, no, but I did see all those missile ports."

"Good call," Alby replied. "Keep those repeaters ready to take out any missiles that thing launches."

Alby climbed out of his seat, as ill-advised as it was, and eased in next to Jaq, balancing on Brad's chair.

"What are we going to do, Jaq?" he asked quietly.

"We're going to buy time for Brad and his people, and we're going to give our people leverage by beating that ship into next week. The Malibor's ship wasn't ready. It's got a screen and has at least one energy weapon available. We're not sure what that weapon will do to us, so we're going to avoid that."

Alby leaned close. "How are we going to do that?"

"By flying fast. We'll accelerate shortly, but we're still picking up the pieces from the last time we took off without everyone being secure. Doc Teller is one of those injured. He's farther from a seat than anyone else."

"How are we doing, Jaq?" Alby asked.

"We're doing fine as long as we're still alive. We're not running away. We're staying here. We worked way too hard to get this far to only go this far. We're here to win this war. Right here. Right now." Jaq punched her fist into her hand.

"What if they run?" Alby asked.

"Do you know something I don't?" Jaq twisted out of her seat and perched on it, holding herself with one foot on the mid-rail and both hands clinging to her chair.

"It's something to talk about while we're not engaged. Do we go after them or not?"

"Not as long as we have people on the station," Jaq replied. "We owe them our support. Getting pulled away would play into the Malibor's hands. We take the station, we can order that ship to stand down. Flying away doesn't save it. We saw fifty bodies on a ship three times the size of *Chrysalis*. It's not finished. The only thing it has going for it is its power generation. Next time it tries to fire at us, we'll hit that weakened screen with a billion obdurium projectiles. It'll die and die ugly."

"What about Bec?" Alby asked.

"He should have never boarded that ship. I'm sorry, but he's on his own. I doubt they even have escape pods, so every member of that crew is going to pay the price unless they surrender."

"Can we take them?" Alby whispered.

"Don't even think that question, let alone ask it out loud. And it's running from us. That makes me believe that *they* don't think they can take us. I doubt their weapons are aligned and calibrated. Maybe that's what that one shot was about. The next one will be better aimed."

Alby nodded. He launched himself and somersaulted toward his position.

Jaq frowned. The worst-case scenario was the big ship heading toward deep space, reducing the obstructions behind which *Chrysalis* could hide.

Bec studied the four walls of the small office where they'd put him. The brig wasn't ready, according to the chief engineer. They had more pressing concerns with the ship, like *Chrysalis* after it first appeared on a high-speed pass months earlier. They knew they'd have to launch *Epica* before it was ready. They rushed to activate only those systems needed to fight the Borwyn cruiser.

Bec had listened while the chief talked. He hurried away once Bec was pushed into the office. Another crewman was assigned to watch the door, but he didn't want to be there. He had other work to do.

"Stay in there. I've disabled the lock," the crewman said. Footsteps pounded down the corridor.

A panel next to the door was hard-bolted to the wall. He couldn't get it to move.

The power plants vibrated the whole ship before the engines kicked in. Bec's stomach heaved with the competing forces. He was pulled toward the deck because of the artificial gravity, but he was simultaneously pulled sideways with the acceleration.

He wondered how the crew responded since this was the first time the ship had left the dock. The crew wouldn't be experienced with the orientation or the rigors of artificial gravity.

Bec had no way to guess how fast the ship was accelerating. He couldn't feel like it like he could on *Chrysalis,* where it was patently obvious. He needed the secrets of the artificial gravity. This ship was so technologically advanced, he had a hard time believing it was a product of Malibor research.

The furniture in the office wasn't welded to the deck because it didn't need to be. He picked up the chair. "Percussive shock, my friends." He aligned the chair rail while holding it tightly to his chest. The legs wrapped around his body. He rotated at the waist and missed the bolt. He did it again and again until he'd repeatedly hammered the bolt and the paint cracked around the connection.

He gripped it but couldn't move it. He wrapped part of his shirt around it and pushed while twisting. It turned. A little bit at first, then it unscrewed freely.

"That's how it's done." He removed it. With only one more bolt, he expected to rotate the plate down, but it wouldn't budge.

He repeated his efforts hammering the chair against the bolthead, but it wasn't responding. He stopped after a while, never wondering if anyone heard him. The guard was long gone, and no one was near. He'd seen the scan data. There were only fifty Malibor on board. That wasn't enough for the ship to fly and fight.

Bec wasn't worried. These were engineers like him. No, not like him. Lesser engineers, except for the ones who masterminded the breakthrough technology.

He put the chair down and sat in it to rest. He was used to working, but not in such a way. He thought through everything he'd seen from the second he arrived, which made him wonder if the lander was still attached to the airlock. He expected it had been torn off with the rapid acceleration, although he guessed at the last part. He wasn't sure how fast they had gone or were going, but he was certain they were moving.

Bec returned to hammering the chair on the bolt, redoubling his efforts to hit it harder and harder.

His chest heaved from the exertion. He put the chair down and sat. A crack had opened between the bolt and the paint. Bec dove at it and grasped it with his fingers. It wouldn't turn. He again used his shirt to aid his grip.

Then he turned to the chair. If he could hammer a slot into the back support, he would have all the torque he needed. He dropped the chair on its seat and put the back brace against the deck. He kicked at the back pad from behind to break it free.

With that opening, he slid the back support along the wall and rammed down to punch into the square support metal. It was hollow, but sturdy. The best he could do was create a sharp edge. Using the first bolthead to wedge between the intransigent bolt and the chair back, he pushed. The bolt turned a little and then more. He dropped the chair and unscrewed it the rest of the way with his fingers.

The panel plate came free. Bec dropped it to the deck, careless of the noise he was making. It was too big a ship with too few people. There were things to worry about, and noise wasn't one of them.

Inside were standard wires and relays attached to a circuit board. A quick study suggested he could short it by pulling one quick-connect free and tapping it on a second. The door opened.

Bec shook his head. The ship hadn't been made with security in mind, but it would be far easier to help himself if he had a toolkit. That would be his first action—find a toolkit. The next would be to figure the ship out, which would be easier if he had access to a computer terminal. He suspected there would be no security on that system either. The ship was completely untested. As an engineer, he was appalled at the captain's lack of understanding about how systems needed to be independently checked and then reverified while incrementally integrating them. There would be cross-contamination from power sources and radiation that could have detrimental effects.

He closed the office door and strolled down the corridor, stopping to look before crossing intersections. He had no intention of getting locked up again. He had his insatiable desire to understand the energy screen and the artificial gravity. He wouldn't let the Malibor workers take that away from him. Who were they to deny him knowledge?

Bec opened doors as he passed. None of them were labeled. The ship wasn't finished. The cosmetics were missing. Not that Bec cared whether the ship was beautiful or not on the outside. He cared that it did things it shouldn't have been able to do.

And that's what he needed to understand. He wanted to get back to Engineering and have free access. That was a priority, too. Computer, toolkit, Engineering, and power generation system.

Yes. They were all top priority.

He hurried down a corridor with a number of doors to give himself the best chance of finding one with an active computer terminal. He stopped before opening the first he came to.

"Dammit! I just did to myself what Jaq has been doing to me her whole life. Giving me multiple pri ones. There can only be one!" Bec laughed at his revelation. "Computer terminal first."

He opened door after door to find unoccupied and unfinished crew quarters. He turned around and headed the other way. He needed to find workspaces. As big as the ship was, they had to be prevalent.

Bec scowled as he searched. *Why aren't there any maps?* he thought. *Even construction crews would need maps. Malibor are morons.*

CHAPTER 10

Support for what you do is critical, especially from your boss.

"I'm going to have to go to the mountain and smooth things over. If the elders denied the military operation, then we're all on borrowed time," Glen said softly.

Crip was less than amused. "We're in the middle of a war. They have no choice but to continue supporting us as we fight it."

Glen raised his eyebrows at Crip's reply. "They absolutely have the choice not to support us. We've remained hidden for fifty years, although those of us who serve are happy to not be trapped inside. The elders have made the final determination on our operations the whole time. They will not be happy with the usurpation of their power."

"Even if they're wrong?" Crip couldn't believe it. He wanted Jaq to be in charge. She did what was right, even if it was hard.

"*Especially* if they're wrong. In their minds, they've never been wrong before because they're still alive and the mountain is undiscovered."

"Maybe the mountain has been discovered and as long as you kept to yourselves, the Malibor didn't invest the resources to attack it. It would not be an easy target, even with massive bombs. It's a mountain—a big one, at that." Crip was angry, but he had a reason to be happy. "Max, Deena, and Tram are okay. It's good that Evelyn is, too. It sucks that we lost Kelvis and Sophia. I better tell the team." Crip stood. "Which squad is going after them?"

"I've already sent Corporal Tenaris and his people. They'll find them and bring them back."

Crip wanted his team to go, but they didn't know the woods as well as the Borwyn who'd been born to them. "I'll let my combat team know about the gunship. I won't tell them that we might be fugitives from our own people."

"Probably best not to. That's why I have to go. I'll leave Eleanor and you in charge. Listen to her, Crip. She knows what she's talking about, and she's a good person."

"I know. I'm glad you found us," Crip told him. "You showed us that we're doing the right thing fighting for all Borwyn. We deserve Septimus. We have every right to reclaim it. There's only one way to do that, and that's by defeating the Malibor in combat. It's the only thing they understand."

"I couldn't agree more, Crip. I'll take one soldier and two horses. We'll head out and get there tomorrow. Then the fun begins. If you and Eleanor see a tactical advantage, take it. The mountain stopped directing us when they lost sight of the possibility that the Borwyn flagship had returned and was systematically destroying the Malibor fleet. They buried their heads. Peace, in their minds, was nothing more than living in the mountain, unmolested. That was never my idea, but I have to answer to them. I'm going to do that. I hope to return as soon as possible."

"You're like us, Glen, not big on hope as a plan."

"They could throw me in their jail or strip me of rank and assign me to a menial labor position. Hope is the best I can do."

Crip couldn't reply with words. It made no sense to him and hadn't since the first time he met the elders. They seemed to live in their own reality, uninfluenced by the momentum of the opportunity that Jaq and *Chrysalis* had given them. For once, the Borwyn had the upper hand. The thought of the elders punishing Glen was beyond contemplation. He nodded tersely. "You better go, my friend. You have two days to think of what you're going to tell them to root them out of their gold-plated cage."

"I might use that." The two shook hands, and Glen walked away, slowly, not like a man with a purpose.

More like a man on the way to his own funeral.

Chrysalis came around the moon. The sensors painted the space station and surrounding area. Seventeen cargo shuttles streamed toward the planet.

Jaq clenched her jaw and stared at the icons that populated the main screen. "Stay the course, Mary." Jaq had lost the leverage of the civilian population. "I'm sorry, Brad."

"Trying to contact the boarding party," Amie announced. She had her face nearly touching her screen as she hunched over it. She mumbled into her microphone with her persistent efforts to reestablish contact.

Jaq wished Brad had taken a radio operator with him, someone whose sole job was to stay in contact with *Chrysalis*.

The ship continued around Alarrees.

Amie tried until the moon blocked the direct signal. "No contact," she said.

"It's okay, Amie. It's not like we could do anything for him anyway. It's more for our edification." Jaq chewed on her lip more out of frustration than anything else.

"What if something happened to them?" Amie asked.

Isn't that the question? Jaq thought. "Then we'll never know, and now that they've evacuated the station of civilians, we can add the complete destruction of the station to our tactical options."

Brad took aim at the sound of footsteps padding toward the door. He kept his pulse rifle leveled in the direction of the sound, following it with the business end, finger on the trigger.

The door slid open and an individual wearing stained coveralls stepped through, only to be thrown backward by a short volley of blaster fire that hit him in the chest. His body lay on its back. The damage done to it was enough to kill him.

Two Malibor soldiers stared at the dead man. In a moment, they would see Brad. He fired at the soldier he could see half of. Their training materials said to take the hardest shot first when he had the element of surprise on his side. The soldier full in the doorway started to raise his rifle, but Brad's was ready. He fired the second shot, hitting the soldier in the chest. The shot sent his heart and lungs through the gaping hole in his back and splattered them across the bulkhead on the far side of the corridor.

Brad jumped out of his crouch and peeked out the doorway. No one else was out there. The corridor was blocked off where he was trapped with three dead bodies. He removed the soldiers' weapons and hid them in the room, taking the worker's toolkit. He needed it to access the bulkhead control.

Then again, wherever the soldiers were was probably a remote access. He worked his way down the corridor and into the room from which they had emerged. Inside, he found food wrappers and drink containers. This was their checkpoint, where they'd been waiting for Brad and the soldiers from New Septimus in a poorly designed trap that locked hunters and prey together. It hadn't worked out for the Malibor.

Poorly designed and even more poorly executed.

Brad stepped over the body of the Malibor he'd killed.

There was a computer terminal inside that Brad accessed. The control screen for the bulkheads was still up. He tapped a button, and both bulkheads lifted into the overhead. Brad rushed to the door and checked the corridor ahead. It was empty. Behind him, he heard the cries of happiness from the four he'd been cut off from. He stepped back and faced the others.

"Did you have a nice break?" He threw his hands up.

"We heard rifle fire."

"Three down plus one. These idiots killed the maintenance tech thinking he was me. Let's go, people."

He waved for them to follow. They jogged once again, but this time, Brad slowed to let them hit the video globes without creating as much separation as last time. By the time they reached the access up to the next deck and ring, they'd transitioned from Q1 to Q2.

"Block it." Brad pointed to the hatch. He eased forward and took a knee to watch up the corridor ahead. Crombie broke out a small torch and dropped a few beads around the door, then he placed a boobytrap to explode if someone forced it open.

"It's good," Crombie confirmed. Gristwall double-checked it and gave the thumbs-up.

Brad popped to his feet and headed out. The more he ran, the more the side accesses bothered him. They didn't need to come down the four stairwells. They could come in from the sides. He slowed.

"Check to make sure there are no side accesses. There's more than one Ring Nineteen."

"But they're not connected out here. The design plans showed that the only lateral accesses were on Rings Sixteen, Thirteen, Ten, Seven, and Four," Pickford replied.

"They could have been modified. Who wants to go up and then back down to get ten meters to one side?"

"The original designers had a reason to do it that way. Maybe the lateral accesses created stress points. There are nineteen rings vertically oriented and then twelve horizontally oriented. I'm sure there was a reason." Pickford's eyebrows plunged as he descended into deeper thought, looking for the meaning behind the station's design.

"Check the side doors. Make sure the Malibor didn't modify the station."

Gristwall, Crombie, and Zin worked their way forward, checking the doors on both sides of the corridor. They found offices, workshops, storage, and even quarters. All had been recently abandoned, a testimony to the fear of the Borwyn boarding party.

Brad had brought thirty-five newly minted soldiers to a fight encompassed within nearly a million cubic meters of space station.

"Stay sharp. They had to expect a lot more of us. Now that they've seen our real numbers and know our objective, they'll be coming."

"What about the civilians?" Pickford asked.

"They must be sequestered away from this ring. We're far more isolated than they are, but that's good for us. Let's get going. We're delaying."

"We're catching our breath," Zin offered, even though he was the youngest and arguably the most fit.

Brad saw it as deference to him.

"Now that we're well rested, we have two more stairwells to block off." Brad jogged toward the rising horizon of the corridor.

A bulkhead fifty meters away slammed down in front of them. Brad slid to a stop and dropped prone, aiming up the corridor. Another bulkhead dropped toward him. He flinched in anticipation of getting cut in half.

A hand stuffed a pulse rifle into the gap. The bulkhead hit it and stopped.

Brad rolled back into the space with the others. The pulse rifle bent and broke under the pressure.

"Sorry," Zin said. "I lost my rifle."

Brad stood and clapped him on the back. "You saved a life with that rifle. We'll call it a wash. Use one of the Malibor weapons."

"If they keep dropping those bulkheads, we'll never get to Q-Three or Q-Four," Gristwall complained.

"Change of plan. Weld this bulkhead to the deck, then we'll go back to the Q-Two stairwell. We'll take it down and see if we can get at the other side of the command center. Maybe we don't have to go farther."

The team used their small torch until it ran out of fuel. Crombie blew on the end to cool if off enough to stuff it back in his pack. They could get more fuel, but they couldn't get another torch. They embraced the conservation of resources that they'd lived their whole lives with on New Septimus.

The video capture globes had been destroyed. The Malibor wouldn't know what Brad's team was doing.

"You can dismantle the boobytrap, can't you?" Brad asked over his shoulder while jogging toward the Q2 access hatch.

"Of course!" Crombie called back.

Brad swung wide to get around the bodies they'd left in the corridor as a warning to anyone who might try to follow them. The Malibor respected power.

Back at the Q2 hatch, Crombie and Gristwall combined their efforts to undo the boobytrap and cut the welds free. The five men prepared to breach the door and enter the stairs to head down to the next level, where they would be on the far side of the command center.

Pickford went through first, looking over the barrel of his pulse rifle up the stairs. He eased in to where he could see between the railing and stairs.

"Clear," he said softly.

Brad was next. He hurried in and went down the steps, carefully, also looking over the barrel of his rifle.

"Hey!" someone shouted from ahead.

"Hey yourself. Who are you?" Brad called back.

"Nobody. Maintenance personnel trying to fix the damage to the station. Do we have you to thank for that?"

Brad was taken aback. He'd expected a hostile answer from Malibor soldiers or a call from his own people as a remote second possibility. He never anticipated a voice that was Malibor but less confrontational.

"Not our intent to damage the station," Brad replied. He continued down the stairs, aiming over the rail at the single figure wearing coveralls until he reached the landing. When he came around the corner, the individual up front ducked and soldiers behind him fired.

Brad dove to the side. Fire shot through his side as one of the rounds hit home. The others splattered off the bulkhead. Brad landed in a heap. He lost his grip on the pulse rifle to find that he'd been hit in the arm, too. Both grazing shots, but he needed to bandage them to staunch the flow of blood.

"Fire in the hole!" Zin cried and dropped a grenade over the rail, spinning it as he let go so it would bounce away from where it landed.

Brad covered his head with his good arm and curled up in

the fetal position. He felt the explosion through the metal of the landing. The blast shook the stairwell. Zin and Crombie raced down the stairs. They rounded the corner and unloaded their pulse rifles at the space below.

"Control your fire," Brad urged, but he didn't shout because he was still curled up.

Gristwell showed up and helped Brad to sit on a step. "Good. You're not dead."

Brad snorted. "Just in pain, that's all. Secure the stairwell first. I'll catch up."

Gristwell examined Brad's expression but discerned nothing alarming. He followed the other two down the stairs.

Pickford waved on his way past.

Brad leaned back to stretch out the pain. His right side and left arm. The arm was barely more than a scratch. He wondered why he dropped his rifle. He didn't need to bandage his arm. It stung but had already stopped bleeding. His side was a different matter. The bullet had cut through between two ribs, tearing the cartilage, scratching the bones, and bleeding profusely.

He bunched up his excess shirt and pressed it against the wound, pinching it tightly with his elbow.

Weapons fire sounded from below. Brad lurched to his feet using his pulse rifle as a crutch. He hunched sideways to keep pressure on his wound. Sharp pains stabbed through his chest. He nearly fell, catching himself at the last second. The rifle clattered against the bulkhead. He clutched it to himself while fighting to catch his breath. A series of rounds peppered the wall in front of him, sending shards of metal into his face and exposed arm.

He gasped and turned away, but the damage had already been done. Brad moved back to the landing above. He ran a hand over his face and picked out the bits of metal he could feel.

On the decks below, silence returned. A deep silence born of depleted men finished after a hard battle.

He shouldered his pulse rifle and headed down the stairs. The landing had the remains of two Malibor soldiers and the man in coveralls. Brad felt sorry for him but only for a moment.

Brad looked down the stairs into the darkness of the first deck. He couldn't hear anything there or in front of him in the corridor. He backed up and pointed his weapon through the hatch. He stepped through and quickly looked left and right. Two of his people were prone to the left, aiming at a barrier, and the other two were prone to the right, aiming at a barrier on their side. Each barrier bristled with weapons pointed by the soldiers behind them.

Brad's eyes shot wide, and he ducked back as both sides fired at once at a single target. Him.

The hatch sparked and shattered under the onslaught. Pulse rifles barked in response until all weapons fell silent.

The pause reminded Brad of the pain. The lights briefly swam before his eyes. He clenched his side, hoping that the bleeding would stop and he could get his wits about him.

"Fire in the hole," Crombie said.

Pickford repeated it.

Two grenades headed for the barriers. Brad covered his ears.

The explosions were muted, followed by the sound of falling debris. The barriers getting blasted from behind.

"Report," Brad called through the hatch.

"Two good this side," Crombie replied.

"Good this side," Pickford said.

Brad dipped his head out and pulled back. Both barriers had been blasted. "The command center is in front of your pos, Pickford?"

"I can't see it from here. Cannot confirm."

"Crombie?"

"The emergency bulkhead is dropped about thirty meters down. Can't see anything beyond that. I have four doors left and five right."

"Three left and two right. Movement!" Pickford ended his report with a single shot and a curse. He pulled his original power pack and swapped it with a second.

Zin and Gristwall were already on their third packs, Crombie was on his second, and Brad was still on his first.

"Fire discipline, gentlemen," Brad called. He wanted to join them in the corridor but didn't want to die trying. "Tell me when it's clear. Crombie, reorient yourself to join Pickford and Gristwall. You have Tail-End Charlie, Zin. Don't let anyone sneak in behind us."

"Clear for the moment. Get down and hurry," Pickford said over his shoulder.

Brad hit the deck and low-crawled through the hatch. He nearly ran into Crombie, who was doing the same thing. Crombie moved to the left to make room for Brad, and they reached Pickford's defensive position at the same time. They were using bodies as part of the barrier.

"This is pretty gruesome," Brad whispered.

"They came at us in a rush," Pickford explained. "This bunch was armed with axes and improvised weapons. I'm not sure they're soldiers, but that group behind the barrier was. I see their blasters."

"I'm going up there," Brad said.

"No," Pickford replied, nodding toward the bloodstain on his combat vest. "Crombie, are you up for it?"

"On my way," the new soldier replied. He crawled over the two bodies stacked in front of him and worked his way forward. Before he reached the barrier, shots rang out. They pinged off the crates, desks, and chairs of the barrier and ricocheted down the corridor. Everyone ducked.

Brad sprayed a few rounds off the side walls, but they didn't ricochet like the lower-speed Malibor projectiles. "We need their weapons."

Pickford picked up a hand blaster and reached it across his body. "Here you go."

"I thought you said they weren't armed with blasters," Brad wondered.

"Not this bunch, but those at the bottom of the landing were."

Brad took the blaster pistol and fired one round to the right and above the barrier. It bounced off and pinged down the corridor twice before the sound died away.

"When I fire, you two move up to the barrier." After they confirmed the order, Brad emptied the weapon at a variety of angles above and around the Malibor's ad hoc barrier.

Pickford and Gristwall reached their next position without issue.

Brad started to crawl over, and two enemy rounds slammed into the body barely two centimeters from where his head was. He pulled back and dropped behind the bodies. He slipped sideways to where Pickford was. He peeked over the top to find a solid obstruction in front of him where there was a gap where he'd been lying. Brad climbed over and moved forward.

He was tired, bone tired.

In front of him was a hole made by a pulse rifle's obdurium projectile. It was big enough for him to get his eye to. It had a view of the corridor beyond. "I see at least four barrels behind another hasty barricade, but this one seems to be made of metal. Looks like a girder with steel plates attached."

Pickford hoisted the last grenade. "We have one of these little gems left."

Brad checked again through the hole. "They have netting strung above the structure. You wouldn't be able to get it to the other side." He studied the construction. There were small slots every meter from one side of the corridor to the other, and it was from these that the tips of the blaster barrels projected. "I think this is their last stand defensive position. If they only have four soldiers behind them, then they're on their last leg. I bet we surprised them coming down that stairwell."

"I'd say we did. They might have been trying to come in behind us, block us out from this corridor and cut off our access to the command center," Pickford replied. He grinned at Brad. "Endgame."

"I like the way you think. How do we breach that monstrosity?" He moved aside to let Pickford look.

Zin cried out, "Bulkhead is lifting." He unleashed his pulse rifle on fully automatic.

"Fire discipline," Brad grunted as he tried to twist around to see behind him, but he put too much pressure on his wound. Sharp pains rocketed through his chest and straight to his head. He saw nothing but the white light of agony.

"I'm out!" Zin shouted in a panic.

Pickford kneeled behind the main part of the metal barricade where he had a clear view past Zin. He fired one shot at a time at the group that tried to press past the bulkhead. Zin had dropped the first wave who hadn't been carrying weapons besides axes and clubs.

Individuals from behind the half-opened bulkhead had blasters but ran short of motivation to continue their attack under the destructive firepower of the pulse rifles. An impact on a person up front affected everyone behind them as the projectiles tore through the first bodies and continued nearly unhindered.

Fallen bodies behind the first wave testified to that fact. A few random pops sounded as the emergency bulkhead closed, only to get caught on the bodies beneath it. It stopped and started opening.

Crombie and Pickford aimed carefully. Brad forced himself upright.

Malibor soldiers were in a mad scramble for cover. The three Borwyn picked them off with single shots until no one remained in the corridor.

Brad pulled a power pack from his vest and slid it across

the deck to Zin. "Single fire only. That's the last one you get. Make it last. Go get one of those Malibor rifles. I'll cover you."

"I got it," Crombie said. He eased forward to get a better view but not so far that the soldiers at the metal barrier had a shot at him.

Zin crawled forward, keeping his eyes on the doors to either side.

Crombie took aim and fired, blasting a video globe that overlooked the hatch to the stairwell. It could have covered the corridor, too. Zin slammed himself to the deck. He covered his head with one arm.

"Finish up, Zin. We got work to do," Brad said.

CHAPTER 11

Peace does not come from the peaceful.

Max flopped the small deer on the ground between the injured souls he had to care for.

Evelyn scooted to the carcass. "You've done an admirable job cleaning it," she said.

Max was skeptical. The eastern Borwyn villagers were skilled in cleaning game. They had tried to teach the spacers, but generally took over and did it themselves. "I got it," Max replied.

Deena laughed. "That's my man."

"Which means?" Max asked.

"Let Evelyn do it." Deena stabbed her finger at Evelyn. It was more than skill; it was to give her something to do. She'd just lost her husband of only a few weeks. They'd survived the crash, but she had to hold her friend while she died. The tragedies she'd suffered had been plenty. Coddling wasn't what she needed.

"Teach me," Max stated, rotating his knife to hand it to her, handle first. "Well, again. I didn't get it the first five times."

Deena smiled and nodded.

"No, but you did clean it the right way to not spoil the meat. How about you gather firewood so we can cook this and preserve the rest for future meals. How far are we from Glen's company?" Evelyn asked.

"Two or three days, at least."

"Then we're going to need more food." Evelyn made her first cut into the carcass.

"Yeah. I'll go back out." Max prepared to leave.

Deena stopped him. "You don't need to go right now." She nodded toward Evelyn.

"You're right. I need to learn to do this, because once we win this war, I'm digging a hole in the ground and that's where we'll live!"

"Hang on..." Deena scowled.

Evelyn snickered.

Max made himself comfortable where he could watch Evelyn work. He would have joined in, but the deer was small, and they only had one knife. Everyone had been engaged in something else at the time they ran for their lives.

Deena said, "I don't see any more smoke over the city. I wonder how things are?"

Max stared at her. "We don't seem to have anyone in the city to tell us." Before Deena could reply, Max raised his hand. "And good thing, too. Civil war? Shooting people on the streets? I barely made it to the restaurant in time." He laughed. "That was something. You working in a restaurant, and the boss man saying you were his best employee ever."

"We cut up an officer and fed him to the soldiers. Unintentionally, mind you. It's amazing what you can do with a liberal sprinkling of potent seasoning."

Tram opened his eyes and stretched his neck. "Sounds like something the Malibor would do."

"Yeah. The man who did it was a retired cook from the Malibor fleet. The man who got served up? He was vile. I'm not upset about it, well, anymore."

"Delivering justice at the end of a kitchen knife," Max said. "No one's judging you, Deena, especially not me."

"It was a sausage grinder, not a kitchen knife," Deena said matter-of-factly.

Evelyn stopped what she was doing, wiped the blade off on the hide, and placed the knife on top of the carcass. She limped past the first tree and leaned against it to puke.

Tram climbed to his feet and tottered to her to hold her hair out of her face while she sent bile to the ground.

He hugged her to him when she finished, holding her tightly while she sobbed.

Max hung his head and stared at the dirt.

"I'm sorry," Deena called across the small clearing.

"It's not you. It's all the horrible things together. Are we worse than the Malibor?" Evelyn cried.

"Not even close," Max replied. He stood. "What they would do for fun, we do out of necessity and only as a last resort."

Deena joined Max next to the carcass. She pointed toward the city. "There are good people in that city, but none of them are in charge. Everyone in a position of authority is willing to do anything, and all of it is self-serving. No, Evelyn. We're nothing like the Malibor. We're not going to take that city. We're going to liberate the people of that city. Tomorrow, Max and I are going back. We're going to start a revolution."

"We are?" Max asked. He poked Deena in the side, and she nearly collapsed from the pain.

Bec moved quietly through the corridors, looking for that one office to exploit. He found one with a sign taped to the bulkhead outside that said, "Temporary Command Post."

He listened at the door but didn't hear any noise from inside. He moved back down the corridor to a maintenance access crawlway. He popped the hatch and crawled inside, then pulled the hatch closed behind him. Satisfied that it made a decent hiding spot, he climbed out, leaving the hatch open.

Bec casually strolled back to the office. He tapped the access panel and to his surprise, the door opened. He peeked inside to find it empty. There was no dust because of the spaceship's air systems, but it had an aura that no one had worked there for a while. Papers were strewn across the four desks, and the lone worktable contained a cup, half-filled with ice-cold coffee.

He powered up a workstation that was still open to the last thing they'd had on the screen—an outer section that needed physical reinforcing.

That held no interest for Bec. He backed out to a menu with the plans numbered and in alpha-numeric order but without descriptions.

"Not going to make this easy, are you?" He started with one through ten. They were sequential sections in the ship. He then skipped to every five drawings and then every ten. He found nothing that hinted at the innovative engineering within the ship. Most were structural, some held power systems, but nothing showed the energy screens or artificial gravity.

Bec backed out even further to find a parent menu stating that the one he'd been in had been structural. He clicked on the one for the artificial gravity and disappeared into the very first drawing. After his examination, he went to the second, then the third. By the twentieth system drawing, he knew exactly what he needed. He also knew that what he looked at wasn't a Malibor design.

"Who did this?" he wondered.

Bec backed out of that folder and accessed the weapons systems. He cared less about them than the energy screen, but there wasn't a folder for that. He quickly discovered the energy screen was considered a weapon. He leaned back to think about it. He saw it differently, but the Malibor hadn't asked his opinion.

He started with the first drawing and found the math not just complex but incomprehensible. He grabbed a writing instrument off the table and started taking notes, copying formulas that used equations he'd never seen before. It took thirty minutes to copy down a scant amount of detail. Bec stared at the screens to memorize what was on them, same as he'd done for the artificial gravity drawings. He returned to that folder, where he found similar equations but in the background. They'd been translated into standard math that both the Borwyn and Malibor used.

Bec checked the weapons. There was a high-energy laser, a pulse beam, an EMP generator, and smart, stealthy missiles. The pulse beam held his interest until it didn't. He didn't care to produce any weapons. He checked the EMP generator. The first drawing held specs that showed it would eliminate any electronics to a range of ten thousand kilometers. That meant they could send the surface of any planet back to caveman days.

He returned to the artificial gravity design and made more notes until he had so many they wouldn't fit in his pocket, but he wasn't going to leave any of it behind. The technological innovations were lightyears ahead of where he was, and in Bec's mind, he was at the forefront of all engineering. The Malibor had lost their advantage over the previous fifty years.

"So where did you get this?" Bec wondered anew. He didn't expect he could replicate it on *Chrysalis*. He'd need a more robust industrial complex, like the one on New Septimus. He'd convince Jaq to drop him off there.

He only had to figure out how far they were from the shipyard. He dug deeper into the computer system until he found the access to show the screens from the bridge. He casually clicked on the button and found they were rounding the moon, Alarrees. *Chrysalis* and the space station were nowhere to be seen.

Bec checked the navigator's station, which confirmed

what he'd seen on the external views. Bec crossed his arms over his chest and studied the screen before him. There was an icon for the anticipated position of the enemy—a red icon located on the far side of the moon holding a steady course and speed that matched *Epica's*.

He wondered if he could transfer control of the ship, but there was nothing like that. All information coming from the bridge was one-way. It could only be manipulated from the bridge. He dug through other systems for anything that could provide him with the ability to take control. He didn't care how trivial the system. He only wanted to find a way that might help find back doors to access other systems.

Bec admitted to himself that Teo was better with computers. He used them only as tools. Teo expanded how they could be used to be integral to her processes, although the bio-pack was only marginally computer controlled. Bec didn't understand how that worked, even though Teo had explained it twice.

He would have conceded that she was smarter, but it was biological, which meant that it was one step above magic. He preferred hard steel and surging energy.

Bec powered down the computer and stood. The door opened.

"I'm sorry. I didn't think anyone was in here," the Malibor crewman said. He'd stopped in the doorway and was staring.

Bec shrugged. "I was just leaving. Can you tell me where to find gravity control? I got a bit turned around."

"That can happen. You don't look familiar. Did you board before we left the yard?"

Bec hated the inanity of such questions. His eye twitched as he fought against verbally leveling the mentally deficient individual. He lost his battle. "No. I've been aboard for a while. It's a big ship, and I don't have much contact with the crew."

The crewman nodded. "It's that way. Take the first stairs to the bottom deck. Turn left and it's the first space on your left."

Bec nodded and walked out.

"Hey," the crewman's voice called from behind him.

Bec waved over his shoulder and kept walking. He saw the stairwell, dodged inside, and ran to the lowest deck. He popped out and hurried to the space designated as Gravity Control. He didn't expect to find anyone in there since once it was running, it was hands-off.

He aimed to change that before anyone interrupted.

The control panel was straightforward. There were settings for zero to two gees with nothing outside that range, and it was all-or-nothing. It didn't give him the ability to isolate sections. The entire ship enjoyed one level of gravity. The current setting was one gee.

"How do I turn you off?" he asked the control panel, but it didn't respond. It wasn't voice controlled. No one had mastered that, not yet anyway.

A siren sounded and a red light flashed above him.

Bec had expected that. The Malibor crewman he ran across would have called in the chance meeting. It made Bec happy that he powered down the computer so they couldn't immediately see what he'd checked. Maybe they could, but there was no need to make it easy on them.

He also knew that he needed to leave the place the Malibor knew he'd be. The controls had a power input gauge. He backtracked that to the feed. The screen showed him where he needed to go. He hurried to the rear of the system, the opposite side of the gravity engine where the panel was located. The cable was below an access panel in the deck.

Bec pried it open.

Excited voices filled the space between the engine and the hatch that he hadn't heard open.

"He's not here," a recognizable voice said. "I swear this was where he was headed."

"You idiot. It was a diversion. We have to get to Engineering. He's probably sabotaging the engines right now!" Footsteps pounded away. The door closed, and Bec was happy to have heard it this time. He glanced around the corner of the gravity engine to make sure he was alone before getting back to work. He could pull the cable free, but then they'd just hook it back up.

He could short the entire system, which would take much longer to fix. He was perfectly comfortable in zero-gee. Would they be able to adjust? What if they tried to accelerate?

"Aha!" Bec cried. "They won't be able to maneuver."

He braced himself above the connection and pulled the cable free. The artificial gravity ended, and he would have floated free had he not been ready. He jammed the live end against the unit.

Artificial gravity returned. He thumped to the deck. He dropped the cable and hurried around the unit. It was most assuredly offline.

He groaned his dismay. Of course they had a backup. *Epica's* operations were critically dependent upon the gravity working. Without it, they would be unable to maneuver. Such a constraint would make actual combat sketchy. One hit in the wrong place would take the whole ship offline. Or an engineering fault. This was new technology.

Bec left the space. The red lights continued to flash. He hurried forward, staying as far from the nearby stairwell as he could get. He needed to find the second gravity generator or formulate a different plan.

Now that they were aware of what he was trying to do, he had no doubt there would be guards at the backup generator.

Time for a new plan since he had zero inclination to get into a physical brawl with anyone. He needed to outsmart them by taking the ship down without giving Jaq the opportunity to pepper it with E-mag fire. As he thought about it, he knew she had no choice.

She would kill her own brother to advance the Borwyn cause. The Malibor's master ship had to die if the Borwyn wanted any chance of winning this war. They thought they had time to deal with the big ship because it wasn't finished, but it flew at only seventy-five percent because the power and critical systems that made it a warship were functional well in advance of the final structural elements.

Bec couldn't even transmit data to *Chrysalis*. The moon blocked the signal. He had no way to check on the stealth scout ship, *Starbound*, but it was better than no chance at all.

He needed to find a communication terminal with access to an external array. Movement ahead forced him into a side room, where he hid in a small closet. Once inside, he closed his eyes and reviewed the pages and pages of formulas he'd seen. It was innovative and beyond that, it was unprecedented. Even new breakthroughs springboarded from existing technology. The gravity generator didn't do that.

Was it revealed in a dream? he thought. He discounted that. He didn't believe in Septiman. It was something different. He would figure it out once they stopped looking for him.

CHAPTER 12

Controlled application of extreme violence wins battles.
Holding that known violence back wins wars.

Jaq continued scowling at the screen. "It's been an hour and we haven't seen them, which tells me we've matched their course and speed. Good job to the flight control team. Now that we've bought ourselves time, what do we do with it?"

Alby scanned the bridge crew. No one wanted to speak up, not because they were afraid, but they didn't have any ideas. They were in a *safe* stalemate. No one was dying, at least not on *Chrysalis*.

"We're going to have to fight them. Coming up from behind is probably our best option," Alby finally stated.

"We couldn't penetrate the shield before. What gives us an advantage this time?" Jaq asked pointedly.

Alby shook his head. "We don't have a new advantage beside firing at a smaller and smaller aimpoint on the shield to see if we can break through."

"I don't advise it," Slade said. "All the data suggests we broke through not because of finding a weak point, but in finding overall weakness. Unless we can increase our rate of fire on the condensed energy screen, we won't be able to break through. Bec made it through because of the interference from the shipyard structure. Now that the ship is in open space, we don't have that advantage."

"That's the chill of outer space delivered to you through a cold shower," Jaq said. She climbed out of her seat. "Warn me before you accelerate." She pulled herself across the bridge but not all the way to Slade's workstation. "What can we do?"

Slade studied his screens. "We destroy the shipyard so it can't come back."

"We're not going to destroy the shipyard or the station. We need both of those. Any other options?"

"When they fire, their screen is weakened. We hit them at that point. Use the scout ships or a lander filled with explosives. We have one ready to go, don't we, Alby?"

Jaq shook her head. "It would be funny if it wasn't so tragic. Fill the landers with explosives and then don't. We can't blow them up."

"All we have to do is get them to shoot at something that is preferably *not* us. I think that energy weapon would do us ugly times three," Alby stated.

Jaq thought so, too. She expected a direct hit would destroy her ship and end the Borwyn's engagement of the Malibor fleet. They would have no resources remaining to fight with. *Chrysalis* was the only warship in the Borwyn fleet since they lost contact with *Matador*. Maybe the combat team on the ground could force the Malibor capitulation, but

Jaq expected that as long as the Malibor had that warship, they would never surrender.

"*Cornucopia* is requesting to speak with you," Amie announced, looking at Jaq.

"Put them on," Jaq said.

"We are approaching Alarrees. Where do you need us?"

"Away from here!" Alby shouted. "Don't you dare, Jaq."

Jaq had no intention of using the supply ship as a target. "Get me *Starbound*," Jaq said. "Standby, *Cornucopia*, but prepare to divert course away from Septimus."

"*Starbound*, this is *Chrysalis*, please respond," Amie said quietly into her headset. Three calls later, the scout ship answered.

"*Starbound*. What's going on over there?"

"We need someone to draw the fire of the big ship that is incomplete but appears to be operational with an energy screen and a pulse beam and the ability to fly. We're chasing each other's tail," Jaq replied.

"We never picked up on that. Sorry. Just like we missed the cruiser-carrier. Passive systems aren't showing us anything that you need."

Jaq shook off the apology. "What we need is a target to draw fire so we can shoot through a weakened screen."

"I heard that part, but I was ignoring it since I don't want to do that," *Starbound* replied.

"I appreciate your honesty," Jaq said. "I need you over here in case the Malibor start shooting at *Cornucopia*."

"And then what? Is that the trigger to make myself a target? I think you overestimate the ability of my small ship."

"I do not," Jaq replied. "I know that you can make your

ship visible or barely visible, and it is highly maneuverable. I doubt a ship that has never fired its weapons can hit you. They won't have refined their targeting parameters. The safest place to be might be where they're aiming."

"Then you make yourself a target," *Starbound* replied.

"We used to have better manners," Amie muttered.

"It looks like that's what we're left with. Alby, any volunteers to fly *Starstrider*?"

Alby raised his eyebrows. "*Starstrider*?"

"I can fly it," Taurus said.

"Absolutely not. I need you firing our weapons."

"You don't," Taurus replied. "Jaq just said the safest place to be was where they were aiming. We don't have much time, do we?" She looked to Jaq for an answer.

Jaq shook her head once more and confirmed what Taurus was thinking.

"I better get going. Don't accelerate until I'm in the scout ship. I don't want to be splattered across the bottom of the central shaft." Taurus unbuckled her harness and pulled herself out of her seat. She raced down the corridor using the mid-rail to keep herself moving in the right direction.

Alby looked to Jaq to say something. "You have fire control, Alby."

"That's it? You're just going to let her go?"

Jaq moved close to her battle commander. "Yes. We need the decoy so we can destroy that ship. My brother is on that ship, and I'm going to do everything in my power to kill him even though I don't want to. I was starting to like him. I like Taurus, too. If we want to win this war, we have to win this fight. That means we have to do everything we can, no matter the cost."

"Maybe Bec is annoying them so much that they'll surrender to get rid of him."

"We'll call that best-case scenario. I doubt they know he's on board, so we're going to create the conditions where we can get the best shot at that thing. When we do, I need you to be ready. The quicker you can kill it, the more likely we all survive."

Alby nodded. Jaq's tone suggested she was finished discussing it.

"*Cornucopia*, Jaq here. We'll need you to assume a position on the far side of Septimus, away from where we're playing tag with the Malibor ship. You need to be heading the other way. Do not give him a shot at the sides of your ship. Head on or tail only to reduce your target signature. Do you understand?"

"We do," Godbolt replied. "We're currently decelerating at three gees. We're going to be exposed as we hit zero-gee and fire up the other way. We could be your decoy, even though it wouldn't be our first choice. We might be it by default."

"Increase your acceleration to seven gees. You cannot approach the moon."

"We don't have seven gees, Jaq. We have three. That's it. This is an old tub."

"We'll track you and get ourselves into position. Looks like this fight is coming sooner rather than later." Jaq accessed the ship-wide broadcast. "Let us know when you're in the scout ship, Taurus. All hands, prepare for rapid acceleration."

Alby swallowed hard. He clenched his fists and stared at the main screen, but it told him nothing he didn't already know. He was grasping for a solution that would be better, but nothing was there.

"Alby, tell Benjy to launch that lander bomb when we get close to the station. Maybe the big ship will take a shot at it or not even see it in the noise of the station and shipyard."

"Roger," Alby said softly. He made the call barely above a whisper.

Jaq climbed into her seat. She stared at the screen, but it was to figure out the angles and do time-distance calculations. Shaping a three-dimensional battlefield was never easy, but this was the hardest she'd ever looked at. Too many moving parts. A ship that would end them with one shot. A space station with her people and a shipyard that needed to survive if they ever wanted to rebuild. And Bec on board the target of every E-mag that *Chrysalis* could bring to bear.

Her lips turned white, and her jaw muscles stood out as she fought to maintain her composure.

Ordering people to their deaths wasn't what she ever wanted to do.

"Brad." Pickford nudged him.

He roused. "Did I fall asleep?"

"Passed out, more like it. We slapped a bandage on your wound. Here, drink some more water."

"How long was I out?" Brad's brain was fuzzy.

"Not long. Maybe twenty minutes."

"That's a lifetime." Brad fought to gather his wits. The short rest made him feel both better and worse. "Any news from the other side?"

"I haven't turned on the radio, but it's been quiet. I don't think they know what to do because they're like us. Soldiers are a limited resource. Risk nothing. Lose nothing." Pickford tipped his chin at his own wisdom.

The corner of Brad's lip twitched upward. "Then maybe they're amenable to having a conversation." Brad had been lying on his back. He rolled over to push onto his knees, then he crawled forward and leaned against their barrier.

The metal blockage stood less than ten meters away.

"Hey you over there. This is Captain Brad Yelchin of the Borwyn fleet. Anyone willing to talk to me? I don't think we need to kill any more of your people to prove our point. I only want to talk."

"Which means you're desperate," came a gruff Malibor voice. "We will airlock every single Borwyn on this station!"

"Then why haven't you?" Brad countered. "We've been here for a few hours and there's a lot of bodies scattered on the first three decks, very few of whom are Borwyn. You've already lost this fight, and like I said, there's no need for anyone else to die."

"We are willing to die for our cause!"

"You are not," Brad shouted around the barrier. "Because it's not the end of life as you know it. It's the start of a whole new life with new opportunity. I wish you knew how much we long to live on the planet, or even in this station. We've been without gravity for so long, it bears on us like the fire of Armanor. Yet we want to lift our faces to the star's light.

Septimus is a big planet with plenty room for all of us. Let me say it a third time. There's no need for anyone else to die."

"You're desperate." The Malibor forced a loud laugh. "Why would we share our home world with outsiders?"

"About that. The Malibor came from Fristen by way of Sairvor. The Borwyn were born of Septimus. You've been fed lies the past fifty years. That's when the Malibor fleet descended on the Borwyn and destroyed nearly all of them. This station? Built by the Borwyn. Your flagship that you called *Hornet*? It was built by the Borwyn and called *Butterfly*. Have you been to Pridal, the city that you now call Malipride? That was built by the Borwyn, too. Think about it. We're locked and loaded over here, so if you doubt me or want to die for your cause, come on over. We'll accommodate you, but know that we won't be happy about it. I'd rather we all walk away."

"Retreat to the ladderwell and give us this corridor. We'll let you go in peace," the voice replied.

"In return, your people abandon the command center. We'll be happy to walk away if you stop fighting the war. It's time for this to end."

Pickford nudged Brad and whispered, "I agree one hundred percent. It's time to be done with this."

Brad nodded. He struggled to keep his eyes from glazing over. "Who has our last grenade?"

Pickford pointed to himself.

"Think you could get it past their defenses? Maybe scoot it through an opening on the deck."

Pickford looked through the gap. "If we could expand it a

little bit. We'll have to hit it with pulse rifle fire, which would use up some of our remaining power. We're running low."

"Make war so horrible that the alternative is better," Brad quoted. "Peace with the Borwyn. The Malibor are really screwed up in the head."

"Not all of them, only the ones who believed the propaganda they've been fed their entire lives."

"Which is all of them."

"Okay, maybe you're right, but this guy is listening. Ignore his words and listen to his tone," Pickford advised.

Brad spoke toward the opening. "Here's what we're going to do. We're going to hammer your barrier and chuck grenades through. Those who don't get away will be killed. Before you can blink, we'll be there, shooting everyone we see, and you'll get your wish of dying for your cause. We're going to do this in one minute. Get yourselves ready. Any final words to your loved ones? We'll see that they're delivered."

Brad rolled back. "Are you ready? Look lower right. There's something small filling a gap. Shoot everything we have at that, and then Pickford will chuck the grenade through. On my mark. Forty-five seconds and counting."

A scuffle broke Brad's concentration as he counted down. He peeked through the hole to see heads bobbing as the defenders fought each other. No barrels protruded.

He whispered harshly, "Go. Get to that barrier and capture them."

Crombie was first over. He hit the deck with a heavy thud and zigzagged the short distance to slam against the heaviest part of the metal barrier. He thrust his barrel through the netting at the top and shouted, "Surrender or die!"

Pickford ran around the barrier to the other side, making sure he headed for a solid section so he didn't press his body against one of the firing points.

"Don't run," Pickford warned. Gristwall helped Brad around the temporary barrier to the metal one. "Open it up, please."

Crombie tracked someone behind the metal framework as they moved to the front. A screeching of metal on metal signaled a section being pulled aside.

Brad walked through first with Gristwall aiming his pulse rifle past Brad's side.

"Who was I talking to?" Brad asked.

They pointed to an unconscious man.

"Help him up, please. As I said, and this is a promise, no one else has to die." Brad called over his shoulder, "Zin, move in between these two barriers and watch our six."

The Malibor lifted the man to sit on the deck and lean against the bulkhead.

"This is the last defense before the command center," Brad stated and nodded toward a heavy door ahead that opened to the side. The corridor beyond held the cable trap. Brad shouted, "Phillips! You over there?"

He didn't receive an answer, but the pain in his side didn't let him project his voice as he wanted.

"I'll try," Crombie said. He moved forward, training his pulse rifle on the command center access. "Hey! Phillips. You over there?"

A muffled voice replied, the higher pitch of a teenager.

"Keep cutting. You'll be through soon," Crombie shouted in encouragement.

Yellowish smoke roiled from the overhead.

"Get out of there," Brad called, but Crombie was already running. He made it two steps before falling to his knees. His eyes rolled back in his head as he fell on his face.

"Back up, people!" Brad waved toward the barrier. "Come on. You, too." He motioned toward the Malibor. They left the one behind who was sitting against the bulkhead. Brad pulled him to his feet and dragged him toward the barrier.

The yellow smoke cut off, staying close to the command center door as if on guard.

Brad pulled the soldier through and laid him on the deck. Brad fell back against the barrier to catch his breath and hold his side, trying to keep the pain from overwhelming him. Brad muttered, "I'm pretty sure the Borwyn didn't install that."

CHAPTER 13

Victory is a place of mutual acceptance.

Jaq breathed deeply. With the active scanners radiating at one hundred percent, they tracked *Starstrider* as it accelerated into the void. The lander followed it away from *Chrysalis* but at a much slower speed and at an angle to the scout ship's course. The lander took the shortest route to the predicted flight path of the Malibor ship.

Intercept the ship. Alarm its crew into firing. Hit them when they're exposed. That was the entirety of Jaq's plan.

Chrysalis had moved in behind the space station. With the evacuation of the civilians, it was no longer a collateral damage liability. She wanted it to remain intact, but her greater duty was to *Chrysalis*.

How many more sacrifices? she thought.

Jaq remained in her captain's chair. She expected erratic maneuvering would be called for.

"Ship-wide, please," she asked. According to the tactical

view on the main screen, they had less than a minute before the Malibor ship appeared. Four Borwyn vessels would be visible to it nearly simultaneously. *Cornucopia, Chrysalis, Starstrider,* and the lander.

Amie gestured toward the captain, who nodded in reply.

"All hands, prepare for combat. This is the most difficult enemy ship we've ever encountered. We have to take risks to get a shot at this vessel. And then we'll keep firing and maneuvering until one of us is finished. It needs to be that ship. Stay in your seats until damage control is called. I expect we'll be accelerating unpredictably. This is it, people. This is the one that wins the war. Jaq out."

Alby pumped his fist. "E-mags are hot," he reported.

The visual from outside the ship had it half-hidden behind the station. The E-mag batteries stood above the station with clear lines of fire to where they expected the Malibor to appear. They'd circled the moon for over an hour. There was no doubt where the enemy would be.

Chief Ping had his sensors painting a broad swath of space. Thirteen-year-old Dolly Norton leaned forward in her seat with both hands holding the headset earmuffs in place. Her eyes were closed, and she mumbled to herself.

Donal Fleming sat back with his arms crossed. He'd already done as much as he could to calibrate and align the E-mags with the targeting systems to a one one-hundredth of a percent error on a shot not affected by a celestial body's gravity. At extreme distances, that would be problematic, but at closer distances, the margin would be deadly.

The shepherd prayed under his breath. As if he saw Jaq leaning over the edge of her seat and looking at him, he opened his eyes and started to raise his hand. Jaq acknowledged him.

"In His name, we pray," the shepherd droned. "Grant us victory over Your enemies so we may resume our place in this system and worship You from the planet named in Your honor. Septiman! We invoke Your name as a trumpet call to battle."

The shepherd looked like he was going to say more, but Slade cut him off.

"Malibor ship coming around the planet. She wasn't circling the moon."

The lander and *Starstrider* were woefully out of position. The energy screen dimmed.

"Fire! Fire all batteries!" Jaq shouted.

Alby had started slewing the E-mags the instant Slade updated the screen with the big ship's location. An energy pulse launched into space but not at *Chrysalis*.

Cornucopia slowly accelerated away, but she was closer than Jaq expected, coming in at a ninety-degree angle from where the Malibor ship appeared on the planet side of the orbital plane and not the moon side.

The shot blinked into space, missing by a narrow margin.

The E-mags thrummed through the ship as they fired in a cascade instead of a barrage. New barrels joined those that had slewed more quickly.

The energy screen brightened as it returned to full power. The obdurium impacts looked like sparks dancing across the surface of a glass sphere.

"Move us to the other side of the station, Mary, quick as

you can," Jaq ordered. "Come on, Godbolt, find some more speed."

"Continuing to fire at the cyclic rate," Alby called out.

As long as rounds splashed off the energy screen, the Malibor wouldn't risk firing.

"Belay my last," Jaq said. "Close on that ship. Move us in tight where we cannot miss."

Alby agreed but selfishly so. He was willing to sacrifice himself to save Godbolt. Jaq had faith that the E-mags would penetrate the barrier in the one second before the pulse weapon fired. When would they blink?

"How long can we maintain the cyclic rate?" Jaq asked.

"Ten more seconds and then sustained rate of fire, or we can push it until they overheat and power down on their own, maybe twenty seconds."

"Mary, new course, angle us to deliver a full broadside, keep the power plants on the far side. Ferd, prepare to accelerate at nine gees should that energy screen dim. Don't wait on my order."

The flight control team acknowledged the order, fearing to blink and miss the immediate response this battle demanded. One second here or there could make the difference.

The energy screen dimmed.

Jaq held her breath and stared. The E-mags were already firing wide open. Ferd jammed the button for flank speed. The ship lurched.

The E-mag rounds peppered the screen in a tight pattern, but with the movement, the pattern widened.

"Come on!" Jaq shouted at the tactical display and live feed.

"Yes!" Alby cried with the first impacts on the enemy ship's hull.

A wave of energy washed through the screen and over *Chrysalis*. It made Jaq's hair stand on end. Sparks and pops sounded as the lights went off and the screen went dim. The emergency lights came on, bathing the command deck in red.

"Slade, what happened?" Jaq demanded. She felt loose against her harness. The engines were offline, and they were in zero-gee. Jaq tapped her comm button. "Engineering, Teo, we need power."

"Comm is down," Amie replied. "All of it."

"Going to Engineering," Jaq said. She bolted out of her seat and accelerated down the blood-red light of the corridor.

She caught the rail at the entry to the central shaft to slow down before pulling herself more deliberately downward. If power came back on and acceleration returned, she'd be splattered on the bottom. Holding on, she gave herself a chance to escape a long fall into darkness.

Then again, at nine gees, she'd be able to hold herself for microseconds. She let go and pulled herself faster.

The closer she got to the bottom of the shaft, the more she realized it wasn't going to be a quick fix.

She inverted and landed on her feet, absorbing the impact with her knees. She pushed off to go up one level and out.

"Teo!" Jaq called. "Report."

"EMP," Teo replied while standing locked to the deck and wrapping a wiring harness over the control station and into the ion drive. "Bypassing all electronic controls because I don't know which ones are good and which aren't. That could take weeks. I'm sending all the power through the bio-pack directly. If I'm right, it'll deliver what we need to get the ship moving. I'm certain we want to move, don't we?"

"We do. We're nothing more than a big target without propulsion. Are you sure you want to send our full unregulated power through the bio-pack? If we blow that, we're dead."

Teo stopped what she was doing. "Why aren't we dead already? I was watching the bridge display, and they had a clean shot. Are they going to board us instead of kill us?"

Jaq stepped forward. "I don't know anything. The sooner we can restore power to the ship, the better off we'll be. Engines will be good, but only if we don't blow them. Maybe start with the Malibor power plants?"

Teo thrust a wire cutter into the bag hanging over her shoulder. "Let's take a look."

The two hurried up two decks and down the corridor to where the power plants were stored in Cargo Bay Four. Spacesuits hung outside the small airlock. Teo dressed and went through first. Jaq followed as quickly as she could. Teo checked the connections. "We need a lot of replacements," she said, showing a circuit board covered in scorching. "We can't bypass these because they regulate the nuclear reaction within the system." She held up her radiation detector. "Levels are increasing. We need to do something, or this will pollute the whole ship."

"We can't jettison them," Jaq shot back.

"Energy gauge was at ninety-six percent when I last

looked. That's good enough to do what we need to do. Let's look at how we can channel that power where it can be put to the best use, without wasting it."

They left the cargo bay and tossed their spacesuits on the airlock deck. It wouldn't leave them completely radiation-free, but it was the best they could do under the circumstances. They flew back to Engineering, passing two damage control teams along the way. Jaq ordered both the teams to put up any lead they could between the ship and the Malibor power plants.

Both rushed off to find the necessary materials, leaving Jaq and Teo to continue their mission.

Jaq expected the death blow to arrive at any moment. Energy or projectiles or both slamming into her home and ripping it apart. But every second they didn't hit the ship was one more second the crew could invest to save themselves.

The cabling from the workarounds of previous months was scattered over the deck. Teo sorted through them until she found the one she wanted. "This'll do."

Jaq couldn't figure out what made it different from others, but Teo had a plan. "Do you need help?" Jaq asked.

"A couple techie types, yes. You? No."

Jaq laughed. "I like your honesty. I'll find a couple warm bodies with lots of smarts and send them your way."

———

The lights went off. Emergency floodlights snapped on with an audible pop, casting long shadows down the corridor. Brad was instantly on alert, at least as alert as his body would allow.

"What happened?" he asked their prisoners. "Put your arms down."

"We lost power, it seems. Like, the whole station. That's odd."

Brad felt his body lighten as the ring's spin slowed. There was enough friction between it and the other rings that it wouldn't spin into perpetuity. It needed energy to keep it moving.

"We're moving to zero-gee," Brad said. His people were better equipped to deal with it than the Malibor. "Was that meant to stymy us, because it won't."

"No. We don't have zero-gee on the station," one of the Malibor said.

The one on the deck groaned.

"Make sure he doesn't get any wild ideas." Brad waved at the other three prisoners. They pulled the man to his feet and held him tightly until they all started to float. Brad activated his boots to keep him magnetically attached to the deck. The others didn't have the magnetic boots because they had come from New Septimus and had only spent a minimal amount of time on *Chrysalis*. There hadn't been enough magnetic boots to go around, like much of the logistics on the Borwyn cruiser. "Where can we find out what happened?"

"The command center," the grumbling man replied, gesturing down the corridor from his waist because his arms were held.

"You'll want to grab onto something," Brad advised. "What's that smoke?" Brad looked over the barrier where the remnants of the gas lingered in the corridor. Crombie remained where he was, face down on the deck.

"Don't know," the gruff man replied. "What are you going to do with us?"

"You." Brad pointed at one of the other three Malibor. "What is that gas?"

"Don't know," the three said in unison.

"Fine, I'm going to turn you loose, and you're going down there to get my man and bring him back here. Do you understand?"

Brad clomped to the one not holding the prisoner and propelled him toward the barricade. He flailed wildly until he hit the metal. He grabbed the net over the metal obstructions and hung on. Brad tried to pull him off, but he wouldn't let go.

"So, you know what the gas is, don't you?"

He vigorously shook his head.

"But you know what it does. Is he dead?"

The man relaxed. "I don't think so. It's potent. We were told never to breathe it in, even in small quantities."

"We don't have a respirator, so which one of you can hold your breath long enough to get him out so he can stop breathing the remnants of whatever it is?"

The group of Malibor stared at the deck. Brad was the only one who could do it. Without leverage, anyone else would have a difficult time pushing Crombie out and then getting out themselves.

"I know," Brad said. "Keep an eye on these four. I'll be right back."

Brad pulled his coverall up to his nose as he walked

forward. The gas lingered in the air. It had been dissipating into the air-handling system, but with the loss of power, it would remain an obstacle. They needed power to clear the air so he could confront the command center. Brad took a deep breath two steps before the nearest tendrils of the gas. He stepped forward, grabbed Crombie by the collar, and pulled him toward the metal barrier.

Brad figured the total effort lasted ten seconds, but it was all he could do to gasp and pant to recover his breath once finished. He checked Crombie's pulse. It was slow, but it was there.

"You're right. He's alive." Brad was relieved. He faced the cabling beyond the command center. "No power, Phillips. Get those cables out of there but avoid the yellow smoke. It'll put you on your butt."

"Roger," came the young voice.

"Where's your dad?" Brad called.

"He's trying to seal off a section behind us. They snuck some people through."

There was a lot left unspoken. Brad didn't push it. "Cut everything you can while the power is off," he reiterated. "We'll meet in the middle once we can clear the air."

Pickford moved from one Malibor to the next. "We could have the four of you breathe in the gas, knock yourselves out, and then we wouldn't have to worry about keeping you prisoner. When you wake up, this will all be over."

"That's not a bad idea, Pickford. Will they breathe in enough for it to make a difference?"

"If they try to fake being passed out, we can stab them in

the eyeball. If they cry out, they were faking it," Pickford suggested.

"I like it," Brad agreed.

"Hey! You're not stabbing me in the eye!" the gruff leader of the group said. A black eye was swelling into existence from the brief pummeling imparted by his fellow soldiers.

"You're right. We won't do that because we're not Malibor. You should have figured that out by how we're treating you so far," Brad explained. "I don't want anyone else hurt, and I definitely don't want anyone else to die. Our challenge is, how do we talk with the people in the command center when there's some kind of knock-out gas floating in front of the hatch and there's no power."

"We can blow it down the corridor, but we'll have to let Phillips and anyone else know on that side."

"Will they open the door if we bang on it loud enough?" Brad wondered.

"I can't answer that," the lead soldier said.

"Fair enough." Brad pointed at Zin. "Break us off a couple pieces of that barrier so we can use them as fans."

Zin attacked two chairs to rip off the padded seats.

Brad said, "Turn to, young people."

They moved forward slowly, waving the seat cushions before them. By the time they cleared the area right in front of the command center, the yellow clouds had dissipated to where they didn't look like anything was getting blown into the cabling beyond.

"How you doing over there, Phillips?" Zin shouted.

"Doing just fine, whoever you are," the young man

replied. "I'll be through in another five minutes. Make sure the power doesn't come back on."

"If only we had that level of control," Zin replied. "We'll keep you informed. Get Edgerrin up here, if you can manage it."

"Will do," the teenager said and yelled the order into the void behind him.

Brad let Crombie and Gristwall guard the prisoners. He walked forward slowly and deliberately. He was sure the people in the command center couldn't see him without the power on. The air handlers were down. Everything was offline except the battery-powered emergency lights.

CHAPTER 14

A life worth living comes with risks, some greater than others.

Glen hopped off the horse and walked stiffly for a few steps before shaking off the effects of the long ride. He had thought about the arguments he would make with the council of elders, but it all depended on what they said. They could take the conversation in a variety of directions.

He waved at the guards as he passed. They all knew him because they were soldiers retired from the field, now working in the comfort of the mountain while enjoying being outdoors for many shifts.

The best of both worlds, they called it.

Glen stopped at the first guard inside the mountain. "Corporal! Fancy meeting you here. How's it hanging?"

"Good, sir. We figured you'd be back."

Glen had already taken a step away. He stopped cold and turned back. "Why so?"

"When those spacers stole the gunship from the Elders, a

lot of people had their hair on fire. Do you know what happened to it? Because they're out for blood, just to warn you."

"We think they were shot down," Glen replied. He kicked at the dirt of the cave floor before looking into the corporal's eyes. "Do you want this job forever?"

"It's not a bad gig. I have a girlfriend, and we get dinner or breakfast together every day, depending on my shift. But yeah, this is a good life."

"And that's why we're condemned to live it." Glen pointed upward. "Those people came here to free Septimus for all Borwyn. And they're doing it whether we help or not, so we're helping because I'm tired of getting shot at. I'm tired of moving from camp to camp under cover of darkness. What about those people in the mountain? There are citizens within who have never been outside."

"Their loss," the corporal said weakly. "Are we winning? If the ship was shot down..."

"We are winning. Last we heard, Borwyn have boarded the space station between here and Alarrees."

"The station! I thought that was Malibor propaganda."

Glen winced, wondering how the corporal had reached that conclusion. "It's real, and in Borwyn hands once more. We're going to win the war, the one we thought was long over, but thanks to people who survived the harshness of space, we have a chance to be free. *Spacers* is a term that should be spoken with reverence, not derision. Carry on, Corporal. I have to talk with the council."

Glen walked away before the conversation could continue. Not that he minded educating the young man, but he needed to do the same thing with the elders and didn't want to exhaust his mental stamina.

He wasn't used to engaging with people in rhetoric. He talked with his soldiers every day, but that was different. It wasn't verbal jousting with people who were entrenched in their position based on a narrow-minded, risk-averse view.

Glen stopped and leaned against the cave wall. They were doing the same thing as *Chrysalis* and company—trying to survive—but with limited resources on the ship, long-term survival depended upon finding a planet where they could live.

They came home.

Glen clenched his teeth and headed into the maze of walkways and streets that made up New Pridal. He strode unerringly across the expansive main cave to the tunnel where the leadership was located. He found his way to the outer office and made his presence known.

The secretary told him to wait as the elders weren't in session yet.

"How about just the general?" Glen asked.

"You'll have to wait," she told him. There was kindness in her voice, but it belied a hopelessness.

"I'm going to give it an hour, then I'm getting something to eat and returning to the front lines. This fight is already here, whether the elders want it or not. We have no choice but to fight. New Pridal can join us, or they can sit back and wait, but actively interfering by cutting off the front lines is like joining the Malibor. Is that what the elders are doing?"

"Of course not!" the secretary retorted. "How dare you!"

Glen glared. "When's the last time you were outside?"

Her mouth fell open. The fire behind her eyes dimmed. "I'll see what I can do."

"That's all I'm asking. I need to tell them what is happening and encourage more support than we're getting. Abandoning the assault brigade will risk New Pridal's existence. Not supporting us, which is what I see right now, is a higher risk than sending everything we have into the field. We need to win this war, and we're close. Please, help us to help all Borwyn."

"I wasn't aware that the front-line companies weren't receiving the usual support."

"It's not what it needs to be. I'm here to fix that or cut all ties with New Pridal."

Her mouth fell open again, and she stared in disbelief. "You can't be serious."

"Get them to talk with me. I'll explain how critical this situation is. This is it. For all of Septimus to see."

"I think I understand. They stole the gunship," she said softly.

"They can't steal what they brought here of their own accord. Spoils of war. But it was their spoils, not ours. Thinking we could take that away from them was actively countering a strategic plan that had been put into motion years ago. Do you want to take my new pulse rifle?" He held it out to her. She recoiled from it. "Because the gunship, just like this rifle, is how we're fighting this war. And for what it's worth, we think the gunship was shot down after it completed its mission. The Malibor thought it was other Malibor rebelling. Last I heard, the city was descending into chaos. It's time to attack a weakened enemy, torn apart by their own misguided fears."

He left that last thought with the secretary. He had expected to convince the elders, not a go-between who wouldn't bring the argument with Glen's passion.

Then again, he expected the elders to not receive him even though he'd been summoned.

He paced in the small outer office while he waited for her to return. He sat for a while. He wandered the outer hallway, keeping the open door within sight, checking often. After thirty minutes, he chalked a short message onto her note board that he was getting something to eat, a little coffee, and then he'd be back.

Glen walked away, expecting the secretary to return at any moment, but the delay continued. He hurried away, hoping for a quick meal. Despite his current animosity, he respected the elders and everything they'd done to help New Pridal over the long decades in hiding. They deserved Glen giving them a chance.

He tried to relax, but he was fighting an internal war as much as an external one. He was in charge of the elite First Company, which represented the entirety of the assault brigade's combat power. He answered to no one because there was no brigade commander. It was him and Eleanor coordinating with the mountain.

Now, he found himself hanging on, reacting to events well out of his control. People with more to lose were running the strategy for all Borwyn. They had asked for Glen's help, but they were willing to do without it. Go it alone because they believed so strongly in what they were doing.

And that made Glen a believer, too. He drained one cup of coffee, ate fast, and took the second cup with him when he hurried back to the elders' outer office.

The secretary was there.

"They'll see you now." She pointed at his coffee and then her desk.

Glen drank it quickly and walked down the short corridor to the council chambers. He found a single chair in the middle of the open area where a curved table allowed the five elders to look down on him. He opted to stand.

"Esteemed members of the council, I wanted to update you on the advances of the war against the Malibor."

The general raised one wrinkled finger. The translucent skin showed blue veins beneath. He didn't look healthy. Glen stopped talking and waited.

"We could prosecute a war better if we had a gunship, don't you think?" the general said.

Glen looked from one to another, taking in each member of the council. Three men and two women, all silver- or white-haired with pasty, splotchy skin. Their long lives inside the mountain had come at a cost.

"Borwyn forces under the command of Captain Jaq Hunter are prosecuting the war very well with the assets in their control. They have boarded the space station. Borwyn have returned to the station."

"They do not have our approval. It would be best if they coordinated their efforts with ours."

"They have, and we have. New Pridal has produced pulse rifles, based on the space Borwyn design. They have provided us with the hope of victory because they captured a gunship. It was never ours. It was theirs and only became ours because they encouraged us to think on behalf of all Borwyn, not just those hiding inside this mountain."

"Young man," a woman to Glen's left said. "The Borwyn have survived because of hiding in this mountain. Feeding fifty thousand people every single day is a great challenge that people like yourself don't appreciate."

Glen's eyebrows plunged with confusion he was unable to hide. "Where would you ever get the idea that I don't appreciate the logistics required to keep us alive? That's the principle that guides my direction of our forces in the field. Without food, we aren't soldiers. We become scavengers, starving for our next meal. Combat operations depend on well-supplied troops. No, ma'am. You are grossly incorrect in assuming what I don't appreciate."

Glen stood tall, refusing to be put in his place.

"Why are you doing this?" he asked. "The war is being fought out there." He pointed for emphasis. "Whether you like it or not."

"We most assuredly do not. We kept the Borwyn alive. How quickly your war would throw that away. Have you surrendered your command to this Captain Hunter person?"

"I'm sorry, what?" Glen tried to remain calm, but he felt himself flush with the heat that rose through his body. "Have you lost control of your senses?"

"You are treading a fine line," a man to Glen's right said. "The authority of this council is not in question."

Glen bowed his head and stared at the floor. He was getting nowhere. He lifted his head to address the speaker. "The authority of this council has been in question every single day since we were chased out of Pridal. You've always done right by us. But now, circumstances are out of your control. The war is being fought by our fellow Borwyn on our behalf. Is your goal to help the Borwyn or to retain your power? If it's the latter, then yes, I am questioning your authority."

"You're the leader of our military forces in the field," the general said, motioning for calm.

Glen was happy that he hadn't raised his voice. He was disappointed that he had failed to deliver better arguments, because the council had lived down to how poorly he expected them to act.

"As the leader, you will always think in terms of war and combat. It's the only thing you know in achieving a desirable end result. What if I told you that we've been negotiating with the Malibor for a peaceful resolution to the war?"

"Negotiating with the Malibor? I have a hard time believing that."

"We don't attack Malipride, and they don't attack us here," he said, looking down his nose as if he'd just laid the final trump card.

"But they have been attacking us. Two attacks in the past two months. It's not much, but their adherence to any deal is questionable."

"We have allowed their squads to check on us, to see that we aren't a threat to them."

Glen coughed lightly to clear his throat. Was the old man hallucinating, or had he actually negotiated with the Malibor?

"You've been more effective than we expected, but that's

the risk when the Malibor come out here. If you had let them go, they would have walked around and then left in peace."

Glen threw his head back and stared at the ceiling.

"Excuse me, but you said we made pulse rifles for our soldiers? We approved no such use of the manufacturing equipment. All military allocations must go through this council."

Glen looked at the speaker through tired eyes. He suddenly felt more exhausted than he'd ever felt before. He'd been running around the forest, hiding and training and fighting, when none of it mattered. He became more convinced that Jaq Hunter and Crip Castle were right in fighting the Malibor with every fiber of their being.

It was what Glen had told the secretary. The elders were helping the Malibor. It was indirect, but it guaranteed the Borwyn would forever exist in the shadows.

Glen laughed and kept laughing. He looked from face to face again, scanning them and hoping to see that they were joking in some way, that they would roll in more weapons and deliver a strategy that would return the Borwyn to the land under the blue skies of Septimus. But they weren't joking, and they weren't interested in what Glen had to say.

"I'm going to say my piece, and then I'm going to leave. The only support we've gotten from the mountain for this operation is weapons that were made on the sly. We thank whoever believed in us enough to make that happen. The extra food for the spacers and the eastern Borwyn we had to supply ourselves with extra hunting and scavenging. But the change in weather has made this difficult. We'll probably end up killing one of our older horses to help us over the hump, but not for too much longer.

"You see, this war is in the resolution phase. Whoever wins the current battle will win the war. If *Chrysalis* is defeated, then we will have all lost, but I doubt they'll lose because of Jaq Hunter, who will win through force of will alone. Which is something we used to have. I'm taking my company to the city, and we are going to force them to surrender. The gunship hit them hard, where it hurts, but then was shot down. We have to press our advantage while we have it.

"You can sit here and talk, but I beg of you, do not interfere. Any actions you take that prevent us from winning this war will be seen as collaboration with the enemy. History will not just judge you harshly, it will condemn you, no matter how much good you've done for the survivors of the lost fight for Pridal.

"We're going to win this war, and then we're going to offer the free people of New Pridal to join us outside, in the city, in the fields, or in the forest, because they will have the freedom to choose. Many won't go. They'll choose to stay here where they're comfortable. We'll open trade between Pridal and New Pridal, because we all deserve to do something that matters to help our fellow Borwyn, to do right by our families, and most importantly, to enjoy life. There's a lot more to it than what you have inside this mountain. A lot more.

"Now, if you'll excuse me, I'll be on my way. There is no need for further communication with the assault brigade. We'll contact you when it's over. If we don't contact you, then you can assume we've been killed and the war is lost. If that happens, I wish you the best of luck since luck won't have been on our side, just like you aren't."

He waved and walked out before they could reply. He'd made peace with cutting ties with New Pridal on the way in, all the while hoping he wouldn't have to. Hope wasn't his plan. His plan was to do as he'd done. Deliver his news and leave. At this point, best case was that the elders didn't interfere.

He waved to the secretary. He stopped to take his cup. "I'll return this to the restaurant."

"I hope you got what you wanted."

"I didn't, but I didn't expect to. I'm happy not being arrested, but I'm leaving and won't be back. Ever."

He continued down the tunnel to the main part of the city. He hurried through to escape before they could order him arrested. He hoped he had a good enough reputation with the solders on duty that they wouldn't comply with the order if it had been given. As long as he wasn't coming back, there would be no other repercussions. The war would be over by then. They'd have time later to sort things out. He reached the tunnel to the outside and figured he was home free when the corporal stepped in front of him to stop him.

"I'm asking you not to follow those orders. Let me go, please. We'll take care of the Malibor, but only if I can be out there."

The corporal tilted his head. "You don't want us to go with you and bring a wagon train of supplies?"

"I'm sorry, what?" Glen asked.

"That's our orders. We're being sent to the field. Do you

have any idea how long we'll be out there? My girlfriend will get antsy."

"I wouldn't think more than one, maybe three years."

The corporal looked at him in shock.

"I'm kidding. I'm thinking months, though, but to clarify, you received those orders from the council?"

"From the general himself. *Provide all support, both personnel and material.* That was it. I have to warn you, some of our people are out of shape. They've grown accustomed to home cooking and a warm body sleeping next to them."

Glen couldn't help himself as he glanced at the corporal's burgeoning midsection. "They'll get in shape," Glen replied. "Follow me. We have a lot of work to do." Glen's step had an added bounce, and he lifted his head high to walk into the sunshine and stand under the blue sky.

CHAPTER 15

Brace for impact.

Jaq roamed the corridors, looking for damage control teams to put to work. She knew which circuit boards were most critical, which meant the replacement boards they'd stockpiled from *Cornucopia* were in boxes, tethered to the bulkheads in the corridors. The older boards that had been replaced were still in inventory.

"Break them out and start replacing the ones that are fried. One by one, from the energy storage system outward to E-mag Battery Four. Control the flow, people. Let's start bringing systems back online," Jaq told them.

She had gotten over the feeling that they were going to be attacked at any moment. She had no idea why, unless the EMP had fried the big ship's own systems. She found morbid humor in the thought.

Every second they were given was a gift that they would use to get themselves into the fight. The sooner they could get an E-mag functional, the better the chance they could destroy the big ship. They could fire visually.

Jaq found her way to the port roller airlock, where she climbed in to look through the porthole in the outer hatch. She could see Alarrees straight out the window, ninety degrees to *Chrysalis's* orientation, and it was drifting to her right. *Chrysalis* had been on a course to open space. They hadn't been going fast when they lost power, so they continued on at upwards of five thousand kilometers an hour, which was slow compared to what they were capable of.

Jaq crossed the ship to the starboard airlock. This view was more enlightening. The big Malibor ship was drifting without the energy screen radiating around it. In the far distance, *Cornucopia* was tumbling. She couldn't tell if the ship was being affected by Septimus's gravity.

The Malibor's new weapon was powerful, but it had a significant flaw.

It also extended Bec's life, but she had already reconciled herself with his life. He never should have gone over there.

Bec floated free. He activated his magnetic boots and opened the hatch to look down the corridor. He saw one guard in the middle of the corridor, flailing as he tried to grab the bulkhead and missed with each pass. Bec walked slowly toward him.

He stopped when he was out of reach. "Did they fire the EMP weapon?" Bec casually asked.

"I think so. They don't tell us much. I'm installing wavelength propagators to increase the functional power output on the pulse beams. Exciting stuff. But then they told me to watch this door and report if anyone tries to go through."

"Has anyone?" Bec asked.

"No. It's stupid people giving stupid orders."

"Can I see what you're working on? Sounds fascinating. I'm here to work on the artificial gravity. It's exponentially more advanced than anything else I've seen besides the energy screen. That's also extremely advanced. Most impressive." Bec stepped forward and caught the man. "Hang onto my shoulder."

"Why do you have mag boots?"

"I'm working on the gravity generator. I'm good but have trust issues, as my boss has said."

The man started laughing and kept laughing. "You are my hero. The gravity guy wears mag boots. Wait until I tell the engineers in the weapons section."

"No need to tell them anything," Bec said. "It'll be our secret. I'm sure my boss would be upset about projecting an incorrect level of confidence, but you had it right. Stupid people giving stupid orders."

"That works for me," the Malibor engineer said. He pointed, and Bec went in the indicated direction.

"Did the EMP weapon fry our own systems? What idiot designed that thing?"

"Another zinger! You're on fire, my man." The Malibor directed Bec away from a group of people working at the end of the corridor. "It's just in here."

Bec walked into the space indicated. A single structure dominated. It went from one end to the other and continued through the bulkhead toward what Bec assumed was the outer hull.

The emergency lighting in the space was bright, almost as good as the normal overheads.

The man grabbed a handle on the outer case and pulled himself toward a removable panel. He undid the clasps with one hand and pulled the door out and down. It was on a rotating hinge that cleared the opening without the worry of losing the cover to zero-gee foibles.

Then again, they hadn't contemplated zero-gee.

Inside, he pointed to a series of capacitors. "They build the energy one to the other until final discharge. Happens over the course of point-zero-four nanoseconds. It's quite impressive. Total energy discharge is eighty-seven billion megajoules. I couldn't be more proud."

Bec nodded. He had already stopped listening. The weapon was nothing more than scrap. "Having it energized during the EMP discharge didn't do you any favors. Do you have a complete backup system?"

"What?" The man looked where Bec pointed. Scorching and melting told the complete story. He groaned and deflated. "I better see what we have."

"Here's a zero-gee trick. Kick off wall to wall and zigzag your way down the corridor. You'll get where you want to go. Easy does it. Casual pushes. There's nothing like moving in zero-gee. It's effortless, so if you're working at it, you're doing something wrong."

"Thanks, gravity guy. I think it's hilarious that you are comfortable in zero-gee."

"What can I say? I've had more setbacks than breakthroughs. I better get to the second gravity generator. I've already checked the first one. Can you tell me which way to go?"

"Sure. Out the hatch, first hatch on the right. I'm surprised this corridor didn't look familiar."

Bec laughed. "Me, too!"

The pulse weapon engineer pushed toward the door. He landed on the door, tapped the switch with his toe, and pulled himself out when the door opened. He somersaulted into the corridor, and the door closed behind him.

Bec took one last look at the design and decided that he had been correct earlier. It was a waste of his time.

He walked across the space, out the door, and turned right, ignoring the group at the other end of the corridor. In the next space, he found the second gravity generator. He worked his way around the other side of the massive piece of equipment and repeated what he'd done earlier. Whenever they restored power, the gravity generators would not function until the Malibor engineers reattached the power cables. Bec expected he'd earned himself an extra five, maybe ten minutes. What would he do with that wealth of time?

He wasn't sure. He was happy creating chaos since he'd gotten what he came for. Bec's goal was to get off the ship and return to *Chrysalis*.

It dawned on him that they'd fired the EMP weapon for a reason. *Chrysalis* was probably without power, too. And the space station. Anything within ten thousand kilometers.

He who got their power online first would win this battle.

Bec decided that he needed to return to the original engineering space where they first decided he was a threat. He hadn't been at that point, but taking him prisoner? They had made an enemy of him. It was time to sabotage the ship. If they couldn't fly and couldn't fire their weapons, they were harmless. The weapons were fried, but the engines were probably salvageable.

It made Bec wonder about the ion drives on *Chrysalis*. His babies. The core components were protected against an EMP, but the power system feeding them had to be down. Teo could get them up fairly quickly. E-mags were easier to bring up than an energy weapon. He thought he remembered a reference to a laser weapon. He expected that was doubly fried.

He was sure the missiles were hardened, but he could make sure the Malibor weren't able to open the outer doors.

Look at me being a soldier, he thought. *I hate it, but to get back home, it's what needs to be done. Maybe I can call the ship?*

Bec strolled out of the space and to the stairwell not far from the second gravity generator.

"Hey!" someone yelled from down the corridor. "Stop!"

Beck turned to look at them and found two crew standing against the bulkheads on opposite sides, holding a third crewman between them. They propelled the volunteer down the corridor toward him. The man sailed in a straight line, his hands at his side as if he were a missile.

He didn't understand that he would fly at the same speed no matter how aerodynamic he was. The friction from the air had no impact on his slow-motion approach.

Bec returned to the gravity generator space and grabbed a spanner from the tool cabinet. The rest floated free, but he didn't care. He stepped back into the corridor and waved the spanner like a club. The crewman realized the folly of their plan. He started waving his arms frantically, only to realize it made no difference to his trajectory.

He inverted to fly at Bec feet first.

I really hate this, Bec thought. *But needs are needs.*

He swung hard to hit the crewman in the ankle. The bone crunched under the impact. Bec reached for an arm when the man spun after getting hit. Bec caught the man's hand and swung him head-first into the bulkhead. Blood spurted from the impact and the resultant head wound. The man drifted unconscious.

"Don't do that again!" Bec yelled down the corridor. He walked away without looking at the damage he'd done to the Malibor crewman.

Gravity was a great equalizer. Those without it were envious of those who had mastered it. But not Bec. The lowest common denominator was being able to work without gravity. He could, and they were demonstrating that they could not.

The Malibor had been in space for decades and artificial gravity was new. They should have had experience working in zero-gee, even the newest crew members, but these weren't typical crew. They were engineers and technicians, apparently unused to space.

The captain and his people had appeared to be experienced spacers, so Bec needed to avoid them. In the engineering areas, however, he would dominate. That was his wheelhouse, as they would say.

Bec headed up one deck to the level where the lander

was possibly still attached to the airlock and where the original engineering section was located. It was the largest deck in the ship, designed like no other. It was made like an aircraft where gravity pulled the passengers down instead of from nose toward tail, as physics demonstrated under acceleration in the zero-gravity environment of space.

In the extended corridor above, he found more twists and turns as room sizes varied. He wondered if the designers did it for aesthetic reasons. He shrugged his indifference and followed the route he'd taken last time. The crewman was no longer working on the panel in that corridor.

Bec opened it up and tore out what work the man had done. He spun the repaired part down the corridor and closed the panel. He strolled ahead under the emergency lights. Their emergency system was good, much better than what they had on *Chrysalis*, but the ship had not been designed to lose gravity. Bec couldn't get his head wrapped around what he considered to be an epic failure of *Epica* proportions.

He laughed at his own joke, but footsteps from ahead shocked him out of his reverie. They were the heavy clomping of magnetic boots. The professional fleet personnel.

Bec tried a door and found it was secured. He released his boots and pushed off the bulkhead to fly to the next door, which opened when he tapped the panel. He activated his boots as he eased through the doorway. He closed the door and pressed his ear against it to listen.

The clomping approached the door and continued past. Two unique treads. Two crew with mag boots. Were they pushing someone along with them? Bec punched the door release, and the door opened. It dawned on him that the doors were working when they shouldn't have. Were they isolated from the system? Pneumatically actuated? Magnetically? He shrugged away the anomaly and decided not to waste any more brain cells on it. He peeked out to see two men walking away from him.

The captain from his earlier unpleasant meeting and another crewman that Bec hadn't seen before. They turned the corner and kept walking. The sound of their passing faded until it disappeared.

Bec hurriedly bounced back and forth down the corridor, hesitant to make any noise with his boots until he was certain the professional crew wouldn't hear.

He activated his boots when he closed in on the door to Engineering. They pulled him to the deck. He walked gently through to find crew going about their business. The crewman from the corridor was there, digging into a panel where he looked right at home.

He pointed at Bec and opened his mouth.

Bec shushed him with a single finger to his lips and walked over to join the young man. "What do you have going on?"

"Aren't you the enemy?"

"No." Bec shook his head for emphasis. "Are you?"

"No. I'm a systems technician."

"I'm an engineer." Bec nodded toward the panel. "The EMP fried everything. I think that was self-inflicted pain."

"Yeah. I thought it might. It was grounded to the hull, but the projectors for it are inside the energy screen. What did they think was going to happen?"

"Did it affect the enemy ship or the station?"

"No clue," the man answered. "But we're under orders to get the power online. The ship was supposed to be hardened, but I hate to say it, we got the worst of it."

"I'll let you get back to it." Bec clapped the man on his shoulder.

He nodded and turned his attention to his work.

Bec headed for the main control panel, but it was offline. He wasn't sure if this was where he needed to focus his attention. He made a circuit of the space. They were replacing circuit boards at a high rate of speed, testing each element with handheld meters. Bec wanted one of them. He wanted to see for himself how bad the damage was.

He had a good look at the pulse beam weapon, and it was completely burned out. *We got the worst of it,* the man had said.

Bec ran through the scenarios. There was nothing more he could do here without digging deeper into individual systems. Was the damage to the gravity generators enough? The technicians weren't used to working in zero-gee. It would take them forever to bring the systems online.

Time to go, Bec thought. Without the energy screen, he could fly away unimpeded. "Why didn't I think of this sooner?"

"I'm sorry?" a crewman said from nearby.

"Nothing. Just talking to myself because my expert counsel has failed me. I know where I'm needed, and it's not here. Carry on." Bec strolled away while the Malibor crew watched.

Once in the corridor, he released his boots and kicked off

one wall to the next, zigzagging down the corridor. He listened in between kicks but didn't hear the clomping of mag boots. Bec rounded the corner and kept going, all the way to the airlock, which he found closed. The captain and the other professional spacer were in the lander. Bec rushed into the airlock and closed the outer hatch. He yanked the manual release handle. The lander floated free, ejecting one body into the void. The lander's lights were off.

"Since you took my ship, I'm taking yours. Where's that bridge?"

CHAPTER 16

Perseverance is more than physically powering through. It's not giving up even when you can't keep going.

Max jogged at a speed that Deena could maintain. It was daytime and cool, but they'd cover as much ground as possible in the daylight and save the final approach for the darkness.

"The spaceport," Max said.

"It doesn't have a wall, that's something."

"I have wire cutters," Max said. They'd returned to the gunship, where the toolkit was lying on the ground outside.

Deena nodded, breathing heavily. Her side still hurt, but a couple nights' downtime in the cold had eased the worst of it. She clutched Tram's pulse rifle to her. It was heavier than her Malibor blaster but would provide greater firepower against a known enemy. If Tram and Evelyn kept it, they wouldn't be able to use it to protect themselves. They had the lighter Malibor blaster in case a deer wandered into their small camp.

On their way, they saw numerous shuttles dotting the sky, descending from orbit. "What do you think that is?" Max asked. They stopped to squint at the aerial parade.

"Shuttles from the space station. That looks like a lot of them. The Malibor have evacuated. Does that mean Jaq won?"

Max nodded. "I don't see how it can mean anything else."

The revelation boosted their spirits and added wings to their feet. Max and Deena covered ground quickly and stopped a few kilometers short of the wall. They ducked into a shallow depression and disappeared from view.

"Try to get some sleep. I'll watch," Max offered.

Deena refused, offering to watch because she was too sore to sleep, but rest would be just fine.

Max refused, so they both laid there doing nothing. "Is this the best use of our time?" Max wondered. He peeked over the edge at the imposing wall of Malipride. "Was that wall there before the fall?"

Deena took a while before she replied. "I heard it was built by Borwyn slave labor."

"The single greatest Malibor construction project—put a wall around their conquest to make sure no one gets in as well as keep those inside from getting out." Max wrapped his arm around Deena's shoulders and pulled her close. Deena quickly fell asleep. Max had to fight to stay awake, fidgeting with his free hand and staring into space while running through scenarios about once they made it to the spaceport.

He wanted to find the general. If the two of them were

going to cause the most damage to the Malibor military infrastructure, they needed help. If they were going to do it and avoid loss of life, then they needed an insider. The general answered the question in both cases.

After Armanor cast its long shadows of sunset and darkness descended, Max stood. Deena rose with him and punched him lightly in the chest. "Did you get any sleep?"

"I got everything I needed," he replied. He stepped carefully from the depression and walked over rough but even ground at a thirty-degree angle from their previous route. To the right, the south, the spaceport sprawled across tens of square kilometers, offering ships a level site on which to land.

They maneuvered much more slowly in the dark. Didn't highlight themselves. Sudden movements stood out to anyone who might be watching the darkness. They encountered the field of boulders that had been placed as an additional barrier around the city. They'd crossed it once on the way out. It provided some cover and concealment for those who approached on foot. A force using ground vehicles would have been prevented from moving through.

No enemy had ground vehicles to use against the city. The Malibor were fighting a war against an enemy that only existed in their minds. They thought they were safe when they were their own worst enemy. The gunship attack had exposed that paranoia.

It was time to pick up the pieces.

Max worked his way through the boulders, stopping to check for tripwires, mines, or traps, but the ground was clear with just weeds and undisturbed rocks. At one point, there may have been a multi-level anti-personnel system in place but not any longer. The way was clear. The Malibor had prepared for enemies from within. They'd learned over the course of five civil wars that the Borwyn weren't the greatest threat.

Until the Borwyn returned and they still believed it.

Max climbed over the boulders he couldn't work his way between or around. He stopped at the final obstruction before a ten-meter space that was clear to the fence line.

It looked foreboding in the pale darkness, backlit by distant floodlights. Lights along the perimeter were dark.

"Is the power out?" Max wondered, even though lights were on in the city.

Deena shrugged. "Who knows why they aren't using these lights, but look at all those shuttles. I think you're right. They had to evacuate the station. I rode one of those to the station and then to the shipyard to join *Hornet's* crew."

Random thoughts. Nothing gelled.

Max watched for a long while. It was dark but still early. The silence was as deep as the night.

"Maybe the evacuees are taking all their attention?" Max suggested.

He waved for Deena to follow. He kneeled next to a light pole with its floods facing up and down the fence but not directly below, in case they came on while he was working. He counted on the pole's shadow to hide him from instant observation.

Using his wire cutter, he started working on the fence links. The cutters weren't made for something the thickness and strength of this fence. He had to use both hands and make an effort with each cut. The tool's edge dulled quickly, making cutting harder and harder.

He had to take a break.

Deena watched while he studied the fence to minimize the number of cuts remaining.

Finally, he grabbed the cut section with both hands and yanked it hard to one side. It opened a gap big enough for Deena to crawl through. On the other side, she held the fence up while he worked his way under it, pushing his pack and pulse rifle before him. He left the wire cutter on the ground. It was useless. It was also a Malibor-made tool, so it didn't give away the fact that the infiltrators were Borwyn.

"Carry your rifle at the ready," Max said. He stood straight and walked along a path carved next to the fence line. "We're patrolling."

Deena followed him toward the city side of the spaceport.

"Make like we belong. You better let me go first. You look like the anti-Malibor."

"And you're beautiful, so they won't look anywhere else. Good plan. I can shoot over your head if need be."

"Don't shoot over my head. These things make too much noise." Deena ran her hand along his arm as she passed. She glanced back once she was in front and caught Max looking at her butt. "You won't find the Malibor there."

"No, but I like to stay motivated," he replied.

They strolled the perimeter as if they belonged there. A vehicle approached on the road to a shuttle pad. The passenger waved at Max and Deena. They waved back.

"Was this your plan all along?"

"I like how you think I had a plan with this much detail. The only plan I have is that we need to talk with the general. We need his help if the Malibor are going to survive this. We're not going to level the city, but innocent bystanders will get killed regardless if we can't get the Malibor to capitulate."

"The two of us are going to force them to surrender?"

"No," Max replied. "The two of us and whoever we can get to join us are going to approach whatever leaders remain and show them that their hold on the population is over."

"I figured. I think he has the respect of the front lines. They generally hate the officers, I've discovered, unlike the Borwyn," Deena said over her shoulder, winking at her husband.

Max nodded. "Me, too."

They approached the buildings from the military compound on the edge of the spaceport. Deena slowed. "How do we play this?"

"Walk straight through. This place looks abandoned."

"Maybe they're on the streets," Deena offered.

"Let's hug the wall. There's still a path until we can climb on top. We'll cut imposing figures up there."

Deena shook her head, but soldiers were expected to be on the wall patrolling. In the darkness, only the outline would be visible, and no one would take much from nebulous blobs carrying rifles.

"Halt. Who goes there?" a voice said from the deep black of a crevice near a stairway ahead.

"Lieutenant Deena from Space Fleet. I came down on a shuttle, and those bastards pressed me into service. Do you believe it?"

The voice from the darkness broke into a throaty laugh before stepping into the dim light of a distant lamp. "We need people. Not enough to man our posts."

"Why is that?" Deena asked, walking forward while Max eased to the side and leaned against the wall. "Like I said, I just got here."

"Borwyn attacked the space station. Borwyn attacked the spaceport. Borwyn attacked the city. Borwyn attacked our troops that we sent to the forest. The Borwyn have waited all these years to catch us at our weakest."

"Are you sure it's the Borwyn?" Deena eased closer to the man.

"That's what everyone is saying. We haven't gotten word from anyone inside headquarters because that facility was leveled and dropped on the six levels beneath the ground. We're not sure there's anyone alive above the rank of major."

Deena stopped to rub her chin in thought. "Someone out there was saying the Borwyn have already won. They're laying down their arms."

"I knew it!" the man blurted. "That's why my replacement is two hours late. This sucks! We're going to get tortured to death." He dropped to sit on the ground.

"What if I told you that you're not going to get tortured to death?" Deena smiled and shrugged. "Maybe you should just go home. Leave your weapon with me so you don't make yourself a target."

"Wait..."

Deena aimed her pulse rifle at him. "Leave your weapon on the ground and walk away. You've already lost, Malibor, but we're not taking prisoners because the war is over. Now is the time to live in peace."

"Hey, I recognize your voice. You worked at the restaurant."

"Guilty as charged," Deena replied. She approached the man but stayed out of arm's reach. Max moved in.

The Malibor soldier's face fell.

Deena continued, "We all want the same thing. You know me. Why would I want to hurt you? Why would I want to hurt anyone? We're going to have a huge banquet and party, celebrate the war being over, celebrate the end of hate."

The man stood, leaving his blaster on the ground. "I can go home?"

"Home-home. Not the barracks. Go and tell your family that with the dawn comes a new era where people can make the most of themselves through their own worth and not the value they provide to those in charge. The days of privilege based on position are over."

"I hope you're right." The man walked away with shoulders hunched. He glanced back. "That would be nice."

"The world is what we make of it, my friend," Deena said softly.

He walked between two buildings and was gone.

Max picked up the blaster. It had four rounds and the bolt stuck. Max wasn't sure it would fire. He broke it down, tossed the worn parts over the wall, and tucked the ammunition into a vest pocket.

"Nicely done. I prefer the not-fighting part. It's good to see the soldiers demoralized. This might be easier than we thought."

Pounding feet announced that a group of people were incoming.

Without a word, Deena and Max both ran along the base of the wall rather than choosing to expose themselves above. They dodged behind a building before the soldiers arrived. A squad of four stalked through the area where Deena and Max had just been.

Max raised his pulse rifle and followed the soldiers as they searched. He cued in on the corporal in charge, who looked to be more wary than the others. Max slowly squeezed the trigger. The pulse rifle barked once, but the corporal's head was gone before the soldiers could react to the sound. Max fired at a second soldier and took him center mass. The soldier spun around, hit the wall, and fell. Two dead and two to go, but they were already surrendering with arms raised and weapons held overhead.

"Put your weapons on the ground," Max ordered.

Deena ran forward, staying out of Max's line of fire. She relieved the soldiers of their weapons. More customers.

"The war is over, gentlemen," she told them.

"You're a Borwyn?" one asked.

"I'm a lover of peace and being kind to my fellows. That's it. I challenge you with the same. Now, go home. Don't stop to talk with other soldiers. You will get them killed."

"That dude was right. The war is over." He hovered his head over the corporal's body and spit. He nodded to the other soldier, and with their hands half-raised, they scampered away.

"Let's head to the restaurant. We'll take the high road," Max said, gesturing toward the wall.

They tossed four more Malibor blasters over the side after relieving them of their firing pins and ammunition. Max walked briskly with Deena close behind him. "Remind me where we want to head down, although I suspect it'll be any time after that blockhouse up ahead."

Deena looked around him. "That's where the military compound is separated from the city."

"The wall of shame," Max uttered. They approached the blockhouse that required anyone going from one side to the other to pass through the doors on both sides. It was dark inside the building, but Max expected it contained at least one soldier. He walked behind Deena, not using her as a shield, but she was far less intimidating. "Be careful."

She increased her pace, bouncing a little as she approached. Max hunched over to make himself look smaller.

Deena tapped on the glass, and the door opened.

"Stop where you are," a gruff voice called.

"Why?" Deena asked. She kept walking, and Max tensed.

"Because I need to verify who you are."

"Do I sound intimidating? Am I going to beat you up? Holy crackers, what's gotten into you?"

"I'm... What?"

Deena strolled up to the door. "Did you hear that rifle fire earlier?"

"No. Where was it?"

Deena confirmed he was alone. "Right here if you don't drop your weapon and raise your hands."

"You..." He never finished his verbal assault. Deena fired through the open door. The pulse rifle round ripped through his body and crashed through the glass on the far side of the blockhouse. She stopped the door from closing with her foot.

Max ran up to join her, but she was inside.

"I guess he wasn't vulnerable to suggestion," Max said.

"He wanted to be a hero. Now, he's neither a hero nor alive to regret it." Deena stepped over him and worked her way to the other door. It was made like a mini maze to keep people from running straight through. It was another obstacle to repel an enemy from a different era. Deena blocked open the other door. "Are we ready?"

Max watched Deena. She'd become desensitized to killing. He'd talk to her later, but for now, they needed to keep moving.

"The battle is joined," he told her.

She glanced over her shoulder to look at the body that Max had propped up in a chair. "May Septiman give you peace in the afterlife."

Max relaxed. Military necessity didn't mean Deena had become heartless. The revelation gave him hope.

"Why are you looking at me like that? I don't want to kill any of them. I probably knew him from the restaurant."

"Neither do I, my love. Can we still be us once we get through this?"

"I'm counting on it," Deena replied.

"Good-looking and smart! I married up. Go me."

Deena snorted and smiled. "We have to go, my overly emotional husband."

She took off before he could respond. They should have been long gone. Max weaved his way to the other side and jogged along the top of the wall after her. The first stairway was barely a hundred meters away. She headed down before Max caught up.

The dim lighting from a nearby building allowed him to take the steps two at a time.

"Hey," Deena called from the cutout below the stairs.

Max swooped around and into the space. "Did you see something?"

"Nothing. No noise, either."

"No need to wait," Max suggested. "To the restaurant."

"It's close." Deena walked away with her rifle at the ready. She took two alleys, sticking to the shadows and staying away from the main street. She reached a door and turned the handle to find it unlocked. Inside, the cook was playing with a spatula.

"Deena!" he cried out. "You're back."

"We're here to save the world," she said. "Is everyone else out front?"

"No customers. Curfew and all, so we haven't been able to leave. It's been four days."

"Come on. Let's have a chat." Deena pointed toward the dining room.

Max made sure the chef went first and then followed him in. They found the boss, the general, and Lanni lounging around.

"You're back!" Lanni ran in for a nearly bone-breaking hug. Max stayed back and watched. He was taken by how much they liked Deena even after she revealed herself as a Borwyn spy. He would have been angry to find a Malibor spy on his team. She had won them over, just like she'd convinced the soldiers to lay down their weapons and walk away.

"We're looking for a little help to save the lives of every Malibor soldier out there. They will die if they try to fight," she said. She looked purposefully at the general.

"When armies fight, people die. It's what war is about," the general said, taking a slow drink of his ranji juice.

Max stepped forward. "That's not what war is about. It's imposing your will on another in order to get what you want, or in this case, get back what was taken."

"Are we going to argue political positions, young man?" The general stood and straightened. He had once been an imposing figure, but he was older now and not as fit.

Max was at his physical best. He took another step forward. "That would be a waste of time, General. We're both playing on the front lines of this battle. We're beyond political conversations. Soldiers are dying out there. I suspect civilians are, too. We can stop it if we remove those who are happy ordering others to their death. We need your help to get in contact with the right people."

"While these others may be enamored by Deena, I find myself torn. She is dynamic and says the right things, but she's also the enemy. This city has been in Malibor hands for fifty years. People are not going to give up their homes easily."

"That's the conversation we need to have. We're not asking anyone to give up their homes, only to give up the fight. We're going to find that the only enemy is the Malibor government. The people are okay," Max explained.

"You sound like her. You make a good couple." The general nodded toward Deena. "How many people have you killed, Max? And I'm talking Malibor. How many Malibor?"

Max held the general's gaze. "I'd be flippant and ask if you meant today or all time, but I'm not going to answer that. Don't let the past ruin a bright future."

"How many Malibor have no future because of you?"

"Are you going to be bitter about your ignorance? How many men did you send to the forest to their deaths? There was nothing to gain there, but they went anyway."

"We were still fighting the war." The general looked down at his ranji juice and decided it wasn't strong enough. He pulled a bottle from below the bar and added a dash to it.

"I was just following orders," Max quipped.

"Something like that, yeah." The general drained his glass and poured himself more, adding another dash of the clear alcohol.

Max slung his rifle and stepped to the bar. He held his hand across. "Nothing matters but today and what we do for a better tomorrow."

The general shook his head but took Max's hand. "May we see a better tomorrow. You two are something. You're making it hard to think of you as the enemy."

"Because we're not." Max gestured toward the military compound. "They are."

"We better go in with a plan and in full daylight," the general said. "Are you sure about this? We could all die."

Deena and Max looked at each other. Max replied, "A worthy cause to die for, don't you think? Freeing your people."

"I'm good with it," Deena added. "The plan is, if they take aim at us, we kill them. If they are willing to talk, we'll talk. We've already told a number of soldiers that the Borwyn have won the war, and they were to put down their weapons and go home. Most complied."

"Those who didn't?" The general raised his head. He knew the answer.

"Like I said, if they draw down on us, they don't make it to morning." Deena shrugged while giving her answer. It was a fact, not a threat.

The group continued to talk late into the night. The morning would see if their plan was any good.

CHAPTER 17

Don't look at the end until you're there. Focus on the steps to get there.

Jaq floated down the corridor, neither pulling herself nor kicking off the bulkheads. She was exhausted after racing around the ship for the past six hours motivating the crew, helping carry, delivering food and water, and replacing fried circuits. The problem was they had everything energized, so everything had parts that fried. Much was protected from the pulse because of Bec's insistence during the construction and upgrade process, but finding where the failures resided outside of those was a tedious process.

Everyone was on shift working to restore power, with the focus on a single E-mag that could be fired manually from the station on the fourth deck—the same station where they'd manually launched the missile. It had been repaired and placed inside a dispersal cage. It had a scope to the outside.

They could fire manually. They needed the E-mag tied into the station and powered up. Tying it in was taking forever.

Jaq was drifting. Her emotional energy was spent.

The ship lurched, rotating around the long axis. Jaq bounced off the bulkhead and was pulled back as the ship continued to rotate. It wasn't tumbling, and it wasn't spiraling. That meant at least one lateral thruster was operational. The acceleration stopped, but the ship kept spinning.

Jaq was pulled toward the outer bulkhead from the centripetal force. "This is inconvenient," she told the bulkhead. The central shaft would be a nightmare to traverse, but she needed to get to Engineering. Jaq hurried down the bulkhead, new energy hastening her stride. She jumped into the central shaft, pulling herself downward as close to the middle as she could, where the centripetal force had the least influence.

The spinning slowed to a stop and then started the other way for a few seconds before that stopped.

Jaq raced to the bottom of the shaft. If power was restored and they accelerated forward, she'd be nothing but a splatter. She inverted and used two hands to push herself downward as if descending a rope. Jaq held on tightly.

She reached the right deck and stepped out, happy to activate her magnetic boots. She walked briskly into Engineering.

"Report," she said to announce her arrival. She hadn't bugged Teo in four hours, so Jaq felt she wasn't intruding.

Teo looked at her through dark eyes with heavy bags beneath.

"Someone's manually firing thrusters. It's not me. I'm

getting close to bringing the engines online, though it'll be in a limited capacity. But it'll be all thrust and no vector."

"Last I saw, we were heading toward the inner system."

"We should be fine."

"Once you get the engines online, can you double-check the E-mag progress? It would help us immensely if we could destroy the Malibor ship. I thought that was our priority."

"Have you ever heard that too many chefs spoil the soup?" Teo replied.

"We don't have soup. We have bags of microgreens and algae protein seasoned with a limited supply of, well, seasonings."

"You know what I mean, Jaq. There was nothing I could add. *Our* team was doing everything they could already do. That's why I came back here to keep moving forward on the engines. If we can't shoot them, we can escape. I wanted you to have options. Do you have any idea how the Malibor are doing in bringing their ship back online? I would think they'd have better hardened systems than us, but after four hours..."

"Six," Jaq corrected.

"...six hours, it's clear that they didn't. Surprising. But then again, you said they only had fifty people on board a ship three times our size. They've got issues and can't surge crew to make the repairs." Teo chewed the inside of her lip. "Have you heard anything from Bec?"

"No, but our comm is offline." Jaq scowled.

Teo replied, "Now that we're spinning, we get to see the Malibor ship no matter which porthole we look through but not for very long. Same goes for Septimus, Alarrees, the space station, *Cornucopia*, and the shipyard."

Jaq nodded. "We're not spinning any longer. We need to find who is operating the thrusters so we can make adjustments. Who has radios? By the way, what's your oxygen sensor say?"

Teo blew out a breath and shook her head. "I was hoping you wouldn't ask that. Are you feeling abnormally tired? It's probably because we're at eighteen-point-three percent and dropping. CO_2 is climbing. Neither is surprising. We've got a team working on the air handling, but it's the scrubbers. They had more integrated circuitry than I would have thought necessary. It's painful to watch them dig into one after another in such a small space. We only have four maintenance techs diminutive enough to do the work, plus the Malibor stowaway, that young boy. Who has the radios? There are four with maintenance teams to call for supplies and two with scavenger teams to find what the teams need. That's all we have for handheld radios. Most of the spacesuits have radios."

"The circuitry in the CO_2 scrubbers was Bec's idea to increase efficiency. They were energy drains before he upgraded them. They worked great up until they didn't," Jaq said. "We need air more than we need anything else. I thought we'd be up by now so didn't give it much thought since we needed to survive before we needed to survive, if you get my meaning. The spacesuits. Why don't we have people in suits using the radios to keep in touch?"

"Those will run out and we won't be able to recharge them. There aren't enough for the whole crew," Teo countered.

"Not that. If we get power to the E-mags, we can use the

calibration unit to control it from outside the ship. We can fire by using the Mark One Eyeball."

"Going out there will expedite the process. That's maniacal but also genius, because the one firing the cannon will have a clear mind. I'll do it."

Jaq shook her head. "We already have our volunteer. Get power to one of the cannons. I'll do the rest." Jaq took a step toward the hatch. "I'm going outside."

She released her boots and pushed off. She had to make one trip to the bridge then return to the port roller airlock, where there should be a suit, otherwise she'd use the aft airlock and the suits stored on the lower level. She had options.

Teo stopped what she was working on and followed Jaq out.

Jaq headed up the central shaft, pulling herself along and coasting for as much as she could to conserve energy. She caught the rail at the command deck and headed down the corridor. She found one person on the bridge—Amie. "Tell Alby, if you see him, that I'm going outside to fire the cannon using a manual interface."

"Is that smart? Isn't there residual discharge that might be detrimental to a living being's health?"

"Letting that ship get up before us would be detrimental to all our health. The risk of one person versus all of us. I have no intention of getting my face melted off out there, for what it's worth. I'll take a couple jumpers so I'm not right on top of the cannon."

"That would look more impressive," Amie suggested.

Jaq briefly visualized sitting astride the cannon while it

pumped rounds downrange. It made her laugh. "That would strike fear into any Malibor heart. Alas, no one would see it since none of us have any scanners or enhanced visuals. We'll stick with functional. Do you know who is operating the thrusters?"

"I think that's Ferd. He said he had an idea and flew off the bridge about two hours ago."

"Please find him and tell him to put on a suit with a functioning radio. I might need him to use the thrusters to help me aim the cannon. At this point, we're about thirty thousand kilometers away from the big ship. Hitting it while firing manually could prove problematic."

"Is that so? I thought it was closer."

"We were moving at upwards of five thousand kilometers per hour when we lost power. At least, that's what I think we were doing. My last look shows we're still relatively close. Relatively. Space is a big place."

Amie smiled. "I'll find Ferd and Alby and pass the word that we're ready to start shooting things."

"I like your brevity." Jaq left the bridge. She found the port roller airlock devoid of spacesuits. She pulled herself back to the central shaft and headed down to the lowest level, where she donned the first suit she could find. She used the port access shaft to climb up to the aft airlock.

Jaq had to operate it manually. She secured the inner hatch and started pumping the air out with a crank lever. There was a central wheel for manually releasing the outer hatch. Jaq spun it until the hatch released.

She eased outside. Her boots were magnetically attached to the hull. Jaq hadn't bothered with a mobility pack. If she lost contact with the ship, she'd drift into space. She took small, controlled steps. She kept the Malibor ship in view as she walked. It was out there, dark, just like *Chrysalis*.

The nearest battery was number fourteen. She moved to it and accessed the manual calibration panel. It would allow her to do everything she needed except fire the weapon. To do that, she had to short-circuit the safeties.

Jaq had brought the tool she needed. Two pieces of wire and a knife.

The panel was dark. She attempted to cycle it, but it didn't come to life. "Engineering team working on the E-mags, I'm at number fourteen. Can you bypass everything and send power directly to the cannon, please?"

"We're working on it, Jaq," Teo responded after relieving one of the teams of their handheld radio. "We're close to energizing all the cannons. Targeting systems are offline because they're tied in with navigation and sensors. We have to get all those systems back up before we can aim a single cannon."

"Don't worry about aiming. I just need power to number fourteen, do you hear me? Soon as you can," Jaq pleaded.

"Yes, ma'am." The channel went dead, leaving Jaq to her own thoughts.

Why did you go over there, Bec? she wondered.

Jaq climbed onto the pedestal mounting and leaned on the cannon, thinking briefly about sitting on it and making rude gestures toward the Malibor ship, the space station, and anyone else who'd crossed them, but she kept her boots attached to the cold metal of the outer hull.

A dark shadow passed beside her. She stared at the spot

and then searched the sky behind her for anything that might have blocked Armanor's light, but she saw nothing. She started to think space sickness was getting to her, even though her O2 showed over twenty percent. Her brain should have been working better than it had been inside the ship.

CHAPTER 18

An ambiguous truth is better than a lie.

Bec slowed his approach to the bridge. After his initial bold maneuver in airlocking the captain and a second man, he'd started to second-guess his plan of taking over the ship. By his count, there were still forty-eight crew on board.

He was fresh out of landers to lure them to. Even with the advantage of his familiarity with zero-gee, he was grossly outnumbered. If any of them had a weapon, he'd be done for.

Bec hung his head. He didn't have the answer, but he knew the person who would. As much as it caused friction on his very soul, he needed to call Jaq, but how? The radios would be out of service.

Jaq would be keeping an eye on the enemy. That meant she'd be able to see the ship.

He returned to the engineering space and grabbed a tool bag. The crew stared at him. "I need this if I'm going to be of any help, and that means I'm going to save all your lives, because that's what I do." He clomped toward the hatch and called over his shoulder as he walked out. "You're welcome."

He needed to get to an airlock. He just so happened to know where one was.

Bec released his boots and flew down the corridor. He stopped along the way to pull a glass insulator from the panel where the technician had been working and where Bec had removed the circuit.

It was rounded like a lens, which was what he needed. Bec continued unhindered to the airlock, only to find that it wasn't facing *Chrysalis*. He needed to be on the other side of the ship. He walked a transverse corridor that crossed from starboard to port on the same deck.

And he kept walking. "This ship is huge," he said to himself and mumbled the sequence he'd need to send with his maintenance light. The airlock on the port side was unfinished. It was blocked by a steel plate.

"You people are starting to make me angry," Bec grumbled.

"What people?" a voice asked from nearby.

Bec nearly came out of his skin. If his boots hadn't been attached to the deck, he would have jumped into the overhead.

"The ones who put this plate in my way," Bec said when his heart slowed enough to let him speak.

"It's keeping the evil vacuum of space out there and the niceties of warmth and air in here. I wouldn't be so hard on them. Nice boots. Where'd you get them?"

"Supply section, one of the lower decks. Everyone was supposed to get them." Magnetic boots were standard equipment on board *Chrysalis*. Bec had no need to make anything up, only to change the reference. "Since you're here and I'm lost, where is a nearby porthole? I'd like to look outside. I'll need a reference for when I bring the navigation system online."

"Nav is nearly up? Damn! We'll need thrusters. I thought I had more time." A lithe technician popped out from behind an open panel door. "Come with me."

He bounced back and forth off the corridor walls as he flew ahead. Bec released his magnetic clamps and followed.

The young man stopped to puke, ejecting bile into the open air. "Sorry, this zero-gee is something. I'm sooo not used to it. I thought gravity was a given on this ship."

"What else did they tell us that wasn't true? I've been putting up with that for too long," Bec added.

The man wiped is mouth on a sleeve and strained to reach any surface. Bec activated his boots and moved him along, keeping the young man between him and the floating puke.

"In here." The technician pointed, and Bec pushed him toward the hatch. He tapped the panel and it opened into a long, thin meeting space with a table but no chairs. The backdrop was an oversized screen to space.

Chrysalis had nothing like it, nor did any other Malibor ship. The materials needed for such a screen didn't exist, not for a warship, but then again, a warship with an energy barrier could have windows. They were counting on the screen as well as the artificial gravity. They never believed that both technologies could be offline.

"That's magnificent," Bec said of the view.

"I sneak in here to look when I'm on a break. There used to be a chair..." He glanced around and then nodded toward the overhead where the chair had floated and seemed to be stuck on a light fixture. "They call it a chandelier, a taste of the fancy from back home."

"We could all use some fancy," Bec agreed. He wasted no more time on it. He had to contact *Chrysalis* and tell them not to shoot.

From the window, he had a beautiful view of the dark spot moving in the distance. He aimed the work lamp at it and started flashing. He tried to aim it through the insulator, but that only diffused the light. He tossed it aside and dialed the lamp to its tightest beam.

"What are you doing?"

"Contacting the ship that attacked us and telling it not to attack us again," Bec said matter-of-factly. He found telling the truth much easier than trying to manufacture a story when there was no need.

"You can do that?"

"Yes. I can do that. We're all going to die because that ship will be operational before us. How many railgun strikes would it take to penetrate this window and decompress this entire section? Are the emergency bulkheads working?"

"Now that you mention it, no. Default should have closed them all, making it impossible to move around the ship."

"We left the yard much earlier than we should have. This ship is not ready for combat, not in the least." Bec nodded toward the window. "That ship is."

"How do you know that?"

"How many Malibor ships have been destroyed by the Borwyn fleet in the past few months?"

"How would I know?" The technician clung to the table, gripping so tightly that his knuckles turned white.

"We deployed because *Epica* is the very last combat vessel of the Malibor fleet. The Borwyn have won the war."

"That's impossible!" the man replied angrily. "Who are you?"

"I'm the captain of this ship, and I'm saving your lives."

The technician let go of the table to fold his arms across his chest and float free. "You're not the captain. I've met him. He's gruff and mean like every captain. You look different. Are you a Borwyn?"

Bec waved him away. "I need to concentrate. This is critical to both our survival, and then we're going to bring this ship back online and take everyone home."

"You're a Borwyn!" the technician declared. "I don't know how to feel about this. I want to live, but you're the enemy. I think I'm going to have to fight you."

"I think you'll puke yourself if you tried to fight me. Now please, be quiet."

Bec turned his attention back to the window and sent a series of short and long flashes. He liked the way the beam powered into the void. "D. O. N. T. S.H.O.O.T.B.E.C." Bec said each letter as he sent it, then he started repeating.

"Is Bec over there or are you Bec?"

"I'm Bec. Pleased to meet you," he said emotionlessly. He looked over his shoulder at the young man floating beside the table. He had hooked one foot beneath it to hold himself in place. "You were working on the thrusters?"

"Don't shoot Bec. Will that work?" He ignored the question as Bec would have. The technician had already told Bec what he'd been doing.

"It had better, or we're all going to die."

The man shook his head, which started him spinning. He uncrossed his arms and windmilled them until he regained his purchase on the table. "If you're Borwyn, why would they kill you?"

"I stole a lander to come over here because I wanted to see the engineering for the energy screen. That is something that shouldn't be possible, yet here it is, and then I get over here to find artificial gravity, something else that shouldn't be possible. I want to understand the technological breakthroughs you've achieved. I have to know."

"They don't know you're over here?" was the first thing the man deduced from Bec's revelation.

"They know I'm here. And they'll kill me to kill this ship, which is the only threat left to them. Once we're out of the way, they can restore Borwyn rule over Septimus."

"Damn! I'm from Septimus. That's my home. No! We need to fight them."

Bec stopped sending. "Aren't you supposed to be smart to be a technician working on advanced systems?" Bec glared at him. "They're going to get their systems online sooner than us. We've been diddling around for six hours with the fifty crew, now forty-eight. I've just come from Engineering. They're not very close to fixing this ship. I can't believe the systems weren't protected from the EMP weapon."

"They will be when the ship is finished."

"It'll never be finished because we'll all be dead if I can't get through to my ship." Bec started flashing the light once more. They remained silent through three iterations of the code.

"It's alien engineering," the man said softly.

Bec continued to send the pattern he'd established while looking over his shoulder at the technician. "You found aliens?"

"We found an outpost on Deltor, or that's what I heard."

"That's unbelievable," Bec replied while simultaneously believing it. It made far more sense to him that alien technology was used to advance this ship than a Malibor genius had emerged from the masses. "Can I see any of the documents recovered? I'm intrigued, and that means it's even more important that we don't get destroyed."

"You don't want to die because you're intrigued? Do all Borwyn think like you?" the technician asked. He wasn't trying to be a jerk. He had never met a Borwyn before, and Bec did not live down to his expectations.

"We should all desire to learn more, so I'm not quite ready to give up on this life."

"Anton."

"What?" Bec asked while he continued to flash the maintenance light.

"You never asked my name."

Bec didn't ask because he didn't care to learn the man's name, but now that he knew, he still didn't care.

"Wouldn't they have seen your signal by now?" Anton asked.

"I doubt they have anyone standing by a window and watching for flashing lights. They'll be working through the systems. Their chief engineer is smart, as smart as me, and they have over two hundred crew working on it, as opposed to our forty-eight."

"Forty-seven, because I'm not working on anything at present," Anton suggested. "I'm just saying..."

"Just saying what?" Bec was getting annoyed at the mindless conversation, and it made him wish he'd left the man working in the corridor.

"I could be working. We're going to need thrusters."

"I suggest we'll need air first. Have you noticed that they're not running?"

The young man looked at the vents and cocked an ear toward them. "Nothing is working except the doors and emergency lights. I didn't think about it. I've been working on the thrusters. Do you think we can fix anything? We specialize, buddy, become experts in what we do. I'd much rather be a kilometer deep and centimeter wide than the alternative." He started to wave his arms to emphasize his grandiose statement but thought better of it when he started to float away from the table. His stomach heaved anew.

"What's the alternative?" Bec asked.

"A kilometer wide and a centimeter deep. You never heard that expression before?"

"No. I'm not a Malibor. We all cross-train because we never know where we'll find ourselves during an emergency. Better to be half a kilometer wide and half a kilometer deep. If you adhered to that philosophy, then you probably wouldn't be in this mess."

"We're in this mess because the Borwyn returned and

destroyed all of our ships except this one! We have to fight for the good of all Malibor!" The young man pumped his fist.

"You *were* listening. I think you'll find that fighting with the sole purpose of dying is a losing proposition. You should struggle to live, which means you're going to help me get this ship functional so we can return to the shipyard. The construction needs to be finished. This is an incredible ship. It needs to fly throughout the system."

"It's a warship," Anton countered.

"Maybe you *weren't* listening. The war is over. This will be an exploration vessel, a technology demonstration ship to show what's possible. I'm sure the captain of the Borwyn fleet will look for good engineering types to crew the vessel. She might not even change the name. *Epica* is pretty good."

"Are you serious? The head of the Borwyn fleet is a woman?"

"Shh!" Bec snapped. "Keep your voice down. She might hear you. That woman's got ears." Bec continued sending his latest sequence before starting over once more.

CHAPTER 19

No one knows for sure how anything will end, and that's why you keep fighting.

Jaq stared in disbelief. The distant flashes were code. It had to be Bec. Her comm training was rusty, but she muddled through it, happy that it kept repeating.

"Don't shoot Bec," she mumbled. She activated her radio. "Get me the most powerful flashlight we have. I need to send a message. New orders. Bec has asked us not to shoot the Malibor ship. I have to think that was meant for me."

"Makes me want to shoot him that much more," Teo replied. "We'll get a light out to you, unless there's a way we can flash him from inside the ship. I'd prefer not to manually cycle the airlock."

"That makes two of us. Port roller airlock has a porthole. Do you know our code?"

"I looked it over. Pretty simple. You can help me if I get stuck. Let me see. *Bec u butthole.* Does that sum it up?"

"That'll let him know it's you. Find out what's going on, if you can. I need some assurances that thing won't launch its missiles at us."

"No missiles, jerk face. Got it. Power's on to your E-mag, by the way," Teo added.

Jaq checked the calibration system and was pleased to see lights flash and the internal diagnostic run. She ran it through its paces and moved the barrel around to practice aiming at various targets, not because she expected to use it but because she was bored. She aimed at the space station, then at the shipyard, then at the Malibor ship, then at *Cornucopia*, which continued tumbling end over end.

The shadow passed nearby again. Jaq stared until she could make out what it was. Brad's scout ship. It angled close.

"Is that you, Taurus?"

"Roger. I tried contacting the ship earlier but hadn't heard anything. I thought your radios had been fried."

"Only the ones in use at the time," Jaq replied. "It's good to see you. Bec is on the Malibor ship, and he seems to be signaling us. Maybe you can go over there and assure him that we've received his signal."

"I can do that. Do you want to ride along?"

"Do you have your suit on?" Jaq asked. They'd come up with the plan so quickly that certain safety protocols had probably not been employed.

"That would be a problem," Taurus replied. "No ride for you. Sorry, Captain. I'll be right back." The ship flipped over, twisted around to change heading, and accelerated away. "This thing is fun to fly."

"I'm sure," Jaq said. Having a functioning ship

improved her mood and lightened her spirits. It had been either shielded from the EMP or too far away. That meant they also had a lander out there they could recover. Jaq didn't want to donate any more of her assets than she needed.

A loud whine reverberated through the ship. Bec looked at Anton. "Did they get their systems online? What is that?"

"Pneumatics," the man answered. "It's a backup to the ion thrusters."

"Your thrusters use ion drive technology?" Bec had been easily distracted, but he needed to focus. "What can they do with pneumatics?"

Anton's face fell. "They can fire the missiles."

Bec let go of the lamp. "We need to get to the bridge. Come on!" Bec released his boots and pushed off the bulkhead, catching the technician on his way toward the hatch. They both went through, hitting the wall on the far side of the corridor and kicking off to zigzag down the corridor to the forward stairwell.

Behind Bec, a light flashed from the ship in the distance.

The hissing continued until it reached a crescendo and stopped. With no other sounds in the ship, every noise took on new importance. "Can they fire the missiles manually?" Bec asked, remembering how *Chrysalis* had launched one missile at the troop transport, which ended up saving the *Borwyn* cruiser.

Anton shrugged. "Don't know, but I would think so. The

missiles are arrayed along the top side. I would think manual control would be up there."

"Then that's where we're going. There's no other power in the ship, so the bridge will be useless. Has to be manual control. If they fire those missiles, I lose everything and everyone I've ever known."

They raced up the stairwell, Bec urging greater and greater speed. He'd just told Jaq not to shoot. If she got that message, then *Chrysalis* would die. If she didn't get the message, then *Chrysalis* would die. If she didn't get the message and the E-mags were powered up, then Bec would die.

He wasn't good with any of the imminent deaths. The only way to stop it would be to prevent the launch, if that's what the Malibor were doing. Bec would know soon enough. He reached the top deck and hurried down a lateral corridor and into a wide main corridor where cabling ran along the deck. It floated with the lack of gravity. Bec followed it with his eyes to two different pairs of individuals working on side panels where the cable ducked in and out.

"Stop!" Bec shouted and launched himself down the corridor. He activated his boots to pull himself to the deck. He grabbed the cabling and started pulling on it, jerking to break it free from providing power to launch a missile. One of the crew seized the other end and held it.

He also had magnetic boots. A professional. Bec lost his momentum.

A woosh signaled the launch of a missile. A second pneumatic discharge sounded from down the corridor. Two missiles were in space, heading somewhere.

"Jaq, two missiles just flushed from their launch tubes. Inbound your position."

Jaq didn't have time for anything except to slew the barrel and hope she could get an eye on their rocket tails. This close, the missiles would be accelerating right up until impact.

"Full speed ahead on my engines. I'll try to draw them away," Taurus reported.

Jaq thought she should talk her out of it, but the scout ship would probably be able to evade the missiles. *Chrysalis* could not. "May Septiman watch over you."

The scout ship reoriented and with full acceleration, it started to pull away from its previous course. The burn was clear as a series of green waves. The missile tails became visible with the reorientation. They had adjusted course to follow the increased energy, a target far more viable for a missile's brain than a big chunk of metal on a ballistic trajectory that could have been nothing more than a meteor.

One missile arced across the void as it fought to change course. The other missile straightened on a direct course toward *Chrysalis*. She checked the alignment by laying on the breech block and looking down the rail. She ripped two wires free and scraped the lines bare before touching them to each other.

The E-mag vibrated with the energy of sending an obdurium projectile downrange. She sat up enough to better use both hands. She had one barrel when a high volume of fire was called for. She tapped the wires together repeatedly but could only manage five times a second while trying to aim the cannon. She settled for close-enough on the aim and as fast as she could touch the wires.

The missile grew larger and clearer. She was running out of time. She adjusted the aim with one hand while rubbing the two wires back and forth with the other.

A massive explosion sent a fireball and debris into *Chrysalis*. Jaq flinched and ducked, but she was as exposed as anything on the outer hull. Shrapnel from the missile peppered the hull around her but left the E-mag alone. She waited, even expected, for her death knell to sound, but it didn't. The blast didn't have the concussion it would have within an atmosphere. Out here, it was trivial. The shrapnel was the killer, but it had dispersed around the incoming fire that had killed the missile. The E-mag won the battle of which system could unleash the most energy.

"Bec, I oughta kill you!" Jaq shouted at the Malibor ship, shaking her fist for good measure. But she knew that he hadn't been the one to fire the missile. The problem was, if he couldn't prevent more missiles from coming her way, she'd have to destroy the ship.

Jaq took aim with the wires in her hand and waited. She couldn't see the outer doors to tell if they were open or not. She worried that she would wait too long.

Bec found where the wires came out of a maintenance shaft. The heavy door was partially open. He arranged the cabling and kicked at the door. As he suspected, it caught on them. Was it sharp enough to cut through the mid-gauge wires? He glanced down the corridor and found four men moving his way.

"Time to go, Anton."

The tech decided they'd already tagged him as being with Bec. In their minds, he was a traitor. Long-term fleet personnel were unforgiving when it came to the contract personnel working on *Epica*. He was already considered incompetent and a potential enemy. Being with Bec confirmed it.

"I'm not with you," he moaned as they flew down the stairway. Bec grabbed him and pulled him to the doorway at the next deck. He shoved him through and followed.

"There. We're going back upstairs." Bec pushed off at a sharp angle and flew down the corridor as quickly as he could, taking longer and longer between impacts with the side. He inverted at the last second and tried to stop at the doorway before the stair. He slammed into it and started to tumble. He activated his boots and quickly snapped to the deck. He swayed like a willow in a heavy wind but held firm.

Anton was coming quickly. Bec leaned forward and jammed the young man to the deck, where he hammered into Bec's boots. Both grunted from the impact. Bec took one step toward the door and then went through. The pursuers hadn't entered this corridor.

They could have been anywhere.

Bec led the way up the stairs to the top level. He peeked into the corridor to find it empty. He didn't bother helping Anton. Bec needed to get to the panel and sabotage it. He didn't expect it would take much.

He activated his boots to land gently at the panel and

immediately dug inside. They'd bypassed all of the automatic controls. The targeting system was rudimentary.

Bec prepared to pull it free but decided not to. He could send all the missiles out of their tubes if only he could target something that wouldn't hurt *Chrysalis*. He tapped the controls for a ballistic course of mark zero and orientation plus ninety. He hoped he was right. He tapped one after another. The woosh of pneumatics sending missiles into space was gratifying.

He headed to the panel for the second bank and repeated what he'd done.

The high whistling started anew as the air repressurized the system. "They can't fire again, can they?" Bec asked when he discovered Anton next to him.

"Yes, they can, but no missiles are loaded. The autoloading system needs power. It's not pneumatic like the launch system."

"Time to go," Bec said. He turned to go back to the aft stairwell, but two men emerged. "Not that way."

He turned to see two men step out of the other stairwell.

Bec turned pale. "Any ideas?" he whispered over his shoulder.

Anton was already speeding away toward the crewmen on the aft side of the corridor. "I'm not with him. He kidnapped me!" he shouted.

"Next time, kidnap someone with a little more backbone," Bec muttered. All the missiles had flushed from the tubes. He'd saved *Chrysalis*.

Again.

But this time, he hadn't saved himself as part of the effort.

I'm not the self-sacrificing type, he thought as he watched Anton slow to meet the professional crew.

They shouted at the young man, but he produced an electrical tester. Made a face as he waved it in front of him. "I got you now! I'm going to fry your 'nads!" Anton screamed maniacally. With his tongue out and mouth wide open, he jabbed the tester at them.

The professional crew bolted away from the crazy man and disappeared into the far stairway. Anton shouted and laughed.

When he turned back to Bec, he looked completely normal.

Bec wasn't sure what scared him more.

CHAPTER 20

In the dead of space, nothing is louder than your own thoughts.

"What is that?" Eleanor asked Crip.

He shook his head, squinting at the streaks marking the night sky. Fireball after fireball, splitting into multiple parts, burning out after a short while.

Eleanor continued looking up at the darkness. "Meteors," she guessed.

"I need to call *Chrysalis*," Crip said, but he didn't have the means to. That was with the rest of the combat team and Larson, specifically.

"That's not your ship, is it?" Eleanor winced as she spoke.

"It was nice when no one said it aloud." Crip frowned and groaned. He glanced skyward. The similarity of the trails suggested it was different from a destroyed spaceship. Crip couldn't figure out what it was, but the realization that it wasn't a ship gave him hope, no matter how slender the tendril. "There's a serious fight happening out there. I hope the Malibor are watching this, no matter what *it* is, and feeling the fear that our ancestors felt fifty years ago. The world they know is crashing down around them."

Eleanor touched her brow in a quick salute. "Here's to you, Jaq Hunter. I hope to meet you some day."

Crip did the same. "The battle is joined." He adjusted his pack. "How much farther do you think?"

"A couple hours if we move quickly. Or we could bivouac here and get it first thing in the morning. I don't see any movement in the open areas. I think the Malibor are sufficiently distracted that they aren't coming after your gunship crew."

"Nothing we can do with them tonight. It'll be easier finding them in the daylight." Crip called into the darkness. "That's it for today. Get some sleep. Set a minimal watch of two at a time. I think we're safe here."

Crip hadn't brought as many people as he initially envisioned. Half his squad, including Hammer and Anvil because he wanted their physical strength in case they needed to drag the injured back to the Borwyn main camp.

"We should call the company and update them."

"Radio silence," Eleanor replied. "We'll call them upon pickup and move immediately thereafter as fast as we can. It's standard procedure."

"If they didn't zero in on Deena or us, I don't think they're using RDF or searching the airwaves for Borwyn signals," Crip suggested.

"Still. Not worth the risk. What would you tell them if you made contact?"

"To call the ship," Crip admitted. "What the hell was that debris entering the atmosphere?"

"And if you knew the answer, what are you going to do differently right now as opposed to later?"

"I know. Nothing. I'm not going to do anything differently, and that means there's no reward even if the risk is extremely low."

Eleanor touched her nose.

"Get some sleep. I'll take the first watch and you take the last. Let me check on my people."

Crip eased into the darkness, walking silently as he'd learned during his time on Septimus. It would take him hours to calm his mind enough to sleep. He used to be in a position where he could control almost everything. Right now, he was in control of almost nothing and was having a hard time with his inability to move events in a direction of his choosing.

A plan was forming in his mind.

"Is anyone out there?" Jaq asked into her radio. She checked to see if it was working, but the small light was out. Another piece of old tech gone belly up. She wasn't surprised. Most everything they used was on its last leg. She continued to cling to the E-mag, unsure of what to do next. She saw flashes of light heading toward the planet.

Missiles, a massive barrage, but they were heading in at steep angles that they couldn't survive.

That had to be Bec's doing.

Jaq smiled. He was fighting to keep the ship alive. She

assumed he'd found the energy screen and needed more time to exploit the information.

She hoped that Teo was signaling the ship. They'd post an observer in the airlock porthole to watch for more signals, especially since they'd stopped right before the missiles launched.

The thought that they could be reloading entered Jaq's mind, but the ship was still dark. They didn't have power restored.

Jaq needed to get back inside. She wanted the engines online. If Bec had control over that ship, then her priority had to be Brad and the boarding party. She needed to find out about Taurus. What happend to *Starstrider*? What about the combat team?

Frustration could have seized her, but it didn't. She clung to the breech block a little while longer, looking at the space within which Septimus rotated. They were close. Everything she had set in motion was racing well ahead of her. She no longer was able to determine the outcome of events. That had been determined well before her time with the actions every Borwyn took each day.

"Victory is ours," Jaq told the universe.

Brad appreciated the zero-gee. He wasn't sure he'd be able to stand if he had to keep himself upright. His boots did all the work keeping him in place.

With one last cut, Phillips Junior removed the last cable

and stepped through. Four Borwyn followed him, taping non-conducting material over the exposed wire.

"Where are the rest?" Brad asked. The teen shrugged. He was covered in sweat with small holes scattered across his clothing from the spatters of the plasma cutter. "Hey!" Brad called toward the others. "Rally the boarding team in this corridor. All hands. This is where we need to be. Get the elder Phillips up here, too. All hands. Make it happen."

Two men pulled themselves down the corridor. They didn't have mag boots, but they were making do.

Brad drifted in and out of consciousness while he waited. His team surrounded him, ready to engage any enemy that would try to encroach. Gristwall, Crombie, Zin, and Pickford. They had seen him at his best and his worst. They knew he'd be there to the end. They'd bandaged his arm, face, and side as best they could. Once they delivered him to Doc Teller, they'd all be relieved.

They could only do that once they secured the space station.

The volunteers from New Septimus trickled in, two by two, until they reported all present or accounted for. Brad had brought thirty-five Borwyn plus himself and the welders onto the space station.

Twenty filled the corridor, and too many of them were bandaged and nursing wounds, just like Brad.

Brad roused enough to urge himself into action. "Give me a spanner," he said, and one was thrust into his hand. He stepped forward and beat on the airtight hatch. "Open up! We'll accept your surrender."

Nothing happened. Brad wasn't surprised. The heavy

bolts were in place from where they'd dogged the hatch from the inside.

"Didn't you live on this station?" Pickford asked. "What did you do when the power went out?"

"Power never went out when I lived here. Twenty years' worth," Brad replied.

"I bet the Malibor can say the same thing. Zero-gee messed them up. If only we had a few hundred soldiers, we could secure the entire station." Pickford nodded toward the command center.

"Cut this hatch open," Brad ordered. Phillips Senior took the left side and Junior took the right. They started melting steel, one slow centimeter at a time. Brad spoke softly. "Get some of that cabling to tie on to that hatch and rip it open, when the time comes."

"I'll take care of it," Pickford replied. He pulled himself down the cable-trapped corridor, looking for the refuse from the cutting. He recruited one of those who had helped the younger Phillips clear out the second half. At the end of the corridor, Pickford found a three-person contingent, aiming their pulse rifles down the corridor.

The Malibor still didn't want the Borwyn on their station. The boarding party's grip was tenuous at best. The biggest advantage they had was that they were armed while most of the Malibor were not.

"Keep us safe for a little while longer," Pickford told them. "We're almost into the command center."

"Finally. This place sucks, and I'm ready to go home," one of the soldiers said over her shoulder. She was one of four women who had joined the team knowing that it was a combat mission. Pickford hadn't seen any of the other three among the survivors in the corridor. Thirty-eight boarded and just over half were still standing.

Pickford returned to the hatch. He looked to attach the cables he'd collected, but both torches were throwing too much molten steel. He had to wait.

"I don't see all our people," Brad said.

Pickford replied, "We have twenty left, that includes you and the welders. We've lost eighteen, Brad."

Brad sighed. His eyes cleared. "This will be the end of it. Once we have the command center, we'll be in charge of the station. That was our premise when we boarded, but without power, I don't think anyone is in charge of anything. Did you notice there's no air flow?"

"Air will get worse, but depending on cubic meters of space and number of people breathing, it could last a long time. The civilian population evacuated. I don't think air will be a hindrance."

"Here's a crazy thought. We clear the command center, issue a statement however we can, and then leave." Brad snorted. "But there's only one minor problem, and that's we don't have a way off the station."

Brad used his radio. "*Chrysalis*. This is the boarding team requesting pickup."

The Phillips family finished their work, high-fived, and stepped back.

Brad moved across the corridor to stand on the same side as the hatch. He directed the others to follow his lead. "Don't give them a shot. Pickford, rip that door out of there."

Pickford tied the cables to the center wheel and backed away. He and two others jerked it free and dove for cover.

Brad leaned close and prepared to yell, but it was silent inside. A horrible smell wafted into the corridor.

"Smells like cesspool," Jin said.

Brad shook his head. "Smells like death." He leaned close. "Is anyone alive in there? Come on out. Get some fresh air."

After a couple minutes, Brad peeked into the space bathed in red emergency light. He stepped in despite strong hands trying to hold him back.

"They're all dead," he said. "That's anti-climactic. We expected a big fight when all it took was cutting the power. They must have run out of air quickly."

Brad stepped aside.

Pickford took Gristwall and Crombie with him to search the space. Zin started to follow, but Brad stopped him. "Stay with me in case I pass out."

"Sir?" Zin looked at the hatch.

"You don't want to go in there. You have a lot of life left and don't need those images to haunt you for the rest of it. I may not like the Malibor, but I don't wish that kind of death on anyone."

Brad looked at the deck. His injuries had taken a lot out of him. He felt every bit his seventy-some years. "Help me to the airlock," he asked Zin.

The young man wrapped his arm around Brad's waist. "Unhook your boots," he said.

Brad tapped the sides and released the magnetic clamps.

He let himself float free while Zin did the walking. "Retrograde to the airlock," Brad ordered.

The others passed the word, and the movement began. The three at the rear became the leads moving forward. They scouted the way ahead. Others fell in behind with pulse rifles raised. In the hours they'd been on the station, the untried volunteers had become seasoned soldiers.

The point fired a couple times but at shadows. No one threatened the retrograde. No Malibor blocked their way off the station.

"Jaq, this is Brad. Come in, please," Brad tried again.

A voice responded, but it wasn't Jaq or *Chrysalis*.

"Brad, Taurus here, in your ship. I'll meet you at the airlock. I can only take three. *Chrysalis*, the station, the Malibor ship, and *Cornucopia* have all been blasted by an EMP. I think each ship is working to get their systems back online. I was far enough away to avoid the worst of it. I also avoided a Malibor missile. My compliments to you on how nimble this ship is. I like it. Can I have it?"

Brad stared at his radio. Taurus was able to distract them from the madness, pain, and loss. He keyed his mic. "No. But link up to the airlock and let's start evacuating our people. I assume that *Chrysalis* is unable to link to the station herself."

"They're literally hanging on by a thread," Taurus replied cryptically. "On my way."

By the time the boarding party cleared the carnage of their initial passing, *Starstrider* was bumped up against the airlock and pumping air into the small void of the connecting ring.

Taurus opened the hatch. Zin and Brad stepped forward.

"I should probably be the last one off the station," Brad suggested.

"No way," Zin said. He looked behind him. "Pickford, Edgerrin, you guys have it, right? We need to get him to the doc."

"That's right," Edgerrin confirmed. "We'll take care of securing this position, although we look forward to getting picked up. I've had as much fun as I can handle."

He frowned, not looking like he'd had any fun at all. None of them had, but that wasn't the reason for boarding the station. The loss of power removed the efficacy of taking over the command center. Without a maintenance and repair crew on board, the station would remain offline, without gravity, and without a purpose.

Brad and Zin boarded. Crombie joined them.

Taurus secured the hatch.

"I can take three at a time in your ship, Brad, or we can recover the lander, kick off the explosives, and take all the rest in one trip, but we're playing catchup. *Chrysalis* is moving away from the engagement area at five thousand KPH."

"That's inconvenient," Brad said. "Take us to that lander. We'll dump the explosives on the station after rendering them inert."

Taurus accelerated away from the station to where the lander was supposed to be.

"How do we do that?" Zin asked.

"Urinate on them," Brad replied matter-of-factly. "Or we could squirt water on them."

Zin started to laugh. "Can you imagine? Everyone lined up at the hatch, peeing into an airlock filled with explosives?"

Brad tried to fully open his eyes but was struggling. "I think you underestimate the ingenuity required to win this fight."

Taurus shook her head. "Don't include me in your inert rendering plan. I'll fly the scout."

"I'll fly the lander," Brad said.

Crombie grunted his discontent. "You need to get to *Chrysalis* and see Doc Teller. Even if he tells you to drink water and rest, it's better than if you keep pushing yourself. If you die, then our victory won't be as sweet. We took over the space station. The Malibor fought back, and in the end, we did exactly what we went there to do. Seize the command center. By the time we lost power, we'd already won the fight."

Brad pressed his lips tightly together.

"I'll fly the lander," Taurus offered. "Brad can fly *Starstrider* in his sleep. Drop me off and then get yourselves to *Chrysalis*. As captain of this vessel, that's an order."

Brad closed his eyes and drifted off. Crombie and Zin looked at each other. His breathing slowed as he slept.

With every other ship out of commission, Taurus activated the radar to help her find the lander. It showed on the screen, and she tapped the accelerator to shorten the trip.

"Crombie, pay attention in case you have to fly this thing." Taurus showed him what she was doing for orientation and acceleration. It was all about making adjustments. She activated the radio. "Jaq, this is Taurus, are you there? Anyone from *Chrysalis*, can you hear me?"

"They're probably out of range," Brad mumbled.

"You were asleep a second ago," Zin said.

"Just napping. I'm old. I take naps."

Taurus sighed.

"Get enough sleep, because if I have to fly this thing, we're going to crash," Crombie stated.

"When is flying not flying?" Brad quipped, keeping his eyes closed.

"We have a problem," Taurus said, pointing at the main screen showing the live view outside the ship.

The lander was tumbling.

"Slow us to match its speed, and then I'll take over." Brad raised his hand to give the thumbs-up.

Taurus complied, accelerating and decelerating, spinning the ship around and back, adjusting with the thrusters to put the ship a static hundred meters from the lander. She unbuckled herself and squeezed into the back to make way for Brad.

He was better in zero-gee, moving easily into the pilot's seat. Crombie helped to buckle him in. "You're a mess," he said.

"I usually get that from my daughter," Brad grumbled. He took two deep breaths, wincing from the pain in his side when his chest expanded. He blinked the world into focus and tickled the controls to maneuver the scout ship close. He adjusted the live view at the last moment to put the nose of the scout under the lander's side. With small thruster adjustments, he slowed the spinning but had to reposition toward the nose to stop the spin.

A small crunch reverberated though the scout's hull with the last maneuver.

Brad ignored it. There wasn't anything he could do about damage to either ship. "Aligning the airlock."

The lander had two access points, but the airlock was at the bow. He angled the scout until it married up. He activated the clamps, and the two ships locked together. He powered down his engines.

Crombie cycled the scout's airlock and opened the hatch to reveal the lander's circular access port.

"I know what was damaged during that last maneuver." Crombie pointed to a metal cage that surrounded the airlock to protect it from impacts. It did its job but was bent over the hatch.

"Axe," Brad said, gesturing toward the equipment locker.

Taurus grabbed the medical kit from the same locker after handing the axe to Zin.

The young man hammered the frame once and nearly deafened them all. They stuffed their ears with anything they could find before allowing Zin to start hammering on the frame. He braced himself and turned to.

Taurus worked on Brad's side. "What is this?" she asked in between metal-on-metal reverberations.

"Just a little shrapnel or a bullet or a knife wound," he mumbled. "It was a little bit chaotic in there."

"Do you want to talk about it?" Taurus asked.

"Not at all." Brad would talk about it with Jaq and Teo, maybe his boys, too, if he got to see them again. His thoughts drifted to the planet that they called home. He'd been dirtside but had been born and raised on the space station.

Zin stepped up his efforts once he started to see progress.

He put his whole body into each swing until Crombie yelled at him to stop.

They opened the hatch, and Taurus crawled inside. "Disconnect and take him to *Chrysalis* as fast as possible." She secured the lander's hatch.

Crombie and Zin closed the scout's hatch.

The ship eased away from the lander, adjusted heading, and accelerated on an intercept course for the Borwyn cruiser.

CHAPTER 21

Freedom is the first step toward peace. The second is recognizing that it applies to all.

"Time to go," the general said. "Assuming you still want to do this."

"Have to do this, is what you mean to say," Deena said.

Max wrapped a blanket around himself that he'd taken off Deena's old bed to hide the pulse rifle he carried.

Deena looked closely at her weapon, made a decision, and held it out for the general. "Take it."

Max stared in disbelief.

The general looked at the weapon and then to Deena. "I have no intention of using this, but by carrying it, I think they may shoot at me instead of you." He pointed at Deena. "You are the link that ties us together. If we're ever to have peace between the Malibor and the Borwyn, it'll be because the people followed you, just like I'm doing. I'll take the bullet meant for you." He took the pulse rifle and held it by the barrel. "I can also use it as a cane."

His other cane hung on the edge of the bar. The mind was willing, but he was far from his prime.

Max felt the swell of pride along with the fear of failure. If the Malibor started shooting when they approached the military compound, no amount of dedication or willpower would save them.

"Courage is doing what needs to be done even if you're afraid," the general said.

Deena had heard similar from Max and Crip. "No kidding I'm afraid. You just put the outcome of this war on my shoulders."

The general smiled and shook his head. He looked at her through understanding eyes. "You did that yourself by coming here as a spy and leaving as a friend and then coming back."

Deena gestured toward Max. "Coming back was his idea."

Max moved to the door. "Are we going to do this thing?"

Lanni and the boss stood up.

"You're not coming," Deena said. "This could get ugly."

"We're coming. It's not up for debate because as you told us, this is what it feels like to be free. We make our own decisions and then we live with the consequences."

Unless you die first, Deena thought. With a glance, she knew the others thought it, too, but none of them said it out loud.

Max opened the door and stepped out. He scanned the street in both directions and then the rooftops. He walked ahead, slowly, allowing the others time to catch up. It wasn't far to the main gate, where the barriers were down and wire had been strung across the widest part of the opening.

The general limped ahead to walk beside Deena with Max on the far side. She looked up at both men and smiled.

"Who would have imagined this when I was freezing to death on board *Hornet*, while my crewmates were implementing every dirty trick they could to kill Crip. I'm not happy I saw it, but they brought it on themselves."

"Focus," the general said out the side of his mouth. "Here we go."

He raised one hand while leaning on the rifle with the other. "Ho! I'm General Max Yepsin, and I need to talk with whoever is in charge."

"That's me." A soldier stepped forward with his hand blaster raised. "Just you, General. Come ahead."

The general looked at those with him and nodded just to them. He limped ahead, using the rifle as a cane. The soldier only looked at the general's face. Two more soldiers behind the barricade watched with interest.

Max noted that they weren't aiming their weapons. He held his rifle in his hand but down along his leg and under the blanket.

Deena crossed her arms and attempted to look indifferent.

The general reached the Malibor soldier, a corporal but older than average. "I know you," the general said.

"And I know you, too. But you're retired, and I don't answer to you anymore."

"Busted down from sergeant for bilking the new soldiers out of their pay. I should have put you in jail."

"Then how would I have been able to be here at this moment in time to face you, old and broken. Take your gang of losers and go."

"Even retired, I still rate a salute. You know that, or has all decorum left the service? For your edification, when I asked to speak to the person in charge, I meant the real leadership president, general, someone bigger than a busted corporal. I saw the smoke rising from what I have to assume was the headquarters building. Who survived?"

"None of your business, General." The corporal hadn't saluted. He lifted his hand toward the general and flicked his fingers. *Go away.*

Without hesitating, the general raised the pulse rifle, aimed, and fired. The corporal was tossed back and landed with a splat, a crater blasted through his chest.

"Come on out of there," he told the other soldiers while holding his aim steady.

Max rushed forward, raising his weapon and aiming at the Malibor soldiers.

The two put their hands up and walked forward. A siren sounded in the distance. "What are you doing, General Yepsin?"

"Rectifying my earlier mistake. This man was nothing more than a criminal. He had no place serving alongside decent Malibor. You can put your hands down."

The two complied, glancing back and forth between Max and the general.

"Who's he?" one of the soldiers asked.

The sirens grew closer.

"Wrong question." The general returned the rifle to its previous use as a cane.

Max tucked his pulse rifle under his blanket.

"The right question," the general continued, "is, who is she?" He waved Deena forward.

"She's a waitress," the soldier said.

"If you only knew. She's the one I answer to. And he answers to her, too." The general nodded toward Max. "Back to my original question. Who in the hell is in charge?"

"That's Major Lafort. He's the only one issuing orders."

The general nodded. "Take us to him."

"Not them." The soldiers watched the four with the general. One pointed at Max. "He's got a rifle."

"Of course he has a rifle. If there are more like the corporal here, then we'll be obligated to conduct more summary executions. This is wartime, is it not? As such, I'm returning to duty as the senior ranking officer. You'll take your orders from me from now on or passed down from me. Is that understood?"

"Can you do that?" the soldier wondered.

"Would you rather take life-or-death orders from a major?"

"I don't know who I want to take orders from, but right now, that's you because you have a weapon and are willing to use it."

"I'd like to think you're complying because of the respect I earned during my time, but I'll take fear for now."

They waited for the vehicles blaring their notice to the world. They didn't have long to wait since they were already close. Two vehicles pulled up and discharged their soldiers. The general waved at a lieutenant, motioning for him to come forward. The other soldiers assumed defensive positions along the barrier. Twelve weapons pointed at them.

The general limped forward, leaning heavily on his rifle. "Lieutenant. I need to talk with Major Lafort."

"He's not available," the lieutenant answered. "Who are you?"

"General Yepsin, at your service. The call of duty was too great. I've returned to service and as the senior officer, I'll need an escort to whatever passes for our headquarters."

The lieutenant looked skeptical. "Can you do that?"

"Are you refusing to follow a lawful order?" The general purposefully looked at the body on the ground. "Remember, this is wartime. Refusing an order is instantly actionable by any senior officer."

"You killed him?"

"Do you think he was complying with orders? Did you like him?"

"No, on both accounts. He showed me no respect, but I'm not sure that rates a death sentence. Then again, he probably brought it on himself."

"Not probably, Lieutenant," the general confirmed. "Shall we?"

The lieutenant looked at the squad of soldiers for support. They showed him nothing, not support and not belligerence.

"Lieutenant," the general said. He looked at Deena. "Maybe you should talk to him."

She stepped forward, deftly dodging Max's outstretched hand.

"Gentlemen. What war do you think you're fighting?" Deena asked to open the conversation.

"I'm just following orders," the lieutenant replied. He was young, but still older than Deena. He looked down his nose at her and then scowled at the general.

"Are you? General Yepsin gave you an order which you have yet to follow, so there's something else going on inside your brain housing group. What is it?"

"How do we know you're not infiltrators? We've lost a number of soldiers right here on the compound."

"Are we on the compound?" Deena gestured around herself.

"You're confusing me," the lieutenant admitted. He looked to his soldiers, but they were no help.

"You're making this a lot harder on yourself than it needs to be. Take the general to whatever passes for a headquarters. Load up your people and provide security for us. If there are infiltrators on the compound, then the general will be a prime target, don't you think? The enemy has already decapitated the government. Soldiers are fighting civilians in the street, and you're here, wondering what it's all about."

The young man sighed, threw his head back, and stared at the morning sky. He raised his arm in the air and signaled for his squad to re-board the vehicles. "If you'll come with me, General."

"And them, too. They're my support team, and if you haven't noticed, I'm not as physically capable as I used to be."

"Your support team is the restaurant staff?"

The general rested his hand on the lieutenant's shoulder. "In war, you take what you can get. They're good people. Can you say the same for those you've surrounded yourself with?"

"I can."

"Good man," the general said, clapping the young lieutenant on the shoulder. The soldiers reluctantly recovered and slowly boarded their vehicle.

"You ride with me. The rest of you on the truck."

Deena looked at Max, then back to the boss and Lanni. They both had wide eyes and closed mouths. Despite their initial motivation and desire to join the group, it was more than they anticipated.

"Hey, boys, how's it hanging?" Max said and strolled into the middle of the Malibor soldiers.

"What are you?"

"I'm with them," Max replied without answering.

"Let's go, people," the general shouted in a commanding voice that they'd not heard from him before. "We'll get this done and be home for lunch."

"What do you think he means by that?" a soldier asked Max.

"He means exactly what he said. This war is over, and the good news is, we all survived."

"What does that mean?" the soldier pressed. The Malibor were confused and angry at not knowing what was going on.

Deena leaned forward from her seat next to Max in the back of the truck. The boss and Lanni were on her other side.

The soldiers recognized Deena, Lanni, and the boss. "You work at the restaurant."

"That's right. Do you like the food?" Deena asked.

"Yeah. It's good. Servers look good, too." The soldiers chuckled behind their hands.

"We're your average citizens fighting to end the madness. Do you think it's right that soldiers were killing civilians?"

"Soldiers were getting killed out there, too!" one of the group blurted.

"It was nonsensical. The fighting is going to stop. The general is going to make sure of it. We're behind him all the way."

"Did we win or lose?" a soldier asked.

"Yes," Deena replied.

"I feel like there should have been more fighting." The soldier looked at his buddies.

The vehicle sped up and then slowed. They hadn't gone far. The truck lurched to a stop with tires screeching.

Max got up and leaned out the back to look around the side to see what was in front of the truck. The car carrying the general had gone through, but a barrier arm had been lowered in front of the truck. Troops were streaming into the area from a nearby barracks. They surrounded the car.

"It's showtime, people" Max shouted. He pulled out his pulse rifle and carried it across his chest. "They seem to be threatening the general, and we're not good with that."

"You know me," Deena snarled.

"I'm going out there to make sure the general is safe." Max dropped the rear gate and hopped out. None of the soldiers moved.

Deena stepped out and glared at the soldiers. "You call yourselves men."

Lanni and the boss followed her out the back and into the road. Max shrugged off his blanket to show the rifle he carried at the ready across his chest.

The general was ahead, and the soldiers coming from the barracks were attempting to cut him off.

Max wanted to switch his rifle to full auto and mow them down, but there were too many. He ran toward the general.

Deena sprinted to catch him. Lanni and the boss were cut off. They pulled up short of the barrier.

"You will stay back!" the general ordered. He raised the pulse rifle and fired two rounds into the air. "You know who I am. You know I'm the ranking officer. Who ordered you out here?"

"I did," a voice from the back of the crowd called. The soldiers stepped aside to give the general a clear view of the major.

"I have to assume you're Major Lafort. I'm General Yepsin, and I'm taking command."

"I don't think so, old man. Your day has come and gone. You had your chance. Now, it's our time."

"To do what, Major? Start a new civil war? Fighting the Borwyn wasn't enough for you, so you want fight other Malibor, too? I said stand down." The general had assumed a neutral voice. He wasn't ratcheting up the tension. It was already extreme with too many soldiers keeping their fingers on triggers.

"Nah, I'm following our rules on the chain of command. Old men are nowhere to be found. What do you think, boys?

Should we secure the base or let an old man and four civilians tell us what to do? You aren't a civilian!" He pointed at Max, who was standing next to the general.

Deena stepped in front of both of them.

"Hiding behind a woman!" The major roared his mockery. He pointed at Deena and lost his smile. He opened his mouth to say something when a mallet-sized fist hammered into his temple. The major dropped like a sack of potatoes. The boss stood over him, fists ready to fight all comers.

"Secure him," the general ordered but to no one in particular.

The boss flipped the unconscious major over and placed one foot in the middle of his back.

"The thing about wielding power is if you lead by fear, the men won't follow you when they no longer fear you. I'm not threatening you, but I am offering you something." The general scanned the crowd, which was nothing more than a mob, a bunch of soldiers milling about in the courtyard beside the ruins of the headquarters building.

The discipline of the military had deteriorated. The general had presided over that, torn between being a dominating individual and a decent one. He'd been the former. It was the only way to move up until he got to the top, then he wanted to be the latter. But he'd already shown a full generation of soldiers that it was better to be merciless.

It was the lesson they'd learned and not the one he'd tried to teach.

The soldiers nervously shifted, holding weapons at the ready in the confusion of the moment.

The general climbed on a nearby stanchion and stood unsteadily above the troops. More filtered toward them.

"Now is our moment of greatness," the general said in a voice that projected without any apparent effort. "The Malibor will finally achieve peace among our own people and with our enemies, too. It's what I spent my entire career working toward."

"Did the Borwyn surrender?" a voice from the crowd asked.

"The Borwyn have not surrendered. They've destroyed all our ships. They attacked the spaceport and isolated this city. They did not turn us against ourselves, however. We did that. We helped them to win."

"Malibor lost?" the same voice said. "You surrendered!"

"No!" the general bellowed, but the damage had already been done. The crack of a Malibor blaster ripped through the air. The general tumbled backward and landed hard on the pavement.

Max and Deena rushed to his side. Blood oozed from his chest where the bullet passed through. Bubbles appeared as he tried to breathe. Max pressed on the wound with the palm of his hand.

The general pushed the pulse rifle at Deena before his eyes glazed over and his chest stopped rising.

Deena took the rifle and stood. She turned to face the crowd that shouted at her. She stormed up to the shooter, slapped his weapon to the side with the barrel of hers, and followed through with a butt-stroke to the head that dropped him to the ground. She backed out of the crowd. Max stood in the small open area with his pulse rifle raised while dozens of barrels pointed his way.

Deena slung her pulse rifle and raised her hands for calm. "Whether you kill us or not, the war is still lost, but no one surrendered."

"Don't listen to her! She's a waitress."

"Lieutenant Tremayne, Malibor fleet, at your service." She bowed her head slightly. "And this is my husband, Sergeant Max Tremayne of the Borwyn fleet."

Growls and murmurs rose to a fevered pitch.

She calmly looked at them while casually moving in front of Max. "We are the future of our worlds."

"You're an abomination!" someone shouted.

"Petty Officer Dintle, Malibor fleet, retired," a big voice boomed from the rear of the group. "If you don't listen to her, you're wrong, and I'll beat you into next week." The boss shook his fists at the most rambunctious of the soldiers. He worked his way toward them.

They backed down.

Unguided. Undisciplined. If they were turned loose, they'd become nothing more than pillagers.

Max was disgusted but fought to keep that expression off his face.

Deena was the calmest of them all until Lanni stepped forward.

"I'm Lanni Moran. Many of you know my husband, Private Moran. Who among you wants to die? Who among you wants to survive while missing an arm? That's my husband. The Borwyn saved his life after nearly taking it. But he's alive, which is what every single one of your wives and girlfriends want. Alive. You won't be tortured. You won't be killed. Listen to Deena. She speaks for you."

"She's Borwyn!" someone snarled.

"She's Malibor," Lanni said and approached the man. She was young and disarming. She stared at the speaker until he looked away. "I want my husband back."

"What do you want out of life?" Deena shouted, now standing on the stanchion where the general had been shot. His body rested on the ground behind her. She glanced back at him. A lump rose in her throat.

When she faced the crowd again, they were pressing in. Soldiers were pushing from behind, but they had stopped aiming their weapons. Max had slung his over his shoulder. If shooting started, the Borwyn couldn't win. The threat of his pulse rifle was gone. There were far too many Malibor soldiers crowded into the space.

"You want to live your lives. Do a job that matters. Raise families or not. You want the freedom to live as you choose. Is your ideal life living in a barracks, cleaning toilets, and getting harassed until you get sent to die?"

The grumbling died down. These were the lowest ranks. She looked over the crowd and spotted two corporals, the one young lieutenant who had escorted the general to the headquarters' rubble, and the rest were privates. These were the lowest ranks who knew only the pain of service and not the glory.

"Serve your fellow Malibor in a different way," Deena continued. "People need to eat. They need to have shelter. They need the power to stay on. They need clothing. And they need entertainment. When's the last time you had a really good beer?"

A couple soldiers laughed and jabbed at each other.

"Who among you is going to provide that service to your fellow citizens? Who among you will offer kindness instead of reprisal? Put your weapons in that truck and go home. I mean your real home and not the barracks. For those who have nothing else, we need your help in returning the spaceport to functionality. We're going to have visitors very soon."

"All those shuttles. They brought the people from the space station, didn't they?" a man up front asked in a soft voice.

"They did," another solder replied. "They're holding them in the sportsball complex."

"We need to turn them loose. They are your fellow Malibor who've committed no crimes." She found the lieutenant and gestured to him. "Take a couple men in the car and release those people. Send them home, and if they don't have anyone, bring them here. We're going to have barracks space available until they can find accommodations in town."

The lieutenant pointed at three men and headed out.

The soldiers watched her and waited. "Go on now. Weapons in the truck. Grab your stuff and go home. Your service in the Malibor military has come to an end. We'll start a job service soon to help you find positions that suit you best. Also, full amnesty for any crimes committed before this moment. We all move forward with a clean slate. No animosity. No blood feuds. No taking what isn't yours." She twirled her arm in the air.

Max grabbed the two closest soldiers. "Chuck the

weapons in the truck and keep them there. We'll put them up in the armory until a new government can determine what to do with them."

"I have nowhere else to go." The soldier turned to Max for answers.

Max looked into the man's eyes. "Then you can help us. Some people may not be so amenable to a war that's over. Keep your weapon and stand over here. I'm sure you're not the only one."

The soldiers filtered through, tossing weapons into the pile. Some never bothered returning to the barracks. They walked toward the front gate, wearing their uniforms and carrying nothing else.

The sorry state of the Malibor military. It had existed on the idea that it was indomitable when it had already failed.

Max helped Deena down and held her tightly.

"Madam President," he said.

Deena smiled. "I don't know what that means, but I'm sure it won't be any fun."

"For starters, you help them keep food on the table and a warm place to sleep, and everything else is gravy, at least in the beginning. After that, they'll need more, a lot more."

"You mean like a two-for-one sale at the restaurant?" Deena quipped.

"Hey! Are you giving my food away?" the boss cried.

"No, but you better get back there. We didn't lock the door when we left." Deena waggled her eyebrows.

"I honestly thought we were going to die, so I didn't care, but now I do." He started running toward the front gate.

Lanni took Max's arm. "When can I see Moran?"

"We'll ask the combat team to bring him to the city." Max looked around for the nearest high point. The wall was two blocks away. "As soon as we're done collecting the weapons, we'll climb the wall and try to make contact."

Deena looked at Max. "Try making contact now." She motioned toward the truck. "Put the set on the roof."

Max pulled the pack off his back as he walked away.

Deena took a knee next to the general. She closed his eyes and looked for something to cover him with. Lanni provided her shawl, even though there was a bite in the air.

"Go home, Lanni. Check on your mom and your baby girl. I know where you live, but then again, so does Moran. We'll do our best to get him here soonest. Freedom. Those weren't just words. They're an ideal that we have to live up to every single day. Our freedom while making sure others have it, too."

Lanni zoomed in for a hug.

CHAPTER 22

The end comes before the beginning.

Jaq slowly worked her way toward the airlock. She found the outer hatch still open. No one had bothered to manually cycle it. Jaq crawled inside, secured the hatch, and started cycling the air by means of the hand pump. It took longer than when she left the ship because she was tired.

The light turned green, showing that the air pressure was stabilized with the inside of the ship. Jaq stared at it, wondering why this system worked when others didn't. She opened the inner hatch and entered her ship, stripping the spacesuit off and tossing it aside. She flew down the corridor to the central shaft and up to the port roller airlock.

Teo had been in the airlock transmitting a message to Bec. She had gotten creative and included "a-hole" in every message at various locations until she found a replacement who took over for her.

Jaq expected to find Teo, but she wasn't there. No one

was. The lamp had been left in the equipment net. Jaq blinked a message toward the Malibor ship, just once. She watched for a reply, but there was none. She replaced the lamp.

When the scout ship bumped against the airlock, she recoiled and slammed into the frame. Pain shot up her arm.

Jaq peeked out to see the familiar airlock of *Starstrider*. There was no way to communicate with it except by waving through the porthole, which was what she did. An unfamiliar face watched her while waving back. She stepped out of the airlock and closed the inner door. It seemed heavier than normal, even though they were at zero-gee. It should have been effortless, but it wasn't.

The air. Outside, she'd enjoyed plenty of oxygen. Inside, she was struggling just like every other member of the crew.

The panel lit up beside the inner lock, and Jaq cycled it to add air to the outer coupling. The light turned green. She realized that power had been restored to some systems. The corridor lighting blinked, swapping the emergency lighting for the standard light panels.

Jaq listened for the sound of the air handler. She eased down the corridor to the nearest vent. Cool air poured out of it. She pressed her face against it, breathing deeply. The sound of the airlock hatch opening barely registered on her dulled senses.

"Brad's injured," a young man said.

Jaq snapped out of her dream state into a semi-conscious wakefulness. "Brad?"

"Yes. We're taking him to Doc Teller. I'm Crombie," he said from the airlock while easing Brad through.

Jaq held the midrail and waited for Crombie to bring Brad closer. "That's a lot of blood," she said after getting a better look at his clothes. With each breath, her head became clearer. "Let's go."

They dragged Brad's unconscious form to the central shaft and up to the deck where Medical was located. They found it empty. Jaq opened the hatch where Doc Teller was in a sleeping bag attached to the bulkhead.

"Doc!" Jaq called out. She attached her boots to the deck so she could shake him.

"Ow!" He woke with a start. "Watch that. It's broken."

Jaq let go of his arm and stepped aside so the doctor could see them arrange Brad on the table and strap him down.

"What happened?" he said when saw his old friend. Doc Teller struggled to get out of his bag. Jaq helped, peeling him out of it like peeling the skin off fruit.

"Shrapnel, bullets, impacts, all of it," Crombie said evenly. "His side took the worst of it."

"I'm going to have to sew him up. Get my assistant."

"I'll send the shepherd to you. Everyone else is busy getting the ship working. I need to go to the bridge. If you need blood, I'll donate," Jaq told him.

"I'll take care of it," the doc said.

Jaq left the space only to plaster herself to the bulkhead to collect her wits. The ship. She needed to focus on the ship. The Malibor behemoth was still out there. The space station was still a threat, wasn't it?

"Crombie," Jaq called through the door.

He leaned out. "You called, Captain?"

"What's going on with the station?"

"They lost power. We got into the command center, but they were all dead. They suffocated with the complete loss of power. We're evacuating on the lander we recovered. Do you know what happened?"

"Malibor EMP weapon did a number on everyone, including themselves, but Bec has the situation in hand over there."

"He does? How'd he get over there?"

"He stole a lander and he's in big trouble, but that's not for right now. Taurus took *Starstrider*. Where is she?"

"Flying the lander," Crombie replied.

"Did you hear from *Starbound*?"

"No. Should we have?" Crombie wondered.

Jaq shook her head. If *Chrysalis* was functional, then they had a lot to do, which started with returning to the engagement zone. *Cornucopia* needed help. A lander filled with Borwyn was out there somewhere. The reality dawned on her.

"You took thirty-eight total people to the station. How many are you evacuating?"

"Only twenty survived, Jaq, assuming the injured don't die on us, but I think Brad was the worst of them."

"We lost eighteen people?" Jaq closed her eyes and sighed. "I need to get to the bridge and send the shepherd down."

"The Malibor weren't so keen on handing over the station to us, but they lost a lot more than we did. It was ugly over there. Every corner. Every room. We didn't know where the next round was coming from. By the time we reached the command center, their will to fight was gone. Zero-gee is something they hadn't trained for. We were little better, but still better. The pulse rifles gave us an edge."

Jaq nodded. "I understand." She hurried away before they could keep talking, which was what she wanted to do most. She wanted to talk to Brad about the boarding, but that wasn't possible. "I need to go. Thank you." She pushed off and flew down the corridor, catching herself to redirect toward the command deck.

She pulled herself along the mid-rail until she reached the bridge. Only Amie was there. Jaq moved to the upper rail to navigate to the rear, where she found a second and a third person. Donal and the shepherd were both sound asleep.

"Shepherd!" Jaq shouted.

He jerked awake, wide-eyed and staring blankly.

"They need you in Medical, something about donating all your internal organs. Go!"

The shepherd mumbled, "Ours is to serve His greater glory."

"Why are you still here? It's Brad down there."

"On my way, Captain." The shepherd tumbled over the workstations. Jaq pushed him toward the hatch.

Donal tried to look awake. "Hey! Computer is back on."

"It is?" Jaq looked over his head. "Hey! Our computers weren't fried. That's good. Better than good."

Jaq climbed into the captain's chair and cycled through her systems. She tried activating the main screen, but it didn't respond. She looked through the status reports on her screen, but no one had been able to update their sections. The status showed the same from before they were hit by the EMP. Jaq tried the intercom, and it appeared to be functional.

"All hands, this is your captain speaking. It appears that we have returned to an operational status before any of the other victims of the Malibor EMP. We've got lots of things to do, not the least of which is thank our engineers and damage control teams for their efforts to get this ship back online, including bringing the air handlers and filtration system up. I cannot express my appreciation. Ferd, Mary, report to the bridge. We need to pick up the boarding team and then save *Cornucopia* from spinning away to deep space."

Jaq closed the channel. "I'll be right back," she told Amie. She raced down the corridor and down to Engineering, where she found Teo within a spiderweb of cabling. "Congratulations and thank you. We only have to get a few more kilometers out of this old girl."

"Funny," Teo replied.

"Your dad's in Medical with Doc Teller patching him up. He took the worst of it from the station."

Teo stopped what she was doing, which Jaq couldn't see. "I trust the doc to do what can be done. I've got more to do. We replaced the key circuits that were fried, bypassed those we couldn't replace, and jury-rigged the rest. It's going to be a rough ride because the integration of systems isn't happening. Nothing is tied in together."

"It'll do. No one is shooting at us."

"Not anymore, that is," Teo clarified.

"I chalk that up to an overzealous crew on board the Malibor ship. And Bec is over there alone."

"We could do something about that," Teo said. She plugged two cables together and then carefully worked her way out of the maze of wires. "We can fly over there and marry up with it. Engines and thrusters are online, Jaq."

"Take over that ship? We have our boarding party to recover. We have *Cornucopia* to save. And then we can think about taking over the Malibor ship."

"I'm not sure how long these workarounds will be operational. We could lose it all in five minutes, five hours, or five days. Prioritize wisely, because I suspect we'll go down when it's most inconvenient. Every fix from here on out will be done by a tired crew, where it gets harder and harder. We'll need a couple months in the shipyard to get *Chrysalis* back to her former glory." Teo raised her hand to hold off Jaq's counterargument. "I know that we don't have months. We'll make do, but try not to stress the ship too much."

"I promise," Jaq lied. She accessed the comm unit on the bulkhead. "Bridge, this is Jaq. Slow us to a stop, all ahead slow, one gee." No one answered her. She repeated her order.

"I'll tell the flight team when they arrive," Amie replied.

Jaq stepped away from the unit. "I better get to the bridge."

"You said my dad is here, but we have to recover a lander. How did he get here?"

"*Starstrider*. It's at the port roller airlock."

"I have an idea." Teo perked up. "We need to recover that lander first."

Godbolt passed out again. The small crew of four had gathered in the far end of the ship, where the spin was too great, but that was where the engines and thrusters were located. They needed to repair them to stop the spin, but the spin was too much to work under. It pushed almost three gees, which was only tolerable for a limited time and when the crew wasn't exhausted.

They had tried working in shifts, retreating to the center of the ship for an hour and attempting to work for an hour, but that was too much downtime. The air was starting to go bad. *Cornucopia* had a massive internal volume, but it didn't maintain twenty-one percent oxygen. It had about eighteen and a half on a good day.

This wasn't a good day.

Godbolt came to. She returned to the panel where she'd been working and fiddled with the bypass on another connection.

Angel leaned in beside her. "We have to look at abandoning the ship," he slurred.

"We've already been through this. There is no way to abandon the ship. If we get the scrubbers online, we can concentrate airflow into the bridge, but to do that, we need the engines online. It all comes down to right here, Angel. We need the engines online and then we can do everything else, none of which looks like abandoning ship because we don't have a lifeboat, pod, lander, or ship of any sort. We have four spacesuits and five people. We've been through this. We can't get there from here. I'm not flushing you four into space. What then? Do you see anyone out there flying around looking for survivors?"

"I need to go."

"Back to the bridge, relax in zero-gee, but whatever you

do, don't flush yourself into space. You'll die when your air runs out."

"We're dying now," the crewman argued.

"We're not great. We'll survive, but we have to keep our heads on straight."

"I have to go," the man reiterated.

"To the bridge. Go to the bridge." Godbolt watched him struggle away. She felt every bit of the three gees weighing her down. Precision work was hard, and the fact that she could barely see exacerbated the situation. She took deep breaths in an attempt to energize herself, but it only served to make her want more oxygen, something better than the stale air she found ungratifying.

She put her tools down and rallied the other three to return to the bridge. They worked their way as a group out of the heavy gees. The relief was significant, except the air was no better.

We're going to die if we don't get the power on, she thought. She left the others behind and returned to the engine room. She passed out but only briefly. The wire cutter along with her whole body was plastered to the bulkhead. She kneeled as straight as she could to put less pressure on her muscles, but she had to reach out.

The tools were so heavy. Her arms shook with the effort.

"One more, just one more connection," she pleaded with herself. Godbolt twisted the bypass together and leaned back.

Nothing changed.

She let go of the cutter and allowed herself to get pressed against the bulkhead. A clanging reached her distant mind. Something going on.

"No!" she tried to shout, but only a grunt came out. She could barely force her eyes open, expecting to see her crew in spacesuits exiting the ship, but it wasn't her crew. A lone individual in a spacesuit appeared but stayed away from Godbolt.

A dream. Calling me to the light. I'm sorry, Alby. It wasn't meant to be.

A heavy metal hook hit her in the chest. She forced her eyes open once more. The figure beyond gestured frantically.

Godbolt grabbed the hook, but it pulled out of her hand. The figure walked away.

Not even Septiman thinks I'm worth saving, she thought.

The figure returned with others. While they stayed back, the figure approached, clomping incrementally and bracing with each step against the forces that held Godbolt down.

The hook reappeared, and the figure ripped it through the back of Godbolt's collar. Together, they pulled away from the ship's end. The figure grunted and cursed. *A man,* Godbolt thought. *Not Septiman.*

With the help of the barely fuddled crew, they reached the zero-gee center point of *Cornucopia*.

Alby removed his helmet and pulled Godbolt to him. "Let's get you on the scout and back to *Chrysalis*. We'll abandon *Cornucopia* for now, but we know where it's headed, in case we need it later."

He herded the five into the scout ship. They had to stand to fit, and the environmental control system wasn't geared for that many people breathing. Alby put his helmet back on and used the suit's air while guiding the scout away from the freighter.

He accelerated slowly to keep from compressing the poor souls behind him.

Godbolt squeezed in next to him. She fought to keep her eyes from rolling back in her head. "Thank you," she managed to say.

"What else was I to do? Sometimes, you have to take matters into your own hands." He nodded toward the external view, where *Chrysalis* was maneuvering toward the Malibor ship.

"I don't know what I'm looking at," Godbolt admitted. Her brain remained muddled.

"We're taking the Malibor ship." Alby grinned. "The space station is useless without power, so we've abandoned that, too, although it cost us a great deal and we didn't even have to go over there."

Alby didn't continue.

Godbolt was in no shape to parse the information. She was an engineer, not the battle commander. Alby reached around her and pulled her tightly against him. "I'm not letting you go."

She mumbled her consent and drifted off.

CHAPTER 23

Fortune favors the bold but not the boldly stupid.

Glen arrived at the camp to find it nearly empty. "Hello!" he called as the rest of the supply train arrived behind him.

"Commander!" the doctor called as he emerged from the chow bunker. "Word from the front is that they're going to the city."

"They are? I have supplies with me. Food, water, ammunition including grenades."

"You better take them with you. And take these two, also." The doctor pointed at two holes in the ground with cage-like traps overtop. "I think they've done their time."

"I'm happy turning them loose to fend for themselves. By the time they return to the city, we'll have moved, and they won't know anything useful," Glen replied. He gestured to turn them loose. The doctor shrugged and returned inside. Glen looked around. He was alone with his pack caravan.

Glen opened the cages. "Come on, get out of there. I'll

take you to the city, and then you leave. Or you strike out on your own ahead of that. If you try to hurt any of us, we'll kill you. We don't have time for any games. Do you understand?"

Deep, dark bags pooled beneath Moran's eyes. He struggled to get out of the hole, fighting briefly with Glen.

The commander pushed him away. The prisoner staggered and fell. Glen released Raftal, who jumped out of the hole and hurried to his friend.

"He needs you to make sure he doesn't die," Glen said. "There's an easy answer to all of this if you can't take the responsibility."

Raftal raised his hands. "I get it. Last time, we were stupid. I thought Moran had more energy, but he doesn't."

Glen shoved the barrel of his pulse rifle into Raftal's chest and snarled. "If you want to be enemies, we'll be enemies. I've helped you survive, and all you've done is spit in my face. No more!" Glen roared.

"Yeah, I know. I told you I get it."

"Do you?" Glen was angry at the prisoners but more so the situation. He hadn't wanted anyone to go to the city, especially without him. Now he'd be playing catchup while dragging twenty horses loaded with supplies and five extra soldiers.

It wasn't much, but it was far more than what they expected.

"Walk or ride?" Glen snapped.

"We've never ridden horses," Raftal admitted.

Glen led them to a horse in the middle of the line and right in front of the corporal who had been guarding the entrance.

"We don't get our own horses?" Raftal asked.

"No. Put him up there first and you climb on behind him." Glen stood back. He'd lost any trust that he'd given the two. Glen looked to the corporal. "If they try anything, kill them both."

Raftal took his seat and looked down on Glen. "You went from do everything possible to help us to a perpetual threat that you'll kill us. What changed?"

"I know you think you're obligated to try and escape. We both know how foolish that was, since we saved your lives. You return without a scratch, and Moran returns with a well-managed amputation. You'll be treated like garbage, where we were treating you like decent human beings. You betrayed my trust and forced me to treat you like Malibor treat prisoners. I despise you for making me do that."

Glen flicked his fingers at them and walked away.

He was tired and angry. He knew that he'd apologize later, but for now, he would do what he could to catch up to the platoons.

"Move out!" he yelled over his shoulder from the lead horse. He urged his mount to trot. They didn't have a great deal of ground to cover, and he wanted to do it quickly.

Too many unknowns. He should have questioned the doctor more, or the radio operator, or whoever was in possession of the information.

It dawned on him that it was like the newer soldiers who were at the bottom of the chain of command. They followed orders without seeing anything that happened above them unless it was explained at each level, which it usually wasn't.

He relaxed into the knowledge of his dismay. He was

following orders when he was supposed to be the one giving them.

"Going to the city. Yes, sir! But what do we do when we get there? What you're told! Sir! Yes, sir," Glen said to the empty forest around him.

What to do in the city? That was the question he couldn't answer. Why would Crip have given that order? It made no sense. He urged his horse to greater speed.

Maybe they left someone behind who had the answers. What was going on? It was the age-old question that every soldier asked because they existed in a perpetual state of ignorance. It had been called the fog of war.

Glen looked over his shoulder at the Malibor prisoners. They were still where they were supposed to be. He nodded to them, but they didn't respond. He was still angry with them and himself. No one deserved to live in a cell that consisted of a hole in the ground. They should have appreciated the freedom he'd given them.

With the increase in speed, much to the caravan driver's chagrin, they arrived at the front line after only a few hours. The entire company was there, minus one of the combat team's two squads. Crip had taken them to recover the crash survivors, Max, and Deena.

Eleanor had gone with them, with the order that no one was supposed to do anything until Glen returned, so they had waited.

Glen laughed at himself. And that was another bane of the soldier's existence. Bad information. When the word wasn't the right word but got passed along all the same.

"Do we have Crip and Eleanor on the radio?" Glen asked.

Larson shrugged. "They haven't checked in because they said that they were going radio silent."

"Break radio silence. Call them, if you would be so kind." Glen took his binoculars and studied what he could see of the city. It looked normal compared to before. No smoke rose. In the fields, the first workers appeared.

"Aren't you tired?" Larson asked.

"The horses did all the work," Glen replied. He was exhausted, and that was no way to be when attacking the city.

"Contact," Larson declared and handed the microphone to Glen.

"Glen here. Is that you, Crip?"

"It is. We were just thinking about calling you. Are you back?"

"Full support from the council. I'm back with a supply train. We're going to eat well. What's your plan?"

"We're going to the city. Two of our people will escort Evelyn and Tram back to you, but you won't be there, will you?"

Glen hesitated.

"Break, break. Max here. We could use some extra bodies, if you can spare anyone."

"What's the fighting like?" Crip asked.

"None. Deena convinced the Malibor army to concede. War's over, but the civilians in the town don't know that. We will be broadcasting the message using local radio. The message is business as usual. Food, shelter, entertainment.

We're going to host a party in Deena's bar later. You're invited."

Glen looked at the radio. He tapped the microphone on the unit to make sure it was real. "The fighting is over?" he asked incredulously. "I don't believe it."

"Come to town but enter at the spaceport just beyond the wall. Cut yourselves a big hole through the fence. Take a left and look for the smoking crater that used to be the headquarters building. Deena is directing the situation from there."

"Deena?" Crip asked.

"That's Madame President to you. And no, I have no idea how it happened, but she obviously was a force to be reckoned with when she was working outside the gate. Everyone knew her. No one messed with her. I'm quite proud, if you can't tell."

"There wasn't any shooting," Crip replied.

"A little. The general made the victory possible. Would you believe that? A Malibor general who realized the greatest mistake was making the Borwyn their enemy instead of an ally. He made up for that and then paid for it with his life. A few people got shot, but that's it. We've collected most of the Malibor weapons, but we have a peacekeeping platoon that we're building. We need Borwyn as well as Malibor, and that's what I see from the assault brigade and the combat team."

"We have the Malibor prisoners with us. We'll bring them in. We're on our way, Max, and I look forward to stepping foot in the city. Thank you for everything you spacers did for us. Like you told me, we all win together."

"Has anyone heard from *Chrysalis*?" Crip asked.

"Negative," Larson responded, since Glen had already moved away and was issuing orders to the company. "I'll try contacting them again."

"We'll be on our way to the city momentarily. It'll take us a while," Crip said.

"We have all these shuttles parked around the spaceport. Move into the open and I'll see if we can send one your way for a pickup," Max offered.

"My heart races at the thought of not having to walk any farther. I'm sure Evelyn and Tram would appreciate a ride, too. Good luck. We'll be in the open along the edge of the forest beyond the crashed gunship."

"Roger. Got stuff to do. Max out."

Larson broke out the satellite radio set. He found a clear overhead to see the sky, but he couldn't see the moon. He had to go into the open where the moon was low on the horizon and getting lower. He set up and tried to call *Chrysalis* until the moon set.

He broke down the radio and returned to the woods to find everyone packed up and ready to go.

"Did you get through?" Glen asked.

"No joy, Commander," Larson replied.

"It doesn't matter. If we can lock up control of the city, then what happens up there is irrelevant." Glen poked a finger skyward. He strolled into the open and faced the woods. "Behind me is the city we've watched for decades. Now, it's our time. If what Max says is true, we won't be shooting anyone. Stay ready, stay cautious, and don't shoot unless they shoot at you first."

Some of the soldiers grumbled. The eastern Borwyn

natives grumbled but were more anxious than the rest. They moved up front, dragging their husbands with them. Larson joined them. "Looks like we're leading the procession."

"As you wish. Head straight across the field, past the cut, toward the right side of the wall as we will see once we get closer. I'll be on my horse."

The combat team took the lead and moved quickly, something they'd gotten used to with the less encumbered eastern Borwyn.

Larson wondered why they weren't sending a shuttle for them.

CHAPTER 24

Change is what people are the most afraid of. The tastiest carrot is the one the consumer is most familiar with.

Bec strode past technicians on his way to the bridge. There weren't many, and they were civilians, uninterested in challenging him. The last corridor was narrower with bulwarks and even a small guardhouse-looking structure. They'd planned the ship around protecting the bridge.

Too bad you didn't plan to protect the ship from your EMP weapon, Bec thought. They had planned it, but they hadn't implemented it, and that had been their downfall. Now they had no missiles in the tubes, no power, and no hope of restoring their systems any time soon. They had too few people, and the damage was too extensive.

They needed Bec's help. He was sure of it.

He walked past the barriers that had they been manned, his plan would have been impossible. The hatch was open, and he walked through.

Behind him, Anton kicked his way down the corridor and pulled himself even with Bec, clinging to the hatch to hold his position.

"I'm here to save your lives," Bec announced.

"Who are you?" a professional asked. He stood. Bec didn't know ranks in the Malibor fleet, but he looked older and acted important. Maybe he was the deputy. Bec didn't care.

"Bec, former chief engineer of *Chrysalis*. I'm the one who kept them from destroying this ship."

"You did, huh? Are you the one who sent our missiles to the planet to burn up on entry?"

"I did, and that saved you. Did you see the two missiles that were sent to the ship? Those were shot down. That ship is functional. This one is not, but we can bring it online. All we need is time."

"You just told us that *Chrysalis* is functional. I suspect that ship is Borwyn, which means you're Borwyn. We should kill you."

"Interesting." Bec turned to Anton. "They resort to threats of violence based on one small tidbit of information while ignoring everything else. Is that selective dissociation?"

Anton shrugged and shook his head.

"In any case," Bec continued, "I can help bring your ship online. Why are your computer screens operational?"

"Is that your idea of help?" the man scoffed. "Systems on the bridge were hardened and are isolated from the rest of the ship, but not having the other systems operational—gravity, energy screen, weapons, and environmental control—has proven problematic. We'll get it right when we finish hardening the whole ship."

"You seem to have missed the point that this ship is finished. If you want it destroyed, keep doing what you're doing. Or we could fix it and bring everything back online."

"That simple, huh? If we're done for, then why bother?"

"Because I'm on board, so it's important that we keep this ship alive to me personally. By virtue of saving me, I'll save all of you, too, but I need you to stop acting the fool."

"Acting the fool?" the older professional said.

"We're up," another said from underneath the console.

"Behold!" The man who was probably the deputy gestured toward the screens as they came up one after another until they surrounded the stations on the bridge. Information populated.

Bec stood with his mouth open. He'd seen the extent of the damage. The systems shouldn't have been online.

"We only needed to bring the hardened backup systems online, but that took longer than we thought. Primary and secondary gravity generators are offline. Do I have you to thank for that?"

Bec shrugged. His mind raced, looking for a new plan. He hated being wrong, and there had never been an instance in his whole life where he'd been this wrong about nearly everything. But the ship was online.

"The Borwyn ship is bearing down on us," one of the four crew on the bridge said.

"Reload the missile tubes," the officer ordered.

Bec reared back and threw the spanner he was carrying with all the force in his body. It darted across the bridge and hit the officer in the face. He recoiled from the impact and would have tumbled backward had he not been magnetically attached to the deck. Blood spurted from a destroyed nose and a gash in his forehead. The man's arms floated from his sides.

Bec grabbed Anton and launched him like a missile at the crewman who had been ordered to reload the missiles. Bec clomped across the deck to engage with the one who had been under the station. The last thing he wanted to do was get into a brawl, but he saw no choice. His mind had failed, so he would use his body as a weapon.

The man at the workstation struggled to get his feet under him. Bec stomped on his hand. The man rolled away, spinning in the zero-gee. He pushed off with his hands but ran into the unconscious body swaying with the flow of air around the bridge.

The air! Bec wasn't getting enough air. That's why he was wrong. It wasn't him. In the nanosecond he invested in finding an excuse for his miscues, he found solace and relief.

Zero-gee was his friend. His target tried to leverage off the acting captain, but the body swayed. Bec grabbed his flailing arm and rotated his body, dipping as he went to accelerate his throw. The main sailed toward the screen, windmilling his arms and legs in an attempt to change direction. He slammed into the screen, momentarily stunned from the impact. Bec was on him. He caught the man from behind and wrapped his arms around his chest.

The man started to fight, but Bec was already bending over backward, dragging the man away from the wall, up, and over, head-first into the workstation closest to the surrounding wall.

The hearty crunch resounded through the bridge. Bec let go, and the man floated free. Bec stepped toward the two Malibor doing little more than arm-wrestling. Neither looked like they wanted to fight. Bec clomped next to them.

"Stop!" he shouted in a way that he'd seen Jaq do. The two relaxed and leaned toward him. "Take him to the gravity generator. The power coupling on the backside has been undone. Reconnect it. Easy as that. Do it now." Bec pointed toward the hatch with his arm. He stayed that way until they were out, and then he secured the hatch shut behind them.

On the bridge itself, it took him no time to figure out the controls. He'd studied the systems on *Hornet*. The graphic interface was comparable, but smoother and easier. It was much improved over the older ship.

Bec breathed deeply, enjoying the fresh air being blown at him. He checked the comm system and found it functional. He dialed up the right frequency. "Jaq, this is Bec, your favorite ship acquisition specialist. Please dock at the nearest available airlock. Gravity should be up shortly. You're never going to believe what I found over here!"

"Bec, you slimy worm!" Teo shouted into the microphone.

"What are you doing? I need to talk to Jaq."

"She's not available, you slack-jawed Cro-Magnon."

"I sense some hostility when all I've done is save your lives—again! I've got the ship, but I need some help with the crew. They may try to take it back over. They've got artificial gravity."

"That's impossible," Teo replied.

"Eight hours ago, I said that, too."

Bec settled to the deck as the artificial gravity returned. It hadn't taken them more than five minutes to get online, and three minutes of that was how long it took to get to the generator.

"It's online. Any airlock will do. Just get over here."

"We're almost there. Hold that ship steady so we can lock our port roller airlock onto yours. We're bringing the soldiers who boarded the space station. They are less than tolerant of the Malibor. Should we shoot on sight?"

"I'd prefer not. There are only a few military types among the crew. The rest are civilian technicians. Leave them because they know this technology. Look for the ones with mag boots. Those are the ones who are being butt-pains."

"Do they have weapons?"

"No rifles or hand blasters that I saw."

"We'll do what we can," Teo replied. "Keep the channel open in case anything else comes up. Do not turn on the energy screen."

"It's alien technology." Bec sat in the captain's chair and kicked back. The feeling of gravity weighed on him. Unlike *Epica's* crew, he was used to zero-gee and preferred it as a default state. Although he thought he could get used to gravity.

"I have to go, Bec, but we'll pick this up when I get over there. Alien technology, you say? That isn't surprising because they shouldn't have what they have, but it's also extremely interesting. I look forward to seeing what it's all about. I'm checking out, but I'm not closing the channel."

"Whatever that means," Bec said. He laced his fingers behind his head and embraced being king of the universe.

He jumped when someone banged on the hatch. He had no way of knowing who was on the other side, but there had to be cameras. He searched and couldn't find a way to see what was outside, so he shouted at the hatch, "Go away!"

A muffled voice replied unintelligibly.

They kept pounding. Although he found it annoying, it would have been worse if he let the fleet pros inside. He couldn't beat them in a straight-up fight. He had surprise on his side before. Without an edge, they would kill him. He was sure of it.

He covered his ear with one hand and pressed his shoulder against the other so he could continue to search the computer controls for access to the outside area.

Bec retreated to the main control screen to start over. The pounding had stopped, but there was something else.

A warning flashed across the screen. Someone was trying to override the main bridge controls. He kept canceling their request, which would time out after a mere ten seconds. He could do nothing but wait and tap the cancel on the override, but he figured there would be another way.

Personal recognition.

You've reached the limit on override attempts. You must now verify your identity.

"Me or them?" Bec wondered.

The screen produced a square where he was to place his

hand. He put his palm on it. After a quick flash of input, it rejected his print as invalid.

It replaced the square with guidance to adjust how his hand was placed.

"Teo, I have a problem. I'm going to lose control of the ship fairly soon."

"Bec, we're going to have words," Jaq replied. "Define *fairly soon.*"

He smiled in relief, even though his situation had not improved. He adjusted his hand placement to receive a second invalid entry notice.

"A minute, maybe."

"Dammit, Bec!" Jaq shouted in the background until her microphone cut off.

The external view showed *Chrysalis getting* close.

When Bec infiltrated the ship, it was because the screen contained gaps throughout the shipyard structure. Would anything partially inside the screen be damaged if the system became operational? Bec knew the answer to that because of how he had entered the ship

Bec didn't know what safeties were built into the energy screen. He could only surmise that maybe *Chrysalis* would be okay if they were docked or simply close enough to *Epica* if the energy screen raised.

The square for him to place his palm started flashing. He put his left hand on it, but it kept flashing until the screen went blank. And then the rest of the screens on the bridge turned black, including the main screens on the bulkheads surrounding the space.

"Sorry, Jaq," Bec said. He searched for where he'd heard

the spanner drop. It was easy to find as the bridge was mostly clear of debris. Only the body of the technician and the still unconscious, bleeding man.

Bec walked to the hatch. Brandishing his spanner in one hand, he released the lock and undogged the hatch. He eased it open to peek through, understanding that someone from the other side could pull it open before he could pull it back, but no one was there.

He pushed it open to find someone on the deck. It was the thruster control technician. He had been beaten senseless but was still alive.

Bec kneeled and carefully lifted his head. "I'm sorry." Bec meant it, as opposed to when he told his fellow Borwyn. He'd saved their lives enough times that he didn't feel he had anything to be sorry for. "I didn't know it was you out here."

The man's eyelids fluttered as Anton tried to wake, but he fell unconscious again. Bec wanted to carry him, but he didn't have the strength. Bec hurried up the corridor, activating hatches as he passed.

Just like with *Chrysalis*, expansive quarters were the third hatch from the bridge. The captain's quarters. Bec knew the captain wasn't using them since he'd been airlocked. Bec returned to Anton and dragged him down the corridor to put him in the captain's unmade bed. He poured water into a drinking vessel that had been on the deck and dabbed water on the technician's face. Bec set the cup next to the bed and stared at the oddity of perpetual gravity on a starship.

Only for a moment. He needed to find where they had overridden the bridge and regain control over the ship's systems. He needed to stop the activation of the energy screen.

But everything was fried! He argued with himself. He'd been wrong about the extent of damage. But the air. His previous defense of his actions didn't find new purchase. He was thinking clearly enough.

Aliens! That was a distraction. He checked his clothes to find the pages still wedged into an inner pocket. Losing the drawings and formulas would negate everything he'd done, which included killing a man with his bare hands and seriously injuring another. Bec the brawler.

He moved into the corridor and strode briskly aft. He found that he was on the same deck where he'd docked over a week earlier. That's what it felt like.

It had been less than twelve hours. Bec wasn't a slave to a sleep schedule. He slept when he was tired or not at all. Whatever suited him best at the moment.

He passed a technician in the corridor, the first one he'd passed when he boarded. "You should get some sleep," Bec told him.

"They're looking for you," the technician said helpfully.

"I know. I'm staying one step ahead of them. They're not very smart."

"But they're angry and mean," the man replied.

"Angry is good." Bec was happy with that. It meant they were preoccupied.

The last he'd seen of *Chrysalis*, it was heading toward the same airlock he'd used. Engineering was on the way.

Being happy that they were angry wasn't the same as wanting to fight them. When Bec reached Engineering, he opened the hatch but stood off to the side to give it a quick look before heading inside.

He saw mostly the same group working in the same area as last time, all except the other tech who had moved into the corridor. Bec strolled in. "Good job on getting the systems up. I appreciate all of you."

"Aren't you that Borwyn who's on our ship?" a man in torn coveralls asked. He climbed down from a ladder and walked toward Bec brandishing a spanner comparable to Bec's.

Bec waved his spanner at the man. He stopped when he realized Bec was armed.

"Somebody call the bridge," he said over his shoulder.

No one moved.

"You freaking traitors!"

"Sorry, Chief. We're not getting hazard pay, so we're not doing any of those ship-at-war drills they keep trying to stick us with. Not playing. I'm here to install circuit boards and tie wires into them. That's it!"

Bec couldn't have been prouder of the Malibor technicians. He'd never been exposed to someone saying that it wasn't their job. On *Chrysalis*, it was everyone's duty to work in the best interests of the ship, although he'd been told plenty of times by the crew that they didn't work for him.

He never understood such attitudes. Jaq would arrive, huff and bluster, and then fix everyone.

She's good like that but nowhere near as smart as me, Bec thought.

"What's the status of the energy screen and the missile reload?" Bec asked.

The chief glared.

One of the techs called from out of sight. "Energy screen is not yet operational. We don't have any visibility of missiles from Engineering. They don't have anything to do with us."

"Thank you," Bec said and backed out the hatch.

He turned and ran toward the aft airlock. Now was the time when help would be extremely helpful, as opposed to the usual result of getting in his way.

"I'll handle the hard stuff," he mumbled while he ran, "and you handle the physical stuff."

CHAPTER 25

Diligence and perseverance will win in life's greatest struggle.

Weapons fire outside the gate continued unabated. It had been going on for a solid ten minutes.

"Think we should take a look?" Max asked.

Deena shook her head. "We don't know who is firing."

"Need the info." Max stood to run off, but Deena grabbed his ankle.

"Where are you going?"

"Get the info," he replied matter-of-factly.

"I'm going, too." Deena stood and brushed herself off. She found her side hurt less and less as the day progressed.

"You are not. You're more important than me, so we have to keep you safe. I'm just a ground pounder. You're in charge of this mess." Max beamed his best smile. "Stay here, and I'll be right back."

He checked his pulse rifle before stepping away, which didn't instill the greatest confidence. Deena continued to stand. A squad of the self-proclaimed homeless milled about without guidance and without purpose.

Max stopped and returned. "All eyes on me," he barked. The soldiers responded to the abruptness of the order. "You are Deena's personal bodyguards. See that no harm comes to her."

"Or what?" one of the soldiers asked. He appeared to want an honest answer and wasn't trying to be confrontational.

"Do I have to threaten you? I would prefer not. If something happens to her because you weren't doing what you were supposed to, then you'll answer to everyone, but if you're doing all you can, then she should be fine, right? See the world that Armanor shines on, not the darkness that hides within all of us."

The soldier casually moved forward. "You guys don't talk like someone who's in charge. Do you ever get anything done?"

"We get it all done," Max replied. "People work harder when they believe in what they're working on. If you force someone to work, then you get a minimal effort. I want you to believe that she needs to be protected."

The soldiers nodded while Deena shyly smiled.

"You probably need people to protect you, too." The soldier looked at the group and selected five. "Are you good with coming along to protect this man?"

Four were, one wasn't.

"You stay. Anyone else?" No one raised their hand. "Four plus me it is. Sir, if I may make a request. Please don't put us in the middle of a firefight."

Max chuckled. "Deal. And thank you. We're going to take a look and that's it. We're not going to engage." Max jogged away with the five soldiers trailing after him.

The soldier who turned down the opportunity to volunteer moved next to Deena. She tensed.

"Aren't you going to ask?" he wondered. "Why I didn't want to go?"

"No. That's your business, not mine." Deena studied the man. He was young, probably younger than her, and unkempt. Scars on his arms suggested he'd had a hard life.

"I wanted to see if he was serious. No repercussions for defying orders."

Deena raised a finger to object. "No one defied orders. He called for volunteers."

"Yes. I've learned that volunteer rarely starts with the word 'I.' Never volunteer is the standard policy among the junior ranks. It always leads to the most unpleasant of outcomes."

"Like, if you do a good job, they keep giving you more work while everyone else does nothing."

"Something like that. I wouldn't know. I never volunteer, and I do exactly like Max said—the absolute minimum to avoid getting beaten."

"We're not going to beat people," Deena reassured him. "Our goal is to help people live freely, to enjoy their lives as much as possible. Sure, you'll still have to work because we need food and shelter, but we hope you do work that you like and find gratifying."

"They said you were a waitress. Is that true?"

"Yes. I worked at the first place outside the main gate. I

served the soldiers. I enjoyed what good food did to make people happy."

"The food was fine," he replied. "They talked about how you challenged them. You're smart."

Deena wasn't sure what he was getting at. She waited, but there was no more.

He nodded uncomfortably and rejoined the others. Soon, they had a watch schedule and posts. Deena leaned against the truck while the homeless soldiers surrounded it.

A cargo shuttle angled toward the edge of the spaceport and settled to the tarmac.

Deena recognized Crip's run right away, and the others, too. It was her people. Tram and Evelyn moved slowly with help from their fellow soldiers.

"Private, we could use a doctor. Is there one nearby?"

He pointed at the rubble behind them. Anyone who was anyone was caught in the collapse of the headquarters building.

"Then we'll have to make do until we can get a doctor here." Deena almost said *our* doctor but caught herself in time. She was walking a tightrope with the Malibor soldiers. She suspected they might turn on her if they thought she was lying to them or setting them up to be second-class citizens, more than they were under the Malibor hierarchy.

Deena waved from behind the truck at the group a kilometer away. They coalesced into a marching order and headed toward her.

The soldiers nervously fingered their weapons.

"Don't shoot at them, please," she told each soldier individually before walking out front of the square they had formed around her. The soldier who had unvolunteered started shouting. The others moved out to surround Deena.

"Gentlemen, hold steady."

Crip led the squad. He kept his pulse rifle across his chest while the others spread out.

"No shooting!" Deena called. "I'm safe. We're safe."

Crip still approached cautiously, slowing as he got close. The soldiers stepped in front of him. "Halt. Do not approach the president," a soldier said.

Deena helped herself out of the Malibor's protective perimeter.

"Good to see you, Crip." She hugged him to show her soldiers that he was okay. "Move Tram and Evelyn to the shade behind the truck."

The shuttle lifted off and headed toward the forest, with three more taking off behind it.

Deena watched them go.

"I told the pilot to pick up the others and take as much help as he could get," Crip said.

"Max went to the main gate to check on the gunfire. There shouldn't be any, but there is."

Crip took her by the shoulders and looked her over. "You've changed."

"Is that good or bad?"

The other Borwyn mobbed in around Deena and Crip. Eleanor was with them. "You're right, Crip," she agreed.

"Not the upstart young officer madly in love with my best friend."

"I'm still madly in love with him," Deena replied. "I feel like there's so much to do, it's overwhelming."

Crip laughed. "That's what it's like being an adult. Welcome to the club." Crip leaned close. "Have you heard anything from space? We're starting to worry."

Deena shook her head. "We don't have any way of knowing what's going on up there. Tram and Kelvis did a number on the comm station. Maybe one of the shuttles can go up and check it out."

Eleanor looked to Crip.

"Best idea we've heard yet. I don't know what will change, but I'd rather know sooner instead of later. We need to contact the mountain, too. We could use reinforcements to help us with the compound first, and then the city," Deena suggested.

"Is it safe to go into the city, or do we need to go out there in force?" Crip wondered.

"That's what Max is checking out," Deena replied. "I'd love to offer you food and drink, but we don't have any of that right here. But you know what we do have?" She pointed toward the front gate. "A restaurant right outside. There's food left. Nothing super fresh, but we're making do."

Deena stepped off, but her Malibor security guards stopped her. "No. Max said no. People are still shooting out there!" the soldier pleaded.

Crip nodded. "I agree. We'll stay here. We're fine on food and water. Glen will bring some if the shuttles pick him up. He's on his way."

Deena knew that. She'd been listening during the conversation between Max, Crip, and Glen.

"I accede to your greater wisdom," she told the soldier.

"Does that mean you're not going?" he asked.

"It means I'm staying here, yes." Deena joined Tram and Evelyn in the shade. "How are you feeling?"

"Good as long as I don't want to walk," Evelyn said. "Tram is still suffering. He took a bad blow to the head. I think it cracked his skull."

"We need to get him to *Chrysalis* so Doc Teller can check him out. It would help for him to sleep in his own bed."

"Would it?" Evelyn asked. "He's been down here for months."

"I'm okay," Tram muttered. "I don't want to go back to *Chrysalis*. I want to stay on Septimus."

"Crip," Deena asked. "Do you think you could fly one of those shuttles?"

"You assume that *Chrysalis* is okay. We don't know that."

"We already agreed that we should take a shuttle up to look. Can you fly one or not?"

"I can," he replied. He nodded to Eleanor. "Shall we? There's nothing like space, although I'm with Tram. I prefer being down here."

"Let's take a look, then. I want to meet this girlfriend of yours." Eleanor pointed at one of the western Borwyn soldiers. "Keep my seat warm because I'm coming back."

Crip checked the space. "I should be able to land that thing right here. I'll be here shortly to pick up Tram and Evelyn."

"We'll go, sir," Hammer offered. He pointed to Anvil, Ava, and Mia.

"Sure. Make sure you have puke bags."

"They'll be fine." Hammer stood up straight and tall in defense of his wife and sister-in-law.

"We'll be back," Crip promised, and the six ran toward the spaceport.

Deena watched them the whole way. She had nothing else to do. She was waiting on everyone else.

The group entered the first shuttle they reached and after a couple minutes, they piled out and headed for a second one. By the fourth shuttle, they finally took off. The shuttle moved slowly and shakily, but it maneuvered toward them on an erratic course.

Tram chuckled.

"You're seeing this," Deena said.

"I don't see what the problem is." Evelyn shrugged. She had no experience beyond her flights in the gunship.

"I shall hold it over his head for the rest of our days," Tram promised.

"Clear the landing zone!" Deena shouted and chased the soldiers away from the open area.

The shuttle slowly adjusted its heading, turning this way and that before descending to softly touch down. The side door popped open, and Hammer and Anvil ran out to help Tram and Evelyn.

Anvil carried Evelyn rather than make her limp. Tram shuffled along with his head down while Hammer held him. They boarded the shuttle and closed the outer door.

It took off and turned skyward, accelerating slowly at first, then faster and faster until it was nothing more than a dot in the sky.

Four shuttles appeared over the spaceport and dropped to the tarmac. When they discharged their occupants, Deena was surprised to see that the cargo included horses.

The Malibor soldiers were all eyes as they watched the strange creatures. None of them had seen a horse before.

"Those things are a treat. Be gentle with them, and they won't stomp you to death," she lied. She wanted them to learn to be gentle with everything. No threats, no anger, and no violence. Peace had to start somewhere.

CHAPTER 26

Space is more comfortable when it feels like you're standing on your home planet.

Crip reveled in the acceleration of the craft. It was more than he thought. Eleanor's eyes showed the whites all the way around her pupils. She didn't blink.

"It's okay. Everything is normal. Our chance of burning up is far less than fifty-fifty. Far less," Crip joked.

Eleanor tried to slug him, but he was too far away. "That's not funny."

"It is," he argued. Crip looked over his shoulder. "All okay back there?"

Hammer and Anvil nodded. Ava, Mia, and Evelyn clenched their jaws while staring at the front screen.

"Stay belted in. This won't take long." They cleared the atmosphere and continued into space. Crip steered toward the station until he saw the ships. The big Malibor ship with its lights on and *Chrysalis* next to it.

Crip activated the radio and dialed up the right frequency. "*Chrysalis*, this is Crip in a Malibor cargo shuttle, please reply."

"Crip, this is *Chrysalis*. The captain is occupied. It's good to hear your voice, but please steer clear at present. The Malibor missiles are hot. Please stay clear."

Crip inverted the ship and slowed to a stop. He powered down the engines.

"Make like a hole in the sky," Tram mumbled.

"Exactly. Don't give them a target to shoot at, although I don't know why they'd take a shot at one of their own. I wonder if *Chrysalis* moved close to stay inside their engagement envelope."

Eleanor studied the geometry of the ships, but it made no sense to her because she'd only been schooled in two-dimensional combat. The ships weren't limited to that. They stood at angles to each other.

A green ball of light appeared and surrounded both ships.

"That's new," Crip said. "Tram, any ideas what that could be?"

Tram released his belt and eased forward. "Plasma shield?"

Crip shrugged. "No clue but *Chrysalis* is inside it. I thought that big ship wasn't finished. How'd it get out here?"

With Armanor's light, they saw large sections of the ship were missing, exactly as Crip remembered from when they'd previously flown past it. The last snippet of intelligence before they'd descended to Septimus.

"The battle is joined, eh, Tram?" Crip said.

"Victory is ours. Did I hear right? Deena is president?"

Tram said more clearly. He opened his eyes wide and stretched his arms. "Zero-gee is good for me."

"Works for me. I got enough politics inside the mountain. I'm happy having nothing to do with those people. Deena's young. She can handle it," Crip replied. "Is the aft airlock outside that bubble?"

"Looks like it," Tram said.

Eleanor didn't know what the terminology meant. She shook her head.

"I say we dock and help out where we can. You ready to fight the Malibor, boys?" Crip called into the back.

"And girls," Hammer corrected. "We're good to go. Just tell us where they are."

Crip powered up the engines and flew slowly toward the exposed aft end of the Borwyn cruiser. He eased the ship close, taking longer than normal because of his unfamiliarity with the finite adjustments of the boxy craft. He bumped against it harder than he wanted.

Anvil was up like a shot. He pulled himself across the shuttle to link up the airlock hatches and cycle the air to equalize between the two ships. When the light showed green, just like it did on the Borwyn ship, Anvil popped the hatch.

"Let's get you two to Medical," Crip said.

"I know the way. You guys head to the port roller airlock and see what's up with the Malibor ship. I'm sure they can use six soldiers right about now." Tram held out his hand, and the two men shook. "I'll let Taurus know you're here with your new girlfriend."

"If we weren't in a hurry, I'd punch you in the face."

Tram pushed off, reached the hatch, and pulled himself into *Chrysalis* on the lowest deck. Evelyn did her best to keep up but quickly fell behind. Tram stopped to let her catch up. He held onto her to show her how to maneuver in zero-gee. Hammer and Anvil helped their wives.

"Hold onto my foot," Crip said. "I'll pull us. All you need to do is relax."

"Not sure about this." Eleanor started coughing, gagged, and puked up Crip's leg.

He looked down at the floating mess and tried to work Eleanor around it. "Lovely," he said. He pulled hard to get away from the smell. They flew down the corridor, past a line of staged spacesuits, and to the central shaft. Crip grabbed the mid-rail to slow down, and Eleanor slammed into him. He grunted.

"I'll give you a warning next time," he promised. He headed upward, and she gripped his leg tighter and tighter until his foot went numb. "You have to let up. You're not going to fall."

It didn't make a difference. She clung to him as if he were a lifeline.

He slowed and exited into the corridor leading to the airlock. Two crew were at the end, carrying a welding machine.

Crip led the way. "Can we give you a hand?"

"Commander Castle!" one cried out. "You're back."

"Just for a little bit. Are they ahead?"

"Captain went in with the boarding party from the space station and about twenty others, including Teo."

"Where's Taurus?" Crip asked.

"She's gone, sir. After she returned in the lander, she grabbed the scout ship and flew away."

Crip scowled. "I didn't know she could fly." He looked back at the five following him. "Come on. We're playing catchup."

He pulled himself along and after passing the threshold into the Malibor ship, he went face first into the deck. He stood up, confused.

Two meters away, Eleanor hovered on the threshold. She threw a leg across and was rewarded when it was pulled to the deck. She stepped through and waved for the others to follow.

She clapped Crip on the back. "Feels like home."

"Artificial gravity?" Crip guessed. "That's impossible."

"Do you want to walk through the airlock again?" Eleanor suggested. "Don't we need to catch up with your captain?"

Crip gritted his teeth and grunted an affirmative. They renewed their journey into the Malibor ship.

"This thing's much bigger than *Chrysalis*, but it has gravity so the decks are perpendicular to the line of flight. So bizarre."

A pulse rifle shot sounded from ahead, and they started to run. "Just like Septimus. We were always running down there, too."

"For fun and fitness," Eleanor joked. She raised her pulse rifle, as did the others. They stormed around a corner to find one of the volunteers from New Septimus aiming down the corridor. Jaq crouched next to him.

"What did you see?" she demanded.

"Movement!"

Jaq and the young man watched and listened. She finally stood. "Don't put your finger on the trigger unless you're going to fire."

"I know," the young man replied.

"Good enough for me," Jaq said before noticing the group behind her. "Crip? Where'd you come from?"

"Septimus," he replied as if it was every day someone from the planet appeared on a Malibor ship. He indicated for his team to maintain their aim down the corridor. "Hammer and Anvil you know. This is Commander Eleanor Todd, and these two are their wives, Ava and Mia."

"Nice to meet you all, but we gotta go. Bec is taking us to Engineering so we can reestablish control over this ship."

"We don't have control?" Crip wondered as Jaq lifted the young man and pulled him along with her.

"Zin," he said over his shoulder.

Crip followed. He was in a good mood, but there was no time for celebration no matter the good things happening on the planet surface. This was a dangerous situation.

He raised his pulse rifle and moved in beside Jaq. "Do you know where we're going?"

"I think so. Big space around the next two corners on this corridor."

Crip helped himself to the front. "I'll take point," he said.

Eleanor moved in beside him.

Crip ducked his head around the corner and back. "Clear." He hurried around and forward, not giving an enemy time to interfere. They repeated their process at the next corner. That corridor was clear, too.

On the left side was an oversized hatch that stood open. Borwyn were inside.

Crip pointed at Hammer and Ava. "Watch that way."

The two soldiers stepped beyond the hatch and crouched, looking over the barrels of their weapons.

Jaq hadn't seen this group work together. She'd never seen the three women, two dressed in deer-hide clothing. She stared at how well they worked. Seamlessly moving, aiming, staying out of lines of fire. Hammer and Anvil were different men from the two adult children who had left the ship with Crip and Max. Jaq wanted to know more. She wanted to hear the stories.

She didn't know when they'd get the chance. For now, Crip was the best choice to take charge of the military operation on board the Malibor ship.

"It's all you, Crip. They are at your command," Jaq confirmed.

Crip nodded and headed into the engineering space, signing for Eleanor to go left while he went right. Anvil and Mia split up and followed. The four advanced, two-by-two, around the Borwyn standing in the open area. Crip blocked them out. They were stopped for a reason, and he needed to see that for himself.

He cleared to the side and saw a Malibor shooter on a catwalk three meters above.

"You'll want to put that down," Crip growled. Mia leaned around him and aimed at a Malibor holding a weapon that looked like a club. "This is going to get real messy real fast if you don't follow my orders."

"Your people will die. You put it down." The man snarled at Crip.

Time is on the defender's side in combat. Crip held his aim at the man's chest. He squeezed the trigger and blasted the Malibor off the catwalk. The gravity generator did its job and pulled him to the deck with a resounding splat.

"Any other heroes ready to die?" Crip shouted as he rushed in front of the group, noting that a few of the Borwyn had pulse rifles but were carrying them at their side. They'd been caught off guard when they entered the space. Bec was right up front looking angry.

Crip ignored him. He had a space to clear.

He pointed at the Malibor holding a club. "On your face."

The man started to raise his weapon. Crip fired again.

"Anyone else?" he barked. Crip lowered his weapon and motioned for his team. "Secure them."

"Those with the mag boots, they're the ones you want. The others are okay," Bec said.

Crip looked over his shoulder. "Bec."

All the Malibor were collected, but only the ones with mag boots got their hands secured.

"What do you mean, they're okay?"

"They're the ones fixing the ship," Bec said as if that answered the question.

"Then tell them to turn off that green monstrosity," Crip said.

"That's not in this space. That's up a level and forward,"

Bec replied. "We have an injured man. He helped me. Jaq! He needs to see Doc Teller."

"Crip's in charge," Jaq replied.

Crip clenched his jaw. "Bec, you drive me insane with your nonsense. Take Anvil and Mia with you. They know what they're doing." He nodded toward the hatch. "They're in the corridor."

"You want me to go? I have stuff to do here."

"Bec, you're the only one who knows where we need to go. Take care of it, then get back here so we can return control of the ship to the bridge."

"We'll regain control of the ship first, and then we'll shut off the energy screen from the bridge." Bec crossed his arms and spread his feet wide.

Jaq stepped in. "Regain control of the ship, Bec, but first, how many other Malibor should we be concerned about?"

Bec looked to the Malibor technicians. They collectively shrugged.

"Once we have control of the ship, we'll consolidate all the personnel on board, then depressurize the rest of the ship. After five minutes, we'll repressurize, and that will take care of it. This thing is way too big to play hide-and-seek," Crip said. He turned and tried to walk out along with Eleanor, but Jaq stopped him with a simple gesture.

Jaq directed the volunteers from New Septimus to watch the four Malibor they'd taken prisoner.

"What are you going to do with us?" one snapped.

"Probably take you to the planet and turn you loose," Crip replied. "If you haven't heard, the Malibor military has capitulated. There's a new president on Septimus, and she's on a mission to return Malipride to prosperity."

The man snorted. "Lies!"

Crip smiled. "You took this half-finished ship out of the shipyard because it was the last Malibor warship available. And would you look at us! A bunch of Borwyn holding you captive. Is it far-fetched to think that we might have taken control of the planet, too? Five civil wars and a deteriorating military have brought you to this point. The Malibor cannot be trusted to be in charge. Think what you want about our lies, but you'll see it for yourself soon enough when we take you to the planet in a Malibor cargo shuttle."

"My family is in Malipride," a technician said. A second chimed in, and then a third.

Crip raised his hands and called for calm. "The civilians are safe from us. We didn't bomb the city. The only attacks were on the spaceport, the main military compound, and the seat of government." Crip turned to Jaq. "Tram won the war when he took out the headquarters building while everyone who was anyone was inside. One strike decapitated the entire leadership. He's in Medical right now. Hopefully, Doc Teller can fix him up."

Jaq nodded but kept her eyes on the Malibor who weren't bound. "Technicians, get back to what you were doing. Let's get this ship out of its funk and operational. We have a lot of stuff to do."

"We can explore the system," Bec posited, staring into the distance.

"Yes, yes. We need to finish construction on this thing first. If you haven't noticed, it's missing a big section of it," Jaq replied. "The good news is that we have plenty of materials to recycle from destroyed cruisers."

The technicians perked up. "Exploration!"

"Yes, and we'll all go together. See what there is to see. Learn what there is to learn." Bec shook himself free from daydreaming and strolled to a panel where two technicians were standing. "Let's get this fixed, shall we?"

Crip whispered to Jaq, "That guy drives me nuts."

"Me, too, but I'm happy he's on our side. We'd be dead if it weren't for him, and that's just today," Jaq explained. "Where's this injured friend of yours, Bec?"

"Captain's quarters, three doors down from the bridge," Bec called over his shoulder.

"Shall we?" Jaq waited for Crip to follow.

Crip looked at the handful of volunteers from New Septimus. "Keep these four in the corner. Don't take your eyes off them. Actually, tie their cuffs together. That'll keep anyone from trying to run off. You guys look like hell."

"Space station. It was an ugly fight," one replied. The dark look behind his eyes suggested he wasn't ready to say any more.

"Understand. Keep your head up. We're on the downhill side of this thing. Just wrapping up loose ends, then we can all get some much-deserved downtime." Crip moved close to Hammer and said softly, "You're in charge. Keep everyone doing what they're doing. Our goal is to get this ship functioning and back to the shipyard. Then, we're going to take *Chrysalis* to Septimus. It's about time Pridal celebrated the arrival of a Borwyn ship."

Jaq met them at the door. She looked back and forth between Crip and Eleanor but said nothing.

She walked down the corridor toward the bow. She slowed at corners, checking before heading around. They found the bridge amidship, although they had walked far enough to make it feel like the bridge was all the way forward. A bloodstain on the deck in front of the hatch marked where the Malibor had been injured. They backtracked along the blood drops to the captain's quarters, where they found Bec's friend unconscious.

Crip threw him over his shoulder. "We'll take him to see Doc Teller and then we'll return. Is this ship secure? It's really big."

"They had fifty people on board. Bec airlocked the captain and another fleet officer, then he killed one and maimed one on the bridge." She stopped and looked toward the bridge. "Let's take a look. Where was I? Forty-six. You killed two, and we took four more captive. That's an even forty remaining, and they're supposed to all be technicians and engineers. You had the right idea. Gather them all together before sending them back out on repair jobs. Can Bec manage that?"

They walked slowly toward the bridge and the hatch that stood open. Jaq glanced inside.

"I'll go," Eleanor offered and raised her pulse rifle. She stalked inside, scanned the entire area, and walked around the outside of the circular room. Two men were on the deck in the center along with a lake of blood. Once Eleanor was certain there was no one else there, she approached the men one at a time, checking each to confirm they were cold and lifeless. "They're both dead."

Jaq strode in. "I would have never thought Bec could be violent. This proves me wrong. What else is he capable of?"

"He's capable of whatever it takes to achieve his goals. Never forget that, Jaq. He wants this ship because it has tech he doesn't understand. He's going to stay on this ship until he does." Crip shifted uncomfortably. "We need to go see Doc Teller."

"Go on. Eleanor can stay here and bring me up to speed. I'll be here when control is returned." Jaq waved Crip away. He hurried down the corridor. He had a long way to go, which would have been no problem in zero-gee, but hauling the injured Malibor in one gee was completely different.

Jaq watched him leave. She helped herself to the captain's seat since none of the screens were on.

"What do you want to know?" Eleanor asked.

"All of it, but that's a little broad. Crip, Max, Deena, and the rest of our combat team have been on the planet for months. Maybe we keep it simple. How are they doing?"

"They're all married! Those guys..." Eleanor laughed for only a moment. She sobered before continuing. "But they're good soldiers and their wives, too. You saw that for yourself. We lost a few. Danny Johns had a heart attack. Age and the strain caught up to him. Kelvis and Sophia, Tram's wife. They died in the gunship crash after shooting up the spaceport. We didn't have the support of New Pridal until the very end, when they had no choice. Maybe they thought they'd be the new government, but they'll have little, if anything, to do with it. Deena has things well in hand."

"Deena? Max's Deena?" Jaq hadn't heard the full story.

"Yeah. She's in charge of the city and all the Malibor. She's got a good head, and she disarms everyone she talks to. No wonder Max is head over heels in love with her." Eleanor inched toward the hatch. "I should check on Crip. It's a long haul, and the Malibor looked heavy."

Jaq nodded, and Eleanor bolted.

CHAPTER 27

The measure of a great leader is found in the quality of their people.

Max hunched behind the barricade. "I still can't see what's going on. Who is doing the shooting?"

"We're going to have to go into the city," a Malibor soldier said. He was unarmed, blocked behind the barricade like everyone else who was trying to get home. They were doing as they'd been ordered. Leave their weapon behind and go home. Many had gotten through the gate before the gunfire started.

The rest were trapped. "You, you, and you. Come with me." Max designated the two Malibor who'd been guarding the gate when he killed their corporal because they had weapons. The other soldier looked wary but unafraid. Max didn't need someone with him who was going to run. "You stay with me. You other two, right flank. Far side of the road."

Max jumped up and ran to the left. He half-expected the

Malibor to stay where they were and was pleasantly surprised when they ran out from behind the barricade. The two armed Malibor went right as he had directed. He and the other soldier ran to the first building on the left side. They hugged the front wall as they moved forward.

They passed the restaurant. Max risked a glance to find the boss inside. Lanni was nowhere to be seen. He expected she had gone home. Max waved and kept going.

The sound of gunfire increased. Max stepped faster, and the two on the far side of the street matched his pace. He kept the barrel pointed at a forty-five-degree angle toward the ground. He didn't want any accidents with the massive numbers of civilians around. Deena had said the Malibor's official number was a million, but he'd seen the city from the air and didn't think it was much bigger than New Pridal. He figured a quarter million at the most, but that was irrelevant to the current situation.

He reached a corner and looked into the open square beyond to see a massive party. Families were frolicking on a grass-filled area between monuments to Malibor greatness. Fireworks shot to a story high before exploding.

Max raised his fist until the team across the street saw it. He slung his rifle and walked into the street, which was blocked to traffic.

A little girl ran up to him, stared for long seconds, and ran off. He watched her run to her mother. The little girl pointed at him. Max waved and walked into the crowd.

He felt an odd tug as someone grabbed at his rifle. He spun around with fist cocked to catch an old man with wide eyes.

The old man stuttered until he became coherent. "I haven't seen a weapon like that, sonny. I used to know them all."

"This is a Borwyn design. It's called a pulse rifle. It uses magnetic acceleration to send a tiny project at hypervelocity. It's highly effective."

"What are you doing with a Borwyn weapon?" the old man asked. He squinted while taking in Max's features.

Max pointed to himself. He looked around to find more people watching. He wasn't ready to take on the entire civilian population. "I took it off a Borwyn soldier."

"Good for you!" the man cheered.

"What's going on here?" Max asked.

"We're celebrating winning the war! Soldiers came from the base. They were happy and said the war was over. That means we must have won."

"We all won," Max said ambiguously. "There's new leadership, of course, but the big change is that you should feel more freedom. Like this event. No one is going to hassle you. No one is going to extort from you. We're going to make sure all of that garbage ends."

"Was this a civil war? Did we fight ourselves again?" The man shook his head, convinced that he had the answer. "I swear, we're our own worst enemy."

"You can say that again. It'll be different this time. Enjoy yourself, my man." Max made eye contact with the Malibor soldiers. He tipped his chin to them. "Back to the compound."

"Can I go home?" the soldier without a weapon asked. The others looked hopeful for a positive answer.

"You can all go home. Give me your weapons, and I'll take them back with me. Go home, relax, and you'll hear from us when the time is right. Which makes me think, do you know where the radio station is?"

"There's more than one," the soldier said, giving Max his blaster.

"Is it close?" Max pressed.

"This way." The man took two steps and stopped to wait for Max to grab the last blaster and shake the two soldiers' hands.

Once they were alone, he asked, "Why'd you do that, and why didn't you correct that old fool?"

Max wasn't sure. "Maybe I don't think of any of you as enemies, although a day ago, you might have been shooting at me. Maybe I appreciate them watching my back while we looked for what we thought was gunfire."

"Makes sense." He chewed on his lip. "What about the old man?"

"I didn't lie. I think we all won today. I don't want to fight you, and I don't think you want to fight me. I bet we want the same thing. Be with a good person who makes us better versions of ourselves. Help others while enjoying life."

"Not sure about the helping others part. That's gotten me nowhere. I'm a private in the Malibor army. That's as close to being a nobody as anyone can get."

Max didn't think as lowly of the soldiers as they thought of themselves, it seemed. "I think you're just like everyone else. No better. No worse. You'll have more opportunities now. For what it's worth, if the Sairvor Malibor try anything, we've already spanked them hard. They're not going to try anything any time soon."

"Did you come from space?"

Max nodded.

"I never had any desire to go out there and live my whole life inside a metal box. That's not for me."

"We live in the prisons of our own choosing," Max said, "whether a metal box or a dysfunctional military or within the walls of this city. Real freedom lets you move beyond that."

"You mean I can walk out of the city right now, if I want?"

"Not yet, because we haven't had a good conversation with the border security. They may not be so keen about your newfound freedom, but they will know soon. We'll get to them now that we have our people to pass the message."

The man stared at the ground as he walked, his brow furrowed while he was deep in thought.

He stopped all of a sudden and looked around to see where he was. "There it is." The soldier pointed to a sign above a windowed first floor. On the roof of the five-story building, a large antenna stretched toward the sky.

"Thanks." Max held out his hand for the other to take.

"I don't feel like I should be thanked for anything. Good luck." He walked away.

Max headed into the building to find most desks cluttered with empty seats. One person was there. "Did you get stuck with the duty?"

She smiled. "Seems like it. No one else came to work."

"I've got the story you want to cover," Max started.

She made a face and shook her head.

"The war with the Borwyn is over. A new leader is now in place to bridge the two peoples, and she's on the military compound. Would you like to interview her?"

"The war with the Borwyn has been over for decades," she replied. "That's not news. A new leader who's a woman? Probably a token. No news there, either."

Max stepped back to make sure he was in the light. "What do I look like?" he asked.

"Different, but we get all kinds trying to sell a story to us."

"I'm not selling anything," Max replied. He moved close and showed her his rifle. "I'm Borwyn, and the war is over because we won. Are you sure you don't want to cover that?"

"You've got a great routine, but I'll bite. Sitting here is as exciting as watching paint dry. We stick to the main roads. No funny business or I'll run you through." She held up a small knife.

Max laughed. "I promise." He walked out the door and waited. It took her ten minutes to join him.

"What's your deal? Why are you involved in this?"

Max had already told her that he was Borwyn. He took a different angle. "The new president is a total babe."

"Men," the woman huffed.

Max thought it best not to match wits with the reporter. He walked fast to make her breathe hard so she wouldn't keep asking questions that he'd already answered.

People were starting to emerge from their homes. With the soldiers off the streets, they were less afraid. They made it to the main gate without issue. They found no one guarding it.

"Where are the soldiers?"

"They went home. Didn't you hear? The war is over." He enunciated each word slowly and loudly.

She sneered at him.

He kept walking all the way to the destroyed headquarters building, where he found a growing encampment that included a stable with ten horses. He was happy to see Glen.

Max waved, but his immediate concern was finding Deena. He looked for armed Malibor soldiers and readily spotted them surrounding a figure sitting in the shade. Deena was drinking a flask of water. Max approached the nervous guard, but a word from Deena relaxed them. They let Max and the reporter through.

"You should let them know that as your husband, I should always be allowed to see the president."

"She's your wife? You rat," the reporter cried out.

"Talk to Deena." Max pushed her forward, then said to Deena, "She's a reporter from the radio station. I thought you needed to speak to the people. I hope it's okay."

"I never said I was a reporter. I'm an accountant," the woman said, thrusting her chin in the air.

Max's mouth fell open. "Who's the rat?"

She smirked. "All right. I'll play." She turned to Deena. "What's the story here that you want the people of Malipride to hear?"

"I hope you have a little time." Deena invited her to sit. "This could take a while."

"I have this neat recording device." She pulled a recorder

with a microphone out of her pocket. It was the size of a portable radio. She pressed the button, and Deena started to talk.

Crip was happy to reach zero-gee. He thought he was in shape, but the trials of the day had worn on him. He'd traveled through the night. He couldn't remember the last time he'd slept. He pushed the young man called Anton through the ship to Medical. In the corridor outside, he found Brad and Tram resting.

The doc took charge of the injured Malibor. "Doesn't look too bad. I'll scan his head to be sure there's nothing permanent."

Doc Teller took the young man into the medical lab.

Crip remained in the corridor. He was too tired to hurry back to the Malibor ship. "I miss you guys," he told them.

"I'm sure they miss you, too," Evelyn said.

"I'm sorry about Kelvis," Crip added.

"It's war. It happens. It's my luck."

Crip rested his hand on her arm. "We've all had a bunch of bad breaks. I'm going to the bridge."

He hurried to it. "Amie, can you connect me to Taurus?"

"The radio is only partially operational," she replied. She fervently tried calling and adjusting and calling some more.

Finally, a voice came over the receiver. Amie didn't move, not wanting to jinx it.

"Taurus, Crip here. I'm on *Chrysalis*. Is there any way you can come back and see me?"

"No, Crip. I've found this is my calling. There is nothing like flying free through space. I'm sorry, Crip, but it wasn't meant to be." She closed the channel.

"I've been hearing a lot of that lately," Crip said. He sulked for two seconds before he decided that he had known it all along. When they were going to die, he was a good choice. When they weren't under an immediate threat, he was an afterthought.

"I better go back to help Jaq, because ruminating on what we cannot change is a waste of time."

"Crip," Alby called and waved him over. Godbolt floated next to him while they held hands. "You did great down there."

"You did well up here. You defeated the entire Malibor fleet." Crip smiled. "That's once-in-history kind of stuff."

"It only matters if we do something with what we've won. Is Deena in charge of Septimus?"

Crip nodded. "She's the only one in the whole universe who knows both sides. It makes sense. There has to be a lot of bridge building."

"You're going back down, aren't you?" Alby asked.

Crip nodded again. "There's more to do down there."

"I'm sorry," Godbolt said. She stared at the deck, refusing to make eye contact.

Crip crouched next to her and Alby. "Nothing to be sorry for. Today's the day the Borwyn won the war, and we did it without firing a shot. When the Malibor's time came, they simply folded, and we were there to gently let them down. Every action we took along the way. Every step we made. Every time we aimed and fired... It brought us closer to today.

Little things add up to big things. Get on the radio and share that message with anyone who has a radio to receive."

He left the bridge to find Eleanor waiting for him. "I heard," she said.

"What do we fight for, Eleanor?" he wondered. "Or is it who?"

"How many times did you talk about fighting for freedom? Would you deny that to anyone, most of all to someone you care about?"

Crip frowned. "You make too much sense. The worst part is, I knew when I left the ship that I wouldn't see her again. I figured it would be because one of us was dead, not that the freedom bird would fly away and not come back."

"Well, now you know. Can we go? I prefer the gravity on that other ship."

Crip gripped her arm. "You know what? I do, too."

He enjoyed the ease of zero-gee for a short while longer. He stopped when he reached the airlock security team. "No one has come back through?"

"Only you two with that injured boy."

Crip nodded and thanked them. He took the greatest care stepping over the threshold into the Malibor ship by using his magnetic boots to move from one environment to the other. He released them the second he felt the pull of gravity.

He strode with purpose but not haste.

Today is the day everything changed, he thought. He looked at his pulse rifle. How much longer would he have to carry it?

In Engineering, he found the Malibor prisoners shackled

together with tie straps. The technicians worked while two Borwyn guarded the prisoners and the workers. The rest were curled up on the deck, sound asleep. Crip had only been gone for ten minutes.

He appreciated a soldier's ability to sleep anywhere and at any time. Even though they were new recruits, they'd quickly learned the value of sleep. Crip waved to them and sidled up to those on duty. "How's it going?"

"Nothing to report. They're working—" The soldier nodded toward the technicians and then to the group of four. "—and they're grumbling."

"What did you do with the bodies?" Eleanor asked.

"We stuffed them in the room next door," he replied.

Crip walked through the space, moving close to the Malibor technicians. He understood what each was working on. They eyed him suspiciously when he looked over their shoulders.

"Go away," Bec told him.

Crip had never gotten along with Jaq's brother. The two didn't see eye-to-eye on anything, and Bec was exceptionally abrasive with Crip. The only one who could deal with him had been Jaq until Teo came on board. He didn't know how either of them did it.

"I shall accede to your demand. You're staying on board this ship when *Chrysalis* departs, right?"

"Yes. Why?"

"We're going to have a massive party, and it would have been awkward since you wouldn't have been invited. It'll be your going away party, which is for us, really, and not you." Crip walked away, feeling slightly guilty at his pettiness. One of the technicians snorted and covered his mouth to hide his laugh.

Crip raised his hand and waved over his shoulder. He made his way to the bridge. The first time into the ship, he knew it was big, but carrying the injured Malibor had showed him the true scale. His second walk along the length of it would keep him in shape as if he were on the planet, where they walked everywhere.

"When are we going home?" Eleanor asked. She took Crip's arm when he didn't stop.

Crip smiled. "Soon as we can, Eleanor. I need some time, and being up here isn't the kind of break I want."

On the bridge, they found Jaq with Dolly Norton and Donal Fleming.

Crip gestured toward them.

Jaq tipped her chin. "Surround yourself with the best people, the right people for the job, and these two are the smartest we have when it comes to data and programming. They're helping us reactivate the systems," she explained.

"I thought they were up?"

"Most were, but they weren't integrated. Those two are programming bypasses to tie the systems back into each other. We've dismantled the EMP weapon. If we ever need to use it again, we're going to need a couple hours to put it back together. That thing is a menace."

"How do you feel?" Crip asked.

Jaq lounged in the captain's chair. "I miss my chair, even though I wasn't in it very much."

"That's not what I mean. I feel like we're missing something."

"That's because we don't know what we don't know. As soon as we have all our sensor systems up, we'll be able to look around, see if the Malibor are hiding other ships. We have a full rack of missiles and functional E-mags because we have the two most powerful ships in the system. No one can stand against us! Ha!" Jaq cried out and then snickered.

"I don't know what to do," Crip admitted.

"That makes two of us. All we've ever known is *Chrysalis*, and now, our home is obsolete."

"It's a big planet, Jaq. Come on down and stay awhile."

"So this is what all the fuss is about?" Teo called from the hatch to the bridge. "This ship is far more complex than it needs to be, while also being simpler. I can't believe they only had fifty on board when they fought us, but we kicked their hairy buttocks all the way into last week."

"Do they have alcohol on board this ship?" Crip wondered, nodding to Teo. It had been a while since he last saw her.

"I bet they do. Artificial gravity! What we couldn't do with some of that," Teo said.

"We could install it, can't we? We have the technology, at least Bec said he did."

Teo threw her head back and laughed with the greatest of humor. "Jaq! *Chrysalis* is done for. It needs a complete rebuild, every single system inside of it. It has one flight left in it. To the planet surface, where we need to park it and make it a museum."

Jaq's lip twitched. Home. Her home.

Emotions pulled her one direction while intellectually,

she knew Teo was right. "A museum isn't a bad idea. Perseverance brought peace to all."

"Jaq Hunter and her vision brought peace. We just came along for the ride." Crip saluted haphazardly. "With your permission, Eleanor and I will return to the surface and prepare for your arrival."

"We have one lander. I could come down," Jaq suggested.

"No. Teo's right. *Chrysalis* is a wreck, but the ship delivered right to the end. It's time has come and gone. See you on Septimus, Jaq. You're going to love it."

Dolly and Donal hadn't even looked up during the whole exchange. They were hip-deep in code.

Teo left with Crip and Eleanor. "Hi, I'm Teo."

"Eleanor Todd, Lieutenant Commander, Borwyn Assault Brigade."

"Formal," Teo replied. "Proteus Yelchin, Chief Engineer, Borwyn fleet's flagship, the cruiser *Chrysalis*, at your service."

"And we're both out of a job," Eleanor said and thrust out her hand.

Teo shook it once and let go. "Back to the planet, huh? Can I go?"

Crip shook his head. "They are going to have problems getting *Chrysalis* through the atmosphere and onto the ground. They'll need you to make sure that happens. We can't crash, not after coming this far."

Teo studied his expression. "We have come a long way. Yes. I agree. I'll see you on the ground. I look forward to it." She took a couple steps. "How long did it take you to get used to the gravity on the planet? Because this is really weird. I'm used to hauling around a metric ton of stuff. I won't be able to do that unless I'm in zero-gee. Maybe we can reverse the gravity generators to produce an anti-gravity system. Ooh." Teo stared at the deck as she walked. "I need to talk with Bec."

"By choice?" Crip joked.

"If you can focus him, he's fine. It's when he's allowed to think for himself that he has problems." Teo peeled off when they reached the engineering section.

Crip told Hammer, Anvil, Ava, and Mia that they'd stay with *Chrysalis* as long as Brad was laid up, but first, to bring the Malibor prisoners to the airlock once Crip moved the shuttle.

They had no problem with that because the old man still hadn't met his daughters-in-law.

Crip and Eleanor continued to *Chrysalis*. On their way through the ship, they ran into a young boy carrying a patch kit. "Who are you?" Crip asked of the obvious Malibor child.

"Zinod Weft. Prisoner of the Borwyn."

Crip looked around to find no one in the vicinity. "Prisoner?"

"Yes, because saying that I work with the Borwyn is traitor stuff, and I'm no traitor."

"Of course. You are a prisoner, but you know the war is over. There are no prisoners anymore, or traitors. We should call them temporary detainees. Where is your family?"

"The station," he replied.

"Civilians?" Crip pressed.

The boy nodded.

"Deliver that and meet us at the aft port airlock. We'll take you home."

"Back to the station, for real?"

"Your parents were evacuated to Malipride. We'll take you there."

The boy hurried away, deftly maneuvering in zero-gee.

Crip and Eleanor continued to the shuttle and prepped the ship. When the boy arrived, they had him belt in.

They detached from the airlock and backed away. The green shimmer surrounding the Malibor ship was gone. The team had shut down the energy screen. That was the biggest step in detaching *Chrysalis*.

"So much work to do," Crip observed.

"Why the long face?" Eleanor asked.

"Who do we share the victory with? Borwyn are few. Malibor are many. We're not going to rub their faces in it. We only want to enjoy our home planet."

"Me, Crip. You share it with me." Eleanor looked at him with wide eyes. "Stop being horse apples and let your hair down."

"Has it gotten that long?" Crip was confused. He wondered if he was getting space sickness. He'd been away for too much time.

Crip circled the two ships to appreciate them both. "Bec secured that ship all by himself. That could be the hardest thing to believe out of all of this." Crip shook his head. He activated the radio. "Big ship, this is the cargo shuttle *Borwyn One* requesting to dock at your upper airlock. Bring the prisoners to us, and we'll take them home."

"*Borwyn One*, this is *Epica*. Permission granted."

CHAPTER 28

We fought for the good of all humanity. We fought for each other. We fought to live.

Max met the shuttle at the spaceport. Crip and Eleanor led the four prisoners away from the small vessel. Max produced a knife and cut their hands loose.

"You're free to go," he told them.

"Just like that? You're the enemy. You killed our friends," one of the prisoners snapped back. He puffed out his chest and snarled.

"War's over, buddy," Max said in an unfriendly tone.

"Yeah, I killed your friends, which saved your lives," Crip added. "If you all tried to fight, then you all would have died. Don't blame me that you saw reason in the frailty of violence. When we're shooting each other, there can be only one outcome. I'd like to think we found another way." Crip spread his arms to take in the cool air and partly cloudy sky of Septimus.

"For some of us, the war will never be over."

Crip stepped back and raised his pulse rifle. "Is death the only choice you're willing to make?"

"Your death, yes." The man bared his chest before the pulse rifle.

"You don't control whether I live or die, sorry. You'll probably never see me again. You're going to answer to Malibor leadership. You're going to blend back into society. You can be angry, but don't act on that anger and you'll be a better man because of it. Now go away. We have no intention of filling the prison with people who are angry because the war is over. Go see your mothers. They'll be happy you're home."

Crip moved aside and waved with the barrel of his rifle. The four left, snarling and snapping like a pack of angry dogs.

"Killing them now is probably the best choice," Max suggested. He took aim at the four.

Crip tapped him on the shoulder and nodded toward the boy. "You know we can't do that. We're supposed to be the good guys."

"Deena gave everyone full amnesty. It was her first official act as president."

"Sounds like she's on the right track." Crip waved at the boy to follow. "Do you know where the evacuees from the space station are?"

"Oddly enough, I do. There's a recreational facility where they were staying, but Deena told them they could go. I'm sure some stayed. We'll start there." Max led the boy away.

Eleanor took in the immensity of the spaceport and city as they walked. They slowed.

"I could sleep for week," Crip admitted.

Eleanor stopped. "Then why don't you?"

"They might need me," Crip replied.

"I'll watch over you in case someone calls."

"I'll think about it, but I'm sure you have stuff to do, too. Let's find Glen." Crip felt uncomfortable, awkward even. "Life is hard."

"You can say that again," Eleanor replied.

As they neared the temporary compound, the smell of horses was nearly overwhelming.

"That's what happens when you put too many animals in too small a space," Eleanor said.

"Then we need to find them more space." They hurried ahead to find Glen giving direction to four-man teams of Malibor soldiers.

They waited for him to finish before approaching. The Malibor teams left on their way to the front gate and city beyond.

The three shook hands.

"Just when the elders were on our side, the battle was already won," Glen quipped.

"That makes sense. All the risk was ours. You know what that means, don't you?" Crip asked.

Glen shrugged.

"The reward is ours, too." Crip smiled. "We're in tight with the new leadership."

"Speaking of which, she's making a speech." He motioned for them to follow.

At the temporary compound, they found her upwind of the horses. The reporter was leaving.

"Looks like we missed it." Crip was disappointed. He wanted to see it.

Max stood next to her and cast the aura of a bodyguard until he rolled her into a tight hug.

"There you are," Max said when he saw Crip. He put on his best contrite face. "Sorry about abandoning you out there."

"All's well that ends well, Max. I feel like I would've done the same thing. Nothing else needs be said, and thanks to you guys, it's a whole new world."

"How's it going upstairs?" Max asked while Deena clung tightly to him.

"Bec helped take over *Epica*, the Malibor ship. He actually fought people, like, hand-to-hand."

Max stared blankly. "I don't believe that."

"I probably should have questioned it more, too. It sounds ridiculous. It's a nice ship, though. It has artificial gravity. It's mind-boggling, and I'm glad we have it. That ship could have caused us a great deal of grief."

"It would have been nice to see, but I'm not going back out there," Max stated definitively. "We have a lot of work to do here. I expect the Malibor will start an underground and actively fight us, but not today. It'll take the old guard a while to get organized, but from what I've seen, even the Malibor were done with being Malibor. It's a hard life to be that angry and mean all the time."

"All we had to do was wait them out?" Crip was incredulous. "All our losses were for nothing?"

"No, not that," Deena interjected. "The Malibor needed a catalyst. The reaction never would have started without *Chrysalis*, without the destruction of the fleet. It gutted their military, which had dwindled but still held power in a death grip. Without the fleet, they had nothing, even though they wouldn't admit it. When the last bits of the foundation were removed, the whole thing came tumbling down." She paused. "You look like you need something to eat and some sleep."

"Both. Is there a place to snatch a few hours?" Crip asked.

"A full day," Eleanor corrected.

"Take a shuttle to the woods. Find a place and make yourselves at home. Come back after you're rested," Deena said with authority.

"You heard her," Eleanor said and took Crip by the arm to guide him away. He didn't have enough energy to resist. Max and Deena waved good-bye.

Crip glanced back, but they were already occupied with someone else. "Winning...and that quickly, everything is different."

Eleanor stopped him and moved close. He tried to step back, but she hung onto his arms. "Everything is different, but none of the people have changed. Look at Max and Deena. They are free to be themselves. They are going to lead these people to a better place. From my perspective, the hardest part about winning is being prepared to deal with the victory. You don't get to give orders anymore. And you don't have to pine away for someone who wasn't there for you during the hard times because she had her own life. Maybe you need to see what's in front of you instead of what's behind."

Crip hadn't been ready. His whole life revolved around fighting the next battle, doing what it took to win. "I traded a pulse rifle for my fur to make peace with a Farslor Malibor tribe. I wonder if Jaq airlocked it."

"What?" Eleanor shook her head and let go of his arms. "Is that how your mind works? Fur?"

"Yes. My fur. We lost two people in making that contact, Andreeson and Gilmore. You say not to look back, but I think we need that to understand what we did to get here, so we don't forget that this was worth it, and we do everything possible not to regress. We have to look forward without forgetting our past, without forgetting who was there for us through it all."

Crip took Eleanor's hand and together, they walked to the shuttle. An individual was prepping the shuttle next to theirs.

"Are you a pilot?" Crip asked.

"I am. I'm supposed to pick up the rest of Glen's unit. They're waiting."

"Can you drop us off first? There's a village to the east. We'll show you the way."

"Crip. If we don't have a shuttle, then we'll have to walk back," Eleanor whispered in his ear.

"Which will make us think long and hard about it." Crip winked.

"No problem," the pilot said in the way that pilots did because extra flight time was never a bad thing.

Jaq swam through *Chrysalis*. She hadn't grown either accustomed to or enamored of the artificial gravity on board *Epica*.

As damaged and jury-rigged as *Chrysalis* was, she still preferred it.

"Prepare to undock," she said. Alby and Godbolt were there. Ferd and Mary were flying the ship. Amie was on the comm, and the shepherd droned away at the rear of the bridge. Chief Ping worked the sensor systems by himself. Gil had stayed on *Epica,* while Taurus had flown toward Sairvor.

They'd lost contact with *StarBound*, and she was looking for it.

"Undock and take us to Septimus, all ahead slow." Jaq's heart felt heavy. The moment she had spent her life reaching, and the words came hard.

"Undocking complete. Setting course. Engaging ion drives, all ahead slow. Ship is sluggish."

"Because the systems are working independently. They won't be integrated again until we undergo major repairs," Jaq explained, even though they all knew the reasons. It was an incredible feat that the ship was flying at all. It was a testament to the indomitable will of the crew.

And the Borwyn. Fifty years.

Jaq settled into her seat. All ahead slow was a quarter to a half-gee. She could have walked around, but for once, she didn't feel like it. She simply sat and let the tears stream down her face.

Septimus filled the screen. The ship bumped into the

upper atmosphere before forcing its way down, a little at a time. Friction still created a fireball around the ship. Jaq wondered what kind of damage it was doing. *Chrysalis* had hit the atmosphere of other planets pretty hard but hadn't gone intra-atmospheric.

She held on, teeth clenched to keep them from chattering due to the buffeting and the vibrations. Suddenly, it stopped, and the ship felt like it was freefalling.

"We're through," Mary announced. "Inverting to slow."

The view stayed the same while Mary slewed the bow toward space and Ferd fired the engines to slow them down. He used thrusters to angle *Chrysalis* toward the city.

They came in slowly and had to keep the ion drives surging as gravity dragged the ship downward and winds threatened to topple it.

"Wahoo!" Mary shouted as she worked the controls, never in doubt about her ability to maintain the ship's orientation. The spaceport appeared. An area had been cleared between the fleet of cargo shuttles from the space station. *Chrysalis* descended and with a final surge from the ion drives, the ship settled on its tail skids, nose toward the sky. The engines powered down, and silence settled over the bridge.

"You should be the first off, Captain," Alby said.

Jaq worked her way to perch on the edge of her seat. "I don't know if I want to get off at all."

"Of course you want to get off," Brad said from the hatch.

"What are you doing up? You look terrible." Jaq smiled at him.

"You need to get out so you can get right back on. We're moving to the space station."

"Station's broken. And what do you mean *we*?" Jaq didn't know what she wanted.

"I'm going home. I was born on that station. We can coordinate the exodus from New Septimus. We can coordinate the completion of *Epica*. We can do all the things that need doing."

"*We*? You keep saying that word."

"I'll make an honest woman of you, Jaq. My boys agree. Teo, too."

"My only family is Bec, and I am absolutely, without reservation, completely sure that he doesn't care. But the rest of my non-biological family probably has opinions on the matter now that they have time on their hands for idle gossip."

Brad gestured for her to join him. "You need to be the first off the ship," he told her. He walked slowly. He hadn't had enough time to recover properly, but he wasn't going to miss the highlight of Jaq's life.

It was everything she'd worked for.

Together, they waited for the elevator. Brad's eyes drooped, but he fought the fatigue. "I love you, Jaq."

"I figured. My charm is undeniable. Yours is okay, too." Jaq wrapped her arms around Brad's neck.

The elevator arrived, and it was full. Someone thrust an arm out. "Everyone off," a voice called from inside. They left the elevator without a word, giving it exclusively to Jaq and Brad.

"I don't know what to say." Jaq scanned their familiar

faces. She knew them all. It was her crew, first and second generations of those born and raised on the ship.

"I heard there's this thing called shore leave where we get off the ship. Is that real?"

"Yes," Brad confirmed, "but only after the captain approves. We better go so you can get your blessing and run off the ship like crazy people. It's a tradition."

They boarded the elevator and at each stop, no one joined them, deferring to let the captain lead the way.

Jaq walked slower and slower toward the aft airlock. She wasn't sure if the ramp would deploy. It had been more than fifty years since it was last used, but Teo had already thought of that. She stood in the open hatch and directed a portable ramp that was being maneuvered into place.

"Gotta know your limitations," Brad joked.

Teo stepped aside. "Where are you going?" She glared at her father.

"Septimus. It's the second-last stop for this tired old body of mine. We have a station to repair. I hope you'll join us."

"Sure. There's too much dirt and spore-laden air out there for my taste." She frowned and squeezed past the two on her way back to Engineering.

Jaq stood at the hatch while a growing group of people waited beyond the bottom of the ramp. Jaq closed her eyes and breathed deeply of the fresh air. Tears streamed once more.

Brad kissed her on the cheek. "Go on. They're waiting."

Jaq straightened and stepped outside her ship. Above her, hugging the outer hull, was the E-mag battery she'd fired manually at the incoming rockets. The scarring and battle damage on the outside of the ship was all too evident under the bright blue sky.

She set her jaw and strode down the ramp until she reached the last step. She hesitated before stepping to the ground to stand on Septimus.

The end of Starship Lost

Please leave a review on this book as well as the whole series, because all those stars look great and help others decide if they'll enjoy this book as much as you have. I appreciate the feedback and support. Reviews buoy my spirits and stoke the fires of creativity.

Don't stop now! Keep turning the pages as I talk about this book and the overall project called *Starship Lost*.

You can always join my newsletter at https://craigmartelle.com or follow me on Amazon https://www.amazon.com/Craig-Martelle/e/B01AQVF3ZY/ so you can be notified when my next book comes out.

AUTHOR NOTES - CRAIG MARTELLE

Written January 25, 2024

And there it is, the sixth and final book in the Starship Lost series. I can't thank you enough for sticking with me for all six books. This is pure space adventure, which means we have characters doing character things while interacting with other characters. There is conversation and banter, which accounts for about seventy percent of these books.

And a fight to win. In my time in the Marines, we won many fights, but we were rarely prepared for what victory looked like. We always focused on the battle at hand. No counting chickens before they're hatched.

It's the hardest part of being in command—keeping everyone managing today so that tomorrow comes out how you want while simultaneously preparing for that very same tomorrow where you won't be doing anything that you were doing today.

Shifting gears is easy in a car. It's not so easy for a large group of people who spend their lives doing one thing only to do another after they've successfully done that one thing.

I hope I was able to convey that. There wasn't an epic battle with more and more ships, more firepower, men and women fighting and dying until only one remained. Both sides were vastly depleted. What was the turning point in the war? Yes, every battle was critical, but when the troop transport commander tried to run down *Chrysalis*, they lost the bulk of their fighting force. Had he done what Jaq directed, the war would have gone on for much longer because taking the city would have been problematic. Defeating the fleet was important to set up the final battle for the city, but the Malibor could never recover from losing their ground combat power.

There are no magic bullets in war. There is only will and determination for those who survive, while sacrificing when necessary. Winning the war means prevailing day after day. No one leaves unscathed.

Maybe there's too much reality in this book. I think that makes it more military than constant action. I served for over twenty years in the Marine Corps and did an inordinate amount of waiting. Hurry up and wait! That's a cliché because it's real. You train for months for an operation that takes two days, then it returns to a logistics exercise. Eating and sleeping are the commander's bane. You have to make sure the troops get enough of both while being ready to fight when called upon.

Aliens built the Armanor star system! Septiman was an alien?

Damn straight.

As a reminder, https://www.omnicalculator.com/physics/acceleration —need to keep that acceleration calculator close at hand.

Regarding structural materials, I quoted *Structural Materials for Fusion Reactors* by M. Victoria, N. Baluc and P. Spätig from the EPFL-CRPP Fusion Technology Materials, CH-5232 Villigen PSI, Switzerland.

That's it, a bunch of rambling thoughts and a finished book, but far from a finished story. More, coming very soon.

If you liked this book and haven't read Battleship Leviathan (https://geni.us/BLo1), then you'll want to read that one.

Peace, fellow humans.

If you liked this story, you might like some of my other books. You can join my mailing list by dropping by my website at craigmartelle.com, or if you have any comments, shoot me a note at craig@craigmartelle.com. I am always happy to hear from people who've read my work. I try to answer every email I receive.

If you liked the story, please write a short review for me on Amazon. I greatly appreciate any kind words; even one or two sentences go a long way. The number of reviews an ebook receives greatly improves how well it does on Amazon.

Amazon—www.amazon.com/author/craigmartelle

Facebook—https://www.facebook.com/authorcraigmartelle

BookBub—https://www.bookbub.com/authors/craig-martelle

My web page—https://craigmartelle.com

Thank you for joining me on this incredible journey.

THANK YOU FOR READING ENGAGEMENT

We hope you enjoyed it as much as we enjoyed bringing it to you. We just wanted to take a moment to encourage you to review the book. Follow this link: **Engagement** to be directed to the book's Amazon product page to leave your review.

Every review helps further the author's reach and, ultimately, helps them continue writing fantastic books for us all to enjoy.

Also in series:

STARSHIP LOST
Starship Lost
The Return

Primacy
Confrontation
Fallacy
Engagement

Want to discuss our books with other readers and even the authors? Join our Discord server today and be a part of the Aethon community.

Facebook | Instagram | Twitter | Website

You can also join our non-spam mailing list by visiting www.subscribepage.com/AethonReadersGroup and never miss out on future releases. You'll also receive three full books completely Free as our thanks to you.

Looking for more great books?

ROGUE STARS
PURGATORY
BOOK ONE OF THE ROGUE STARS SERIES
JAIME CASTLE

Abandon ship, or go down in a blaze of glory. Commander Predaxes, former Marine in the Lazaab military, has been recommissioned to Prison Station 12, known colloquially as Purgatory. On the outskirts of the Centridium, PS12 relies solely on a wormhole for contact with the government -- not to mention supplies. His newest inmate, Samea Malik, is more than a bit of trouble. Son to the Minister of Justice, Malik is the target of both assassination and recovery. When the station is attacked and chaos rains down upon them all, those onboard must abandon their posts for the closest habitable planet, Faebos. With what little planning they could do, Predaxes and crew discover an old, defunct mining colony and quickly discover why the project was deserted. Faebos is home to violent and nasty creatures, but also great beauty. Survival will mean cooperation between PS12's captives and captors. But will it be enough? Faced with hardship no one expected, needing to tap into old skills and new, Predaxes and Malik find themselves in their own form of Purgatory. *Rogue Stars* **is a brand new Military Space Opera series by #1 Audible and Washington Post bestseller Jaime Castle, creator of the** *Black Badge* **series. Perfect for fans of David Weber, Larry Correia, JN Chaney, and Rick Partlow.**

Get Purgatory Now!

ENGAGEMENT 337

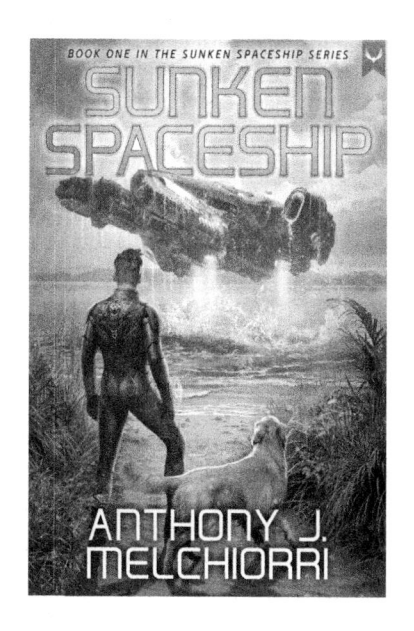

An unlikely hero is swept up into intergalactic affairs when he stumbles upon a crashed starship, Ex-Army paratrooper Griffin "Fin" Brooks thought he left danger behind when his battlefield injuries forced him to pursue a new career in marine biology. But one fateful night off the coast of South Africa a ship nearly crashes into him and his loyal golden retriever, Jacques. Not just any ship. A starship. Though its alien pilot is dead, the rare extraterrestrial animal inside is not. Fin learns the creature is being smuggled across the galaxy when a pair of interstellar visitors respond to the crash. But those same investigators accuse Fin and his dog of crimes he didn't even know existed. The only way to clear his name is to take the strange creature to its home planet and find out who's responsible for killing the starship's pilot. Which means Fin quickly needs to learn how to fly a spacecraft and navigate a galaxy teeming with intelligent life beyond his wildest dreams. And he's not the only one with designs for the crashed starship and its cargo. Fin will need every skill he's honed as a paratrooper and a marine biologist if he—and his dog—are to survive. **Don't miss the next rolicking sci-fi adventure from Anthony J. Melchiorri. It's perfect for fans of JN Chaney, MR Forbes, and** *Hitchhiker's Guide to the Galaxy.*

Get Sunken Spaceship Now!

ENGAGEMENT 339

A conspiracy threatens everyone in the colonized worlds. Only they can stop it. In a distant future where advancements in cybernetics and gene-splicing have resulted in a dozen different variants of humanity, three individuals find themselves entangled in a conspiracy that could doom everyone in the colonized worlds. Paige Angstrom, a fierce and loyal Peacekeeper, yearns to shield her sister Volara from a life of corporate-indentured servitude. Hemlocke Shaw, a gene-spliced engineer, tirelessly searches for his missing eco-activist wife. And Emrald Re, a no-nonsense bounty hunter, embarks on a mission to find a vanished wastelander named Lewis DuCane. Amidst deadly power outages, vanishing civilians, and stalled terraforming projects, the trio unearths a cover-up of epic proportions. The revelation sends shockwaves through their lives, forcing them to confront their own identities and become unlikely heroes in the struggle against the very architects of the Terran race. **From debut authors Matt Conant and Lauren Cipollo, the Parallax series will transport you to a universe teeming with adventure, where ordinary individuals become beacons of hope in the face of oppression.**

Get Origin Now!

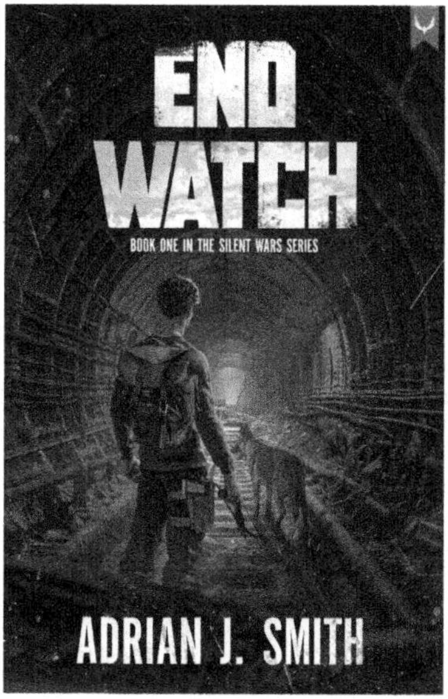
END
WATCH
BOOK ONE IN THE SILENT WARS SERIES
ADRIAN J. SMITH

In the future, freedom is for the modified.
Three centuries after the Genetic War divided humanity, the natural born are slaves. Fated to work in massive subterranean mines, they are expendable. Life is hell. Few escape. Fugitive Recovery Agent Eli Miller and his partner Leylani Haru will never see the sun, breathe fresh air, or taste salt on the wind. They live for the thrill of tracking down criminals and bringing them to justice. When a routine case uncovers a mysterious old journal, Eli is puzzled by its claims of being written prior to the catastrophic conflict and by clues pointing to a way of achieving liberty. Before he can unveil its secrets Eli and his team are sent into the treacherous labyrinth of tunnels to capture the Mayor's runaway wife and stop a precarious political fallout. Reluctant to go, he realises that it is another opportunity to locate the masked criminal known as — Simon. A man he holds responsible for the death of his niece. Following the trail, Eli learns that the two cases are linked and there are those that would do anything to silence his team. But in the unforgiving darkness there's something far worse waiting for him — something which threatens the existence of all natural born. **Don't miss the start of this gripping science fiction thriller from Adrian J. Smith. Set in a gritty, post-apocalyptic dystopia, End Watch will keep you on the edge of your seat from start to finish!**

Get End Watch Now!

ENGAGEMENT 343

For all our Sci-Fi books, visit our website.

OTHER SERIES BY CRAIG MARTELLE
#—AVAILABLE IN AUDIO, TOO

Terry Henry Walton Chronicles (#) (co-written with Michael Anderle)—a post-apocalyptic paranormal adventure

Gateway to the Universe (#) (co-written with Justin Sloan & Michael Anderle)—this book transitions the characters from the Terry Henry Walton Chronicles to the Bad Company

The Bad Company (#) (co-written with Michael Anderle)—a military science fiction space opera

Judge, Jury, & Executioner (#)—a space opera adventure legal thriller

Shadow Vanguard—a Tom Dublin space adventure series

Superdreadnought (#)—an AI military space opera

Metal Legion (#)—a military space opera

The Free Trader (#)—a young adult science fiction action-adventure

Cygnus Space Opera (#)—a young adult space opera (set in the Free Trader universe)

Darklanding (#) (co-written with Scott Moon)—a space Western

Mystically Engineered (co-written with Valerie Emerson)—mystics, dragons, & spaceships

Metamorphosis Alpha—stories from the world's first science fiction RPG

The Expanding Universe—science fiction anthologies

Zenophobia (#) (co-written with Brad Torgersen)—a space archaeological adventure

Battleship Leviathan (#)– a military sci-fi spectacle published by Aethon Books

Glory (co-written with Ira Heinichen)—hard-hitting military sci-fi

Black Heart of the Dragon God (co-written with Jean Rabe)—a sword & sorcery novel

Starship Lost – a hard-science, military sci-fi epic published by Aethon Books

Veracity of Failure – a hard-science technothriller, the race to Mars

End Times Alaska (#)—a post-apocalyptic survivalist adventure published by Permuted Press

Nightwalker (a Frank Roderus series)—A post-apocalyptic Western adventure

End Days (#) (co-written with E.E. Isherwood)—a post-apocalyptic adventure

Successful Indie Author (#)—a nonfiction series to help self-published authors

Monster Case Files (co-written with Kathryn Hearst)—A Warner twins mystery adventure

Rick Banik (#)—Spy & terrorism action-adventure

Ian Bragg Thrillers (#)—a hitman with a conscience

Published exclusively by Craig Martelle, Inc

The Dragon's Call by Angelique Anderson & Craig A. Price, Jr.—an epic fantasy quest

A Couples Travels—a nonfiction travel series

Love-Haight Case Files by Jean Rabe & Donald J. Bingle—the dead/undead have rights, too, a supernatural legal thriller

Mischief Maker by Bruce Nesmith—the creator of Elder Scrolls V: Skyrim brings you Loki in the modern day, staying true to Norse mythology (not a superhero version)

Mark of the Assassins by Landri Johnson—a coming-of-age fantasy.

For a complete list of Craig's books, stop by his website—https://craigmartelle.com

Printed in Great Britain
by Amazon